Selected Praise for

kayla perrin

Erotic Fiction

Getting Even

"This story of exquisitely plotted revenge will have every
woman who has ever been 'done wrong' quietly cheering....
This is sexy erotica."
—*Library Journal*

"*Getting Even* is one wild ride!...Perrin is an author who belongs
on your must read list. Don't miss *Getting Even!*"
—*Romance Reader at Heart*

"[A] writer that everyone should read."
—Eric Jerome Dickey

Getting Some

"A very highly erotic, captivating tale...the sex scenes are
plenty and burn-your-fingers-off-the-page hot & steamy."
—*RAWSISTAZ Reviewers*

"[This] solid, enjoyable novel...takes the reader down
an intriguing emotional path, from sorrow to ecstasy and
back again—it was well worth it."
—Romance Reader at Heart

"Ms. Perrin goes all out with this story as she enters a world of
eroticism...definitely a roller-coaster ride that had me hooked
from the beginning...definitely worth reading."
—*Romance in Color*

D0112274

obsession

kayla perrin

Spice

OBSESSION

ISBN-13: 978-0-373-60520-0
ISBN-10:   0-373-60520-X

www.Spice-Books.com

Printed in U.S.A.

This book is for my editor,
Susan Swinwood.

Thanks for your faith in my
stories and all your support!

prologue

The tip of the feather inched its way along my bottom lip. Such a light, wispy touch, but it sent a jolt of heat through my body, causing me to part my lips and emit a shuddery moan.

Another stroke. This time across my upper lip. My naked body quivered.

Quivered with anticipation of the pleasure that was to come.

The feather traveled lower, over my chin, then crossed the expanse of my neck from left to right. Right to left. All with agonizing slowness.

Then it stopped. Abruptly. Five seconds went by. I held my breath, waiting for what would come next. The blindfold over my eyes prevented me from seeing, but also heightened my sense of excitement. I could hear every sound in the room, smell everything. Mostly, I heard only my own raspy breaths and the whirring of the ceiling fan above the bed. But I could smell the desire in the room, clinging to drops of warm moisture in the air. I could smell the sweat dampening his skin. The scent was musky and heady.

And arousing.

When the feather caressed my left nipple, my body jerked, making my wrists and ankles pull against the ties that bound me to the bed.

"Do you like that?" he asked.

"Yes," I responded, surprised to find my voice faint. "Yes," I repeated, louder this time.

Once again, nothing. My hips writhed. I groaned softly. I was eager for his touch now. Desperate for it.

"Patience, *bella,*" he murmured.

"Easy for you to say," I told him. "You have total control over my body right now." *Total control over my pleasure.*

"Have I disappointed you before?" he asked.

"No," I answered honestly. "Never."

"And I will not disappoint now."

The feather touched down between my rib cage, then traveled south, where it dipped into my belly button. It continued its lazy journey into my strip of pubic hair, then stopped—just when I wanted it most.

I whimpered. "Please, don't make me beg."

He didn't say a word. Several seconds passed and nothing. I strained to hear past the *woo-woo* sounds the ceiling fan was making.

Soft footfalls on the carpet, then the creaking of the bedroom door.

What? Was he leaving me here?

I counted ten more seconds, and when he didn't return, I began to struggle against the ties that bound me. The headboard rattled as I pulled and yanked. Futilely. The knots were too tight, preventing my escape.

And then I heard the sound of footsteps again. He was coming back into the room. I exhaled audibly.

"Look at you," he said. "Your body writhing. Did you think I was going to leave you here while I went and watched a baseball game?"

I didn't answer. I suddenly felt foolish. I *had* been afraid that he'd left me here, totally exposed and helpless to escape until he freed me. I'd been under his complete control before, yet this was the first time I'd felt such a moment of panic.

Why?

Because he seemed different today. From the moment I'd arrived, I could sense a certain intensity level in his looks and his touch.

Something darker.

"I wouldn't leave you," he said. "I would never leave you. You and I, we're connected in a way we can't control."

I swallowed. Did I sense something ominous in his tone? Or was I a little unnerved because I was bound and blindfolded?

How could a person be unnerved and extremely aroused at the same time?

"Do you trust me?" he asked. He was very close to me now. Maybe a foot away. I could tell by the sound of his voice.

I gyrated my hips, a motion that would please him, given the view he had of my pussy with my legs spread the way they were. "Touch me," I said. My chest heaved with each breath. "Touch me before I die."

"Do you trust me?" he repeated, and I felt the weight of his body on the bed, but I couldn't tell where he was.

"Yes. Yes, I trust you."

"Completely?" he asked, his warm breath suddenly tickling my clitoris, and my God, I almost came.

"Yes, yes. Completely, I trust you. Please touch me. Baby…"

I cried out when something cold and wet stroked my clit. What? The sensation had me confused. I'd expected the warmth of his tongue.

The cold and wet brushed against my inner thigh now, and I finally placed what it was. A cube of ice.

He stroked my pussy again with the ice cube. My nub clenched. My hips jerked.

"I wonder if I could make you come like this," he said softly, and stroked me with the ice again.

"I don't know. It feels good, but it's so cold..."

The bed squeaked as he got up. Where was he going now? "Baby, please," I protested.

His lips brushed against mine. They were cold and wet. From the ice. My body writhed, my not so subtle cue that I wanted him. On top of me. Inside me. Fucking me until I collapsed from sheer exhaustion.

He kissed my jaw, then trailed his tongue to my earlobe and suckled. He whispered, "Do you love me?"

"You know I love everything that you do to me," I quickly replied, and that was the absolute truth. I craved this man's touch in a way I wasn't sure was healthy. "Even if you make me wait for it."

The ice cube circled my nipple, and my flesh tightened instantly. A moment later, I felt the flick of his hot tongue. Just a flick though, not nearly enough. I arched my back, pushing my breasts forward.

"Do you love me?" he repeated.

Slowly, I lowered my back. He *was* different today. Why was he suddenly asking me about love, knowing my situation? Knowing the circumstances under which we'd come together?

"I know you love this." He began stroking my clit with his thumb. Back and forth. Back and forth.

"Mmm, *yes*. I love that." I began to pant, close to the edge. "I can never get enough of your hands on my body."

"What about my tongue?" He adjusted his body between my legs, and I bit down on my bottom lip in anticipation. The moment his tongue came down on me, my hips bucked and I started to whimper.

"Baby, I love your tongue. I can't get enough of your tongue. *Ohhh.*"

He suckled me until I was crying from the pleasure and on the verge of exploding. Then he pulled back, denying me my release.

"No, no. *Please,*" I begged. "I need you, baby. I need—"

"Do you love me?" he asked again.

"Yes!" I cried out. "I love you. I love you."

"Oh, baby. I love you, too." Hastily, he untied my legs and hooked them over his shoulders and began to devour me. He sucked, he nibbled, he buried his tongue inside me. He ate greedily, as though my pussy was the last meal he would ever have.

My whole body convulsed as my orgasm gripped me, gripped me harder than anything I'd ever experienced before. It zapped me of my energy. Stole my breath. Left me shuddering as though a speeding train had just rocketed through my body.

Even through my pleasure, I was aware that something had changed between us.

I wasn't sure it was for the better.

I

Six weeks earlier...

I awoke to the sounds of fucking coming from the other room.

For several moments I lay on my bed, my eyes adjusting to the darkness. My right temple throbbed, evidence of too many margaritas that evening, and a general lack of sleep over the past few days.

Yawning, I rolled over and glanced at the bedside clock.

Three-thirteen in the morning.

"Right there...yes, right there. Ohhh..."

Despite my headache, I couldn't help giggling. Maybe Marnie thought I was dead to the world and therefore didn't think she needed to be quiet. Or maybe she didn't care. All I knew, as I lay there, was that she and the guy she'd picked up were screwing like this was their last night on earth—if the loud moans and screams coming from the other room were any indication.

"Yes, yes! Fuck me, baby!" Marnie screamed.

I hugged my pillow and closed my eyes, but I knew I wouldn't be getting back to sleep anytime soon. Not with the sexual Olympics going on in the next room.

I heard a consistent banging on the wall—likely the headboard. At least, I hoped it wasn't someone's body part hitting the wall. And how thin were these walls, anyway, that I could hear their every grunt and moan?

I debated getting out of bed and going to Marnie's bedroom door. But the last thing I wanted to do was embarrass her and the stud in the room with her.

So I stayed where I was, keeping my eyes closed and hoping I'd somehow be able to get back to sleep.

A loud crash in the next room had me bolting upright, alarm shooting through me. What the—

Laughter.

I lay back down. Whatever had happened, Marnie and her lover weren't concerned. The sounds of their lovemaking picked up right where they'd left off.

The moaning and groaning and occasional giggles had me suddenly missing my husband. Missing the way we were in the beginning. Spontaneous, and frisky, and a lot like Marnie right now—not caring who heard us if we were in a hotel fucking.

It had been four whole days since I'd seen him, since I'd left on this trip with Marnie, my long-time best friend, to Grand Bahama Island. Marnie had been in the dumps because she and her fiancé had broken up, and she needed a getaway.

I'd suggested this trip as a way to get her mind off of her heartbreak. And it had been a blast. Marnie and I had had a fun four days of partying like we were college kids with endless energy, and Marnie hadn't mentioned Brian once. I doubt that between ogling hot young men and downing flaming Sambuca shots she'd even had time to think about him. The trip had gone a long way to mending Marnie's broken heart.

I supposed that after being engaged for a couple of years, she was entitled to get her freak on.

Even if I was in the other room.

I couldn't help but listen to them, and I couldn't help feeling slightly envious. What I heard coming from Marnie's room was exactly the kind of sex I wanted to be having with my husband. After eight years of marriage, Andrew and I had fallen into a bit of a routine. Sex on Saturday nights. Sometimes Sunday mornings as well. It was a good week if we also got in a mid-week fuck.

At the beginning of our relationship, we used to go on lots of romantic weekend trips and screw like bunnies. With both of us working full-time now, that kind of spontaneity was impossible. But I still adored my husband, and he adored me. He could still look at me from across a room and make my body tingle the way he first had ten years ago in college.

I suddenly wanted to talk to him. Call him and have some spontaneous phone sex. Get him in the mood to give me the kind of homecoming I was craving.

Yes, it was after three in the morning, but that's what spontaneous was—not worrying about the time nor the place.

I used my cell phone, having learned that it was more expensive to use a credit card to call from the hotel phone. I punched in the digits to my home in Orlando, then lay back on my pillow as I waited for Andrew to pick up.

My lips were slightly parted, poised to say something dirty the moment Andrew answered the phone. But after four rings, it went to voice mail.

Disappointed, I sighed softly. I debated hanging up and calling him back. I wanted to tell him how much I wanted to touch him, stroke him. How badly I wanted him inside me. And while I was at it, I'd even ask if he would take a plane and meet me here, or meet me in Fort Lauderdale, where Marnie and I had boarded the Discovery Cruise Line to head to the Bahamas.

Spontaneity and all that.

But common sense got the better of me when the beep sounded and I heard my voice prompting me to leave a message. It was the middle of the night, and even though I was desperate to talk to him, I couldn't call Andrew back. It wouldn't be fair to him. He had to be up for work in the morning. Besides, I'd be seeing him in less than twenty-four hours.

Real sex would be far better than phone sex anyway.

Though I didn't think I would, sometime during the night I'd drifted off to sleep. I awoke with a start and found Marnie sitting on the edge of my bed.

"Morning, sleepyhead," she crooned when my eyes met hers.

I took a moment to register that she was really there, that this wasn't a dream. I could smell the fresh scent of some sort of floral soap, could see that her short black hair was wet and slicked back. Yep, she was definitely here. And she looked surprisingly well rested for a woman who'd spent most of the night screwing her brains out. Her dark complexion never gave anything away.

"You'd still be sleeping too if you were woken up by the sounds of serious fucking."

"You heard us?" Marnie asked, sounding surprised.

"You've got to be kidding. How could I *not* hear you?"

"Oops," Marnie said sheepishly.

"Is the room a total disaster zone or what? Cuz it sure sounded like you were doing some serious damage to it."

"We broke one of the lamps." Marnie spoke almost proudly.

"What?" But I was really wondering, *how?* "And you're smiling about that?"

"Don't worry. I already went to the front desk to let them know, and I paid to replace it."

"Oh. Okay." Though I was dead tired, I eased myself up on an elbow. Stretching, a yawn escaped my throat.

Marnie grinned from ear to ear. "And trust me, I'm not smiling because we broke a lamp."

I shook my head in mock reproof. "I can't believe you're up already. After the workout you got."

"I know." Marnie sighed happily. "He only left an hour ago, so I knew there was no way I'd be getting any sleep if I was going to make it to that boat later today. I took a shower, had a couple cups of coffee and, amazingly, I feel fine."

"You'd never know. Not with that, 'I've been fucked so hard, I could die a happy woman' look on your face."

"I know." Marnie giggled. "It was incredible, Sophie. Out of this world."

"You don't have to tell me. I feel like I was a spectator. All I was missing was the popcorn and the dildo."

Marnie roared with laughter. "I should be embarrassed—but, what can I say, I'm shameless."

I yawned again, then asked, "So you like this guy?"

"I like his cock. No, I *love* his cock."

Marnie had been my best friend since eighth grade, and we didn't have a problem speaking explicitly to each other. But if the parents of any of our students happened to overhear us talking when we were out on the town, they'd likely be pulling their kids from our classes.

Of course, we didn't have to worry about that here. And we definitely didn't have foul mouths when we were at the front of our grade-school classrooms.

"I do like him," Marnie went on, "but we leave today. Maybe if he lived in Orlando. Heck, if he even lived in the Bahamas. But he's headed back to the Dominican Republic the day after tomorrow."

"It was cute watching you two trying to talk to each other at the bar." What Soriano had lacked in language skills he had easily made up in charm. And that radiant smile of his hadn't hurt.

"At least he served his purpose," Marnie said. "Which was to *totally* get me to forget about Brian. I don't know if it's because this guy was a one-night stand, but nothing Brian did in bed with me was *ever* as exciting as what Soriano and I did."

"It probably was, in the beginning with Brian," I pointed out. "New sex and all that."

Marnie shrugged. "Maybe. But now my body knows that there's life after Brian, and that that life can be quite exciting."

I smiled at my friend. For her sake, I was glad. For a good three months, she had moped over the end of her relationship with Brian, and she'd needed something to get her out of her funk.

She'd already had one marriage fall apart after her husband repeatedly cheated on her, and now that she and Brian had ended things, I knew she was depressed over the thought that she'd never meet her Mr. Right.

I sat up fully and swung my feet off the bed. "I'm gonna go take a shower. Is there any coffee left?"

"I'll make another pot."

"Thank you, babe. I'm going to need it."

2

It was a little after nine in the evening when I pulled into the driveway of my Orlando home. My husband's Cadillac Escalade was there—as I'd expected on a Sunday evening—and excited, I sprinted inside. I wanted to throw my arms around his neck and kiss him until we ended up naked on the living room floor.

I was hoping he would have heard me pull up and be waiting for me at the door. He wasn't. But Peaches, our orange and white tabby, was. She purred in greeting, and I bent to give her a quick rub on the head before making my way into the living room.

Peaches followed me, clearly needing more attention. I needed Andrew.

But he wasn't in the living room. Hadn't he heard me? He had to be somewhere in the house, so why hadn't he come out to welcome me home? We hadn't seen each other in five days. Maybe it was a little corny, but I expected him to stop whatever he was doing and rush out to meet me. Sweep me in his arms and not let me go until we were both screaming as we came.

"Andrew?" I called. When he didn't answer, I frowned. Tonight, I wanted spontaneity. And creativity.

And sex all night long.

I wandered into the bedroom, where I found Andrew lying on the bed. My frown morphed into a small smile as I regarded him. He was on his back, his lips slightly parted as he snored softly.

"Oh, baby," I said softly. "At least you're getting your rest, so you should be in full form when I wake you up."

The cat rubbed her body against my legs, purring. I bent down and scooped her up, then put her out the door and closed it.

"Sorry, Peaches, but I want no spectators for this."

I padded across the room to the bed and eased my body down beside my husband's. He didn't stir. I stretched out beside him and planted my lips on his.

Andrew jerked awake, his eyes widening as he saw me.

I giggled. "Hi, baby."

"Hi," he said, his voice hoarse, then cleared his throat.

"Looks like someone had a hard day," I commented. I placed my palm on his belly and kissed his chin. "But hopefully your little nap helped you regain some energy."

"What time is it?"

"A little after nine," I replied. Now, I kissed his lips.

"How was your trip?"

"Fun. Marnie definitely had a good time." I smiled inwardly, re-membering just how good a time, but I'd never share that with Andrew. "The trip was great for her."

"That's good, sweetheart."

Good? Why wasn't Andrew taking me in his arms and *really* kissing me?

I guess he was still groggy, but I was determined to wake him up. Lowering my hand to his groin, I stroked him through his pants. Then I pressed my mouth against his and kissed him deeply.

His cock hardened, and I purred, satisfied. Feeling a surge of feminine power, I eased my body onto his and straddled him. His hands went to my breasts, gently squeezing.

I gyrated myself against him, feeling his cock through my shorts. I moved my mouth from his, to his jaw, then to his earlobe, where I nibbled gently.

"I was having some naughty thoughts last night," I whispered.

He snaked his hands around my waist. "You were, were you?"

"Mmm-hmm." I pulled my head back to face him. "I even called. But you didn't answer."

Andrew's hands stilled and he looked at me as if he wasn't sure he heard me correctly. "You called last night?"

"Yeah," I said.

"What time?"

"Late," I answered. "But either you were sleeping, or you were out on the town partying."

I was joking, but the quizzical look he gave me told me he didn't think I was. "I guess I was extra tired. It's been crazy at work with that convention going on. I ended up going in yesterday, since you weren't here. You should see insurance adjusters throw them back at the bar. And I thought they were dull."

I slipped my hand between our bodies. His cock was no longer hard. "Hey, big boy. What's the matter?" I pouted. "Aren't you happy to see me?"

"Of course I am." Was I imagining it, or did he sound a tad defensive?

"Then why is it taking you so long to get me naked?" With my legs straddling him, I sat up and pulled my blouse over my head. I made quick work of unfastening my bra. "Touch me, baby. Taste my nipples. I want to you to fuck me so hard, you blow out my back."

"Sophie," Andrew said, his tone disapproving.

"Sorry, baby," I said. Andrew didn't like it when I cursed. "I just missed you, and you're playing really hard to get right now."

Andrew regarded me warily.

"Baby, please don't tell me you're too tired for this." I began stroking him again. "I can do all the work. I just need you to be hard."

"What exactly happened on your trip?" he asked.

"Meaning?"

"I don't know. You seem unusually horny."

Now I sat up and looked at Andrew with a perplexed expression. "Meaning there's some crazy reason why I want to make love to my husband?"

Andrew's shoulders moved in a slight shrug.

What was going on? "Do you think I did something wrong while I was away?"

"I didn't say that."

He couldn't have sounded less convincing. He'd never been the jealous or possessive type, and I'd never given him a reason not to trust me. So I had no clue what was really going on here.

"To set the record straight," I began slowly, sliding off his body, "I didn't do a single thing you'd be mad at me for. Yeah, I had a lot to drink, stayed up late, and danced like I haven't since I was in college, but every guy who talked to me knew that I was married."

Andrew gave no indication that he'd heard me. Instead, he got off the bed and walked out of the room, leaving me confused. Did he not believe me, or was he simply itching for a fight? If that was the case, why was he mad? Because I'd gone away with Marnie? He hadn't expressed any opposition to me going on the five-day trip.

I didn't follow him. If he wanted a fight, I wasn't going to give it to him. I put my shirt back on, knowing that for some crazy reason, I wasn't getting any sex tonight.

The bedroom door now open, Peaches trotted into the room, determined to get some affection from me. She jumped up onto my lap. I began to massage her neck, taking some comfort from the fact that my pet would always be happy to see me.

A few minutes later, Andrew returned to the bedroom door. He stood there, resting his body against the door frame and looking conflicted.

"Are you mad at me because I went on this trip with Marnie?" I asked, getting to the point.

Andrew drew in a deep breath, then let it out slowly. "Something happened," he said simply.

So work was bothering him. It wouldn't be the first time that the stress from work continued to bother him when he got home. I was disappointed that his seeing me hadn't pushed any work issues from his mind, but it was a relief to know that he didn't believe I'd done anything to hurt him.

"Is it something serious?"

He nodded.

I don't know why, but I got the sense that this something wasn't a run-of-the-mill work issue. Maybe Andrew had messed something up at the hotel in a big way and head office was pissed with him. Or perhaps he was involved in a conflict with someone on his staff. It wouldn't be the first time.

"It's okay," I told him. "Whatever it is, you can tell me."

He stared into my eyes, then looked away, his face filled with angst.

"Andrew." Just how bad was this? "You know I'll support you no matter what."

"I'm not so sure about that."

I frowned at him. Peaches rolled onto her back, giving me access to her stomach while she luxuriated in the attention I was giving her. "Why would you say that? Haven't I always been there for you?"

When Andrew didn't answer, a chill crept down my spine, leaving a feeling of dread in its wake. It wasn't like Andrew to not get right to the point. My God, something really awful must have happened.

My heart began to beat fast, several devastating scenarios jumping into my head. Had something happened to his parents? Had he gotten some awful news about his health from his doctor while I'd been away? Had he hit a child while driving?

Andrew sighed heavily. He was taking his time, gearing up to tell me the awful news, but I didn't think my heart could take it.

"Please, Andrew. Just tell me!"

"You know I love you, right?"

"Yes, I know that," I replied somewhat anxiously. "But I want to know what happened."

He couldn't look at me, making my fear worse. My eyes misted. Obviously, what had happened had been serious enough that Andrew hadn't wanted to disturb me while I was on my trip.

I croaked, "Someone died?"

"No."

"No?" A relieved giggle escaped my throat. "Thank God, Andrew." I paused. Took a deep breath. "But something serious *did* happen, didn't it?" Maybe he *had* gotten some awful news from his doctor.

"I..."

I waited. Listened. "What, baby?"

"I never wanted to hurt you."

Those weren't the words I'd expected to hear, and they caught me off guard, like biting into an apple and finding it's filled with mold.

I gave him an odd look. "I don't understand."

"I...I did something. Something I'm not proud of."

This had to be work related, some major screwup that had the head honchos breathing down his neck. God, maybe he'd been fired! Andrew was a manager at the Pelican Hotel and Resort in Kissimmee, close to Disney World, and the job had its share of stress. The people at Head Office didn't always agree with how Andrew and his team ran things at the hotel.

But surely whatever he'd done wasn't bad enough to get him fired.

"Jesus, this is so..." Andrew didn't finish his statement.

"So what?" I prompted.

"I had an affair," he blurted, so quickly that I was certain I hadn't heard him correctly. After all, the cat's loud purring could have made me mishear.

"What did you say?" I asked for confirmation, expecting him to say something else. Confirm for me that I'd misheard.

He looked at me now. "I had an affair."

Stunned, I lowered the cat to the floor. As if she sensed the sudden tension in the room, she ran out the bedroom door.

"You—" I couldn't repeat what he'd said.

"I'm so sorry," he told me. He stepped into the room and closed the door. "I never meant to hurt you."

All I could do was stare at Andrew. It was as though he had morphed into a stranger in front of my eyes.

"Please, Sophie. Say something."

This wasn't happening. This wasn't real.

Andrew walked toward me, slowly, as if trying to corner a scared dog. I didn't say a word. Couldn't. I was too numb.

But when he reached for me, I reacted instinctively, slapping his hand away. "Don't touch me." I suddenly heard the ragged breaths coming from my chest. I sounded awful. "Don't you ever touch me again."

"This is the hardest thing I've ever had to do—"

"Shut up. Just shut up!" I covered my ears with my hands. I wanted to block his words, as though not hearing them would make what he'd said go away.

My hands still over my ears, I stared at Andrew, my eyes imploring him to take back what he'd said. He held my gaze, but only for a few seconds. Then he looked down.

"Oh, my God." I shot to my feet. "Oh, my God."

"Sophie—"

Gasping, I stumbled past Andrew. I wanted to run out of the house, escape to a place where Andrew's words wouldn't hurt me. But as I got into the living room, my knees buckled, and I was lucky to collapse onto the sofa as opposed to the floor.

An affair? My husband had had an affair?

Andrew, the guy I'd known since I was nineteen, who had gently pursued me in college until I hadn't been able to say no. The guy who'd given me a plastic ring in a bouquet of dandelions and told me that even though he wasn't really proposing, he wanted me to know that one day he would.

If there had been anyone I could count on, anyone who I thought I could completely trust not to betray me in this way, it was Andrew.

My eyes filled with tears. Why, why, why? Why would he do this to me? How *could* he?

It wasn't like I rolled over in bed at night and complained of being too tired to make love. If anything, I wanted it more than he did. He wasn't as aggressive when it came to sex as he'd been in the beginning, but he also hadn't been the tear-your-clothes-off kind of guy in the first place. That kind of man didn't look for sex on the side when he had a wife ready and happy to please him.

No, what mattered to Andrew—or so he'd always said—was our commitment to each other. Passion could wane, but he'd assured me that our love would always be strong.

"Sophie." He spoke softly, and I whipped my head up to see he was standing near the end of the sofa.

Seeing him standing there with a pained expression on his face was all it took for my confusion to turn to anger. He dared to look pained? After *he* had betrayed *me*?

"What do you want, a medal? You think because you had the guts to confess that I'm supposed to forgive you for fucking around?"

"No," he said softly. "That's not what I expect."

"Then what the fuck do you want?" I was pissed, and didn't care if my foul mouth offended him.

He shrugged. "I wanted you to know."

"Aren't you just the epitome of honor. Go to hell."

I got to my feet and marched to the bedroom. But as soon as I was in there, I whirled around. I wanted answers from the man I'd given my heart to. The man I'd married and promised to be faithful to.

No, I *deserved* answers.

I was fuming, my nostrils flaring with each angry breath. "You fucked someone else. Tell me why."

He said nothing.

"Tell me why! Wasn't I good enough for you? Lord knows you always acted like sex wasn't the be-all and end-all, so why the hell would you end up in someone else's bed?"

"I don't know."

"You don't know?" I gaped at him. "What—were you abducted by aliens who removed your brain?"

Andrew said nothing.

"Was it a one-night stand?" I demanded. "Some slut you met out at some club?"

Nothing.

My stomach sank. "Someone you met at the hotel?"

Andrew didn't reply.

An awful thought hit me, as painful as if Andrew had slapped me across the face. "She wasn't a one-night stand.... Oh, God."

Groaning, Andrew ran a hand over his face. "It's not like...it's not like it meant anything."

"My God, you're a walking fucking cliché."

"Jesus, Sophie. Can we just...can we talk? I know I was wrong. I made a huge mistake."

"I've heard enough bullshit from you." I was cursing like a trucker, but I was angry.

"I'm trying to do the right thing here." Andrew sounded exasperated. "That's why I told you about it. I wanted you to hear it from me."

Several beats passed. I was so livid, I was shaking. I needed to calm down. Not for Andrew's sake, but for mine.

I drew in deep breaths, trying to bring myself to a better place. I wondered if I'd ever find a better place again.

"I thought I knew you," I said. "I thought you loved me."

"You think I don't love you?" Andrew asked. "That's the reason I'm telling you—because I love you. And I want to make this right."

Make this right... As if it were so simple. As if what he'd done could be undone.

"Get out," I told him.

He looked stunned. "What?"

"I want you gone. Out of my life. Forever, you son of a bitch."

But even as I said the words, I couldn't imagine a life without

Andrew. Just a few months ago, Andrew and I had talked about finally having children. After having devoted the first eight years of our marriage to building up a nest egg, we were ready.

I drew in another breath and held it until my lungs burned. I didn't want to cry, but damn it…Andrew had destroyed everything.

The dam broke on my last bit of self-control, and I began to weep. Huge, chest-heaving sobs.

Andrew gathered me in his arms and, though I wanted to, I had no energy to push him away. He held my head against his body and I cried until no more tears would come.

"God," Andrew moaned. He stroked my hair lovingly, as though he were consoling me for an entirely different reason. "This is the last thing I wanted. To hurt you like this."

His words pierced my heart. I took a step backward, wiping tears from my face. Somehow I was calm when I asked, "How did you think that cheating wouldn't hurt me?"

"I know, I know. I sound like a moron. I'm just saying…all I can say is that I'm sorry."

Feeling cold, I hugged my torso. Though I knew my arms wouldn't keep me warm when the cold was emanating from inside me. "Sorry can't erase something like this."

Andrew nodded. "I get it."

"Oh, stop giving me that look."

"What look?"

"That wounded look. As if this is hurting you more than it's hurting me."

"I'm hurting too," Andrew said softly.

"I'm sure it's been tough," I retorted, turning away. I couldn't stand looking at my husband. Looking at him and knowing that the man I loved had betrayed me.

Slowly, I walked toward the wall near the bedroom door. Drained, I leaned against it for support.

Andrew followed me, but he stayed a few steps away from me. "I told you because I wanted to. Because you deserved to know. And because I hoped that somewhere in your heart, you could find a way to forgive me for being so weak. And stupid. I messed up, but this doesn't have to be the end of our marriage."

"Wow. Thanks for the heartfelt, unbiased advice, you asshole. Don't you *dare* tell me how I should feel and what I should do, because *I'm* going to decide what happens next. You don't get to have an affair and still make the decisions about our future. If you cared about our future, you never would have done something so…" My voice trailed off. I stifled a cry.

Andrew reached for me. "Baby."

"Fuck you!" I snapped. The anger was back. Big time. "Now leave. Because I can't stand the sight of you."

3

I didn't ask where Andrew was going. I didn't care. He could be running straight to his girlfriend and planning to serve me with divorce papers, it didn't matter. If he wanted that slut he'd screwed, he could have her.

That's what I told myself, but in my heart I didn't believe my bold words. I might have wanted to hate Andrew for turning my world upside down, but a person can't turn her feelings off in an instant. The truth was, I loved him, and that made the pain infinitely more intense. That and the fact that what he'd done had come as an utter shock. I thought that Andrew and I had a good, happy marriage. And people in happy marriages don't cheat.

I spent the night alternately crying, fuming and wishing I could start this day over. I'd give anything to be back in the Bahamas, hungover and sleep deprived. At least then I'd been sleep deprived because I'd been overdosing on fun.

Now, as sunlight spilled through the blinds signaling morning, I felt nauseous and numb. My throat was parched, and my stomach was lurching. I needed water. Something inside my stomach. But I didn't have energy to even get out of bed.

Why? That was the question I asked myself in the moments I wasn't crying or dozing. Why would Andrew do this to me? To us. And he had the audacity to claim that he still wanted to be with me, wanted our marriage.

I didn't understand.

My head hurt from thinking about Andrew's bombshell, so I closed my eyes. Closed my eyes and willed the pain to dissipate.

I must have drifted off, because I jolted awake when I thought I heard a sound in the house. Slowly, I raised my head. Was that Peaches?

It had to be. She wasn't in the bedroom with me, which meant she was somewhere else in the house. She'd likely knocked something over, but I couldn't be bothered to get up and check it out.

I closed my eyes then whipped them open when I heard the bedroom door open. Now I knew that it wasn't Peaches.

Andrew had come back?

Marnie poked her head through the doorway.

"Marnie?" I asked, wondering if I might be hallucinating.

She rushed into the room. "Oh, honey. What's going on?"

"What are you doing here?" I asked, my voice hoarse.

She plopped down onto the bed beside me, her face full of concern as she regarded me. "Andrew called. And I'm glad he did. My God—your eyes are nearly swollen shut."

"Andrew called you?"

"Yes." Marnie placed her hand on my forehead, feeling for a temperature. "You're not that warm, but I've never seen you look this awful before. I should take you to the doctor."

"Andrew said I was sick?"

"He just said that you might need me."

"Hmm." Gripping Marnie's arm for support, I rose to a sitting position. "I need water."

"Of course." Marnie was on her feet in a flash. She left the bedroom and returned within a minute, holding a tall glass filled with ice and water.

I sipped, then gulped down the entire glass. I'd needed water more than I'd thought.

"I'm not sick," I said, my voice still weak.

"Then tell me what's going on."

"Excuse me." I climbed off the bed. "I need to use the bathroom."

I made my way to the ensuite bathroom, moving slowly. I knew Marnie was concerned and confused, but she'd learn the truth soon enough.

When I saw my reflection in the mirror, I gasped. *Awful* was an understatement. My hair was a mess, my eyes red and swollen. I wore an expression that was beyond dejected. I looked haunted.

Given my physical appearance, including the clothes I'd been wearing from the day before that were now wrinkled, a stranger might look at me and think I'd just survived a rape.

I relieved myself, then washed my face and drank more water. My stomach grumbled, and for the first time since last night, I felt hunger pangs as opposed to nausea.

Marnie didn't just look concerned as I walked back into the bedroom, she looked scared. "I've got to tell you, I'm starting to freak out here, Sophie."

"Andrew..." I paused. Swallowed. "Andrew had an affair."

"What?" Marnie asked, aghast.

I couldn't repeat the words, only nod.

"He's leaving you?"

I sank onto the mattress beside Marnie. "He says he still loves me. Still wants me."

"What?" Marnie was outraged.

Her anger helped fuel my own. I'd spent an entire night depressed over Andrew's betrayal, but I needed to pull myself together. Andrew had hurt me enough, and wallowing in self-pity was simply going to add to my pain.

"Yeah." I nodded. "Shocker, huh?"

"Oh, sweetie. Oh, my God. I'm so sorry." Marnie paused. "Have you eaten anything?" Like that was the answer to my crisis.

"Nothing."

"Let me fix you some food."

"Where's Peaches?"

"She ran outside when I opened the door. Look, the cat's going to be fine. It's you I'm worrying about."

I nodded.

Tugging on my hand, Marnie pulled me up from the bed. "I know what you're going through. Believe me. And I'm going to help you deal with it."

"Thanks."

I walked with her to the kitchen, but she insisted that I sit in the living room and put my feet up. I did, and for lack of anything better to do, I turned on the television.

The *Maury Pauvich Show* was on, dealing with unruly kids who were going to be sent off to boot camp. I'd seen several shows of this variety, with bold and foul-mouthed children balking at any authority, only to end up weeping and begging for their mothers after a few days of military-enforced submission.

"They should have boot camp like this for cheating husbands," I commented.

"What?" Marnie asked.

I could see her working in the kitchen, getting the skillet hot to fry eggs. She already had coffee brewing.

"I'm watching Maury Pauvich, and they've got out-of-control teens that they're sending to boot camp. I think he ought to do a show where they send cheating men to boot camp. I'd tune in for that one."

"Wasn't *he* an unfaithful husband?" Marnie asked.

"I don't know. Maybe they all are," I added softly. Marnie and Brian had fallen apart because they ultimately wanted different things, but her first husband, Keith, had cheated on her as though he'd been going for some kind of world record.

Marnie wandered into the living room with a mug of hot coffee. "Two creams, two sugars—just the way you like it."

"Thank you." With a smile, I accepted the mug from Marnie, then watched as she sauntered back to the kitchen. I was glad she was here. Because she'd shown up, I was no longer in a cold, dark, depressing place. Friends were what helped keep people sane when they went through heart-wrenching experiences. Without someone to turn to, a person could get lost in their grief and be unable to find their way back to sanity.

While Marnie fried eggs, I turned back to the television. A young female was taunting the audience with, "Yeah, so I slept with fifteen guys—what's the big deal?" while they all booed her and her mother sobbed. A caption on the screen identified the girl as thirteen-year-old Cathy.

I actually chuckled as Maury placed his hand on the shoulder of the girl's mother, asking how she felt about her daughter's shocking admission. The mother was a blubbering mess but managed to say, "I can't believe she would do this to me."

I rolled my eyes. I wasn't a parent, but I was a teacher, and I'd seen firsthand the kinds of problems that arose when parents took the submissive role and let their kids get away with everything. When they didn't set boundaries. Or, when they didn't punish kids for breaking the rules.

"You want to eat in front of the television?" Marnie asked. "Because I can bring out a couple of trays."

"No, no." I got to my feet and walked across the living room to the kitchen's dinette area. "Though watching shows like Maury certainly helps a person forget about her own problems."

Marnie set a plate of eggs and toast in front of me, then took the seat to my right. She had only the coffee for herself.

"Thanks so much," I told her. "If you hadn't shown up, I'd still be in bed, half-comatose."

Marnie sipped her coffee. "Ok, now tell me what happened. You got home last night and what—you found evidence of some other woman here or something?"

"No." I lifted my fork and cut into my egg. "He came right out and told me."

"Nice welcome-home present. Sheesh."

"I knew something was wrong, but I never would have guessed…." My voice trailed off, ending on a sigh. Then I continued, trying to recite the facts without emotion. "He was acting weird. I wanted to make love, but he wasn't into it. Next thing I know, he's all serious, saying he's got to tell me something. I actually thought someone had died." Shaking my head at the memory, I stuffed some egg into my mouth.

"I wish I could say I'm surprised," Marnie began, "but I have to say, nothing men do surprises me anymore."

"I was devastated last night," I went on. I still was, but now I was determined to regain control of my emotions. "Mad at first, then devastated. But you know what—I didn't do this. Andrew did. I'm not saying it doesn't hurt, but fuck, if this is the hand that life has dealt me, I am going to deal with it and move on."

Marnie gave me a slightly skeptical look, but God bless her, she didn't voice any doubts. I'd seen her after her marriage had fallen apart, and though she'd seen it coming, it had taken a long time for her to recover.

"It's not going to be easy," I said. "I get that. But you know what, there are other fish in the sea."

I felt emotion welling up inside me again at the thought of a life without Andrew, and I quickly ate more food before I started crying. Clearly, I was lying to myself.

"I'm here for you," Marnie said. "We'll go shopping, clubbing, whatever you need to take your mind off this."

I nodded. "I know." I'd done the same for her. "I mean, I know it'll be hard. I loved Andrew. I still do. But I can't let this ruin my life."

Marnie nodded, sipped her coffee. "Did he tell you anything about her?"

"Not much. But it sounds like she wasn't a one-night stand." I took a bite of my whole-wheat toast.

"What an asshole," Marnie muttered. "Sorry, but—"

"Don't apologize. You're absolutely right. And I can't believe he told me this, expecting I'd just forgive him."

"Word of advice here—and I know it's early, and I'm not trying to tell you what to do—but you forgive a guy when he cheats, and there's nothing to say he won't do it again. In fact, it's almost like they see your forgiveness as a sign to do it again. Trust me, I learned the hard way with Keith."

Would Andrew be that way? I couldn't imagine. Then again, I

never imagined he'd ever cheat. He'd seemed too grounded, too controlled, too stable—opposite of spontaneous—to do something like that.

"I don't know what I'm going to do," I admitted. "Part of me hates him, part of me loves him."

"You'll figure it out," Marnie said. "But you don't have to do it today. How about we hit the mall for some retail therapy. And we can take in a matinée. That new film with Will Smith. Two hours of shameless ogling." Her face lit up. "What do you say?"

"Will Smith? How can I argue with that?"

The retail therapy was fun, netting me a new pair of shoes and a slinky black dress I promised to wear out to a club with Marnie on the weekend. But Will Smith was like two painkillers, easing my heartache for the two hours he appeared on screen. Marnie had cheered loudly when he took it all off in a shower scene, and while I hadn't been as vocal, I'd certainly enjoyed his delicious body.

We pulled into my driveway shortly after five. I collected the bags with my purchases and got out of Marnie's black Nissan Sentra.

"I'm serious," Marnie said. "Call me if you need me, no matter the time."

"You spent the whole day babysitting me," I protested.

"And I'll come right back if you realize that being in the house alone is too much for you to deal with."

"The moment I'm tempted to curl into a ball on the bed, I'll call you," I assured her.

"But if you don't get me at home, call me on my cell." Marnie wiggled her eyebrows, and I knew instantly that something was going on.

I poked my head into the driver-side window before she could leave. "I know that tone, Marnie Kincaid. What's going on tonight that you won't be at home?"

"Well…" Marnie's eyes lit up as she bit down on her bottom lip. "I didn't want to mention it until later—after I knew how it worked out—but I've got a date tonight."

"What?" I exclaimed. "And you kept this news to yourself all day?"

"I didn't think I should say anything. Not with what's going on with you and Andrew."

"You don't have to walk on eggshells around me. If you've got good news, I want to hear it."

"It's not really a date," Marnie explained. "More of a let's-see-if-we-like-each-other meeting. You remember I told you I signed up with a couple online dating sites?"

"Yes, but I didn't think you were serious. You're the one who said you prefer the old-fashioned way of meeting people."

"I know, I know. Which is why I put off TRULYACUTIE's requests to meet me before we went on our trip."

"TRULYACUTIE?" I asked, laughing.

"Yeah, that's the name he gave himself online. It piqued my interest." Marnie paused for a moment. "Hey, if Soriano lived in Orlando, I'd be all over him. But if there's one thing my affair with him taught me, it's that I'm ready to move on. And let's face it, I'm not getting any younger. So I e-mailed TRULYACUTIE and said I'd like to meet him."

"Wow."

"Of course, this is just a first date to make sure the guy's not a creep, and we'll go from there. But if his picture is for real, then his screen name is quite fitting."

"Where are you two going?" I asked. I knew a lot of people were finding love via the Internet, but still, I couldn't help feeling concerned for my friend.

"The Cheesecake Factory. Very public, very busy. Don't worry, I'll be fine."

"And you're driving your car there, right? He's not picking you up, is he?"

Marnie shot me a look as if to say I had to know she wasn't that naïve. "Absolutely, I'm driving my own car there. You know me better than that. And he only knows my screen name and vice versa. This way, if we don't like each other, we can disappear from each other's lives easily. It's perfect."

"All right." I straightened. I was going to stop the mother hen act. Marnie was thirty, a few months older than me, and capable of taking care of herself. "You're wasting gas. I'll let you go."

"Wish me luck."

"Good luck," I said. "Have fun."

Marnie backed out of the driveway and drove off. Waving, I watched her until she made a left onto a nearby street.

Whether I was depressed or not, I would call her later. Just to make sure TRULYACUTIE wasn't a nutcase pretending to be a nice guy.

For the first hour or so after Marnie left, I was perfectly fine. I was able to put my hurt on the back burner and cook a simple meal of grilled chicken and pasta. I ate at the kitchen table with the sounds of hip-hop blaring from my stereo. I didn't want to play anything soft and mellow, because alone with my thoughts, soft and mellow would remind me of the pain I was managing to keep under control.

Peaches sat beside my chair on the floor, looking up at me with dark, pleading eyes. I didn't normally feed her from the table so

as not to spoil her, but I dropped her a piece of chicken nonetheless. What the heck—I was in no mood to obey the rules when
my husband had broken the most important one.

Every so often as I ate, I glanced at the phone. The red light was
flashing, meaning there was at least one message.

Andrew?

I waited until I'd finished my food and had washed the dishes
before I finally placed the phone to my ear and punched in the code
to retrieve the messages. And when I did, my heart faltered at the
sound of Andrew's voice.

"Sophie, it's me. I'm checking in on you, hoping you're okay.
Call me, please. Let me know."

I erased the message and hung up the phone. The food I'd just
eaten turned in my stomach. Did Andrew think I'd spend one
night crying, wake up refreshed, and be ready to forgive him?

"Don't think about him," I told myself. And I certainly wasn't
going to call back.

I found myself walking to the spare bedroom and digging my
easel and art supplies out of the closet. It was a hobby that gave
me comfort, but one I didn't indulge in all that much anymore.
Definitely not in the past few months. Whenever I decided to
create a picture, Andrew complained that the smell of the paint
bothered him. As I stared at the dusty easel and paint-covered
sheets, I had to admit to myself that I painted far less these days
because it bothered Andrew, not because I didn't care for my
longtime hobby.

Well, Andrew wasn't here anymore.

I set to work. Two hours later, I had an abstract painting with
angry strokes of red and black in the center and muted yellows,
browns and oranges around the edges. I'd used a large piece of

paper rather than a cloth canvas, but I smiled as I stared at the painting as though I'd created a masterpiece.

Though the paper was still wet, I took it straight to the living room and taped it over the large wedding photo on the wall. Then I gathered the various framed photos of me and Andrew off the tables, carried them to the spare bedroom and deposited them in a large dresser drawer.

If only it were so easy to erase the memory of what he'd done.

4

Someone was stroking my calves.

Soft, flirty, circular strokes on my skin.

But who…? Confused, I opened my eyes and turned onto my back. In the darkened room, I could see his form at the foot of the bed, but I couldn't see his face. Yet his touch was familiar, and I didn't pull away.

The mattress squeaked as he eased onto it. His hands moved slowly up my legs, the tips of his fingers giving each part of my body they touched an electrical charge. He added his lips, pressing them to my knee. Then higher, on my thigh.

I wanted to protest, but the words wouldn't come. Not when the sensations flooding my body felt so good.

His mouth reached the apex of my thighs. So did his fingers. He fondled my pussy, spread my folds. Curled his fingers around my hips and buried his face in my center.

My eyelids fluttered. As he licked and suckled my pussy, I gripped fistfuls of the bedspread. I arched my hips, started to scream.

Suddenly his lips were gone.

His fingers were gone.

He was gone.

No, he was still here. Soft suckling sounds still filled the bedroom. And moans. A woman's moans.

And then I saw them. Andrew and a woman, beside me on the bed. The woman's breasts jiggled as she writhed around. Her mouth formed a wide *O*, her pleasure intense. Her legs were over his shoulders and he was eating her pussy, slurping and groaning. Loving every taste of her.

My eyes ventured to her toes. Though the room was dark, the red nail polish glistened. My gaze traveled the length of her body, from her arched feet to her bucking hips to her jiggling breasts.

To the perfect *O* formed on her lips.

The woman's eyes flew open then, meeting mine. She smiled.

I bolted upright, a cry escaping my throat. But then she was gone. Disoriented, my eyes flew around the rest of the room.

I was alone. Alone in my bed, my heart beating fast. My ragged breathing was the only sound in the still of the dark room.

My hand went to my throat. I was flushed. Aroused.

I'd been dreaming.

Exhaling slowly, I lay back down. I tried to get my heart to settle, but the dream had been so real. And startling.

For the next hour, I couldn't sleep. The images from the dream haunted me. Andrew pleasuring another woman with his tongue, the expression of pure bliss on her face. I know it was a dream, but the very nature of it disturbed me. Had me wondering exactly what Andrew had done with this other woman. How he'd touched her. If he'd tasted her. The sounds she'd made while coming. The sounds he'd made.

If their connection was more electric than ours.

I needed to know.

I didn't think I'd want to, but as I lay in bed in the dark, I realized there would be many nights like this. Nights when Andrew and this other woman came into my bed, the visions of what they could have done torturing me as surely as if I were witnessing their affair.

My imagination would be infinitely worse than knowing the truth.

That was what fueled me the next morning, got me out of bed early. I showered, got dressed and drove to the Pelican Resort.

Only to discover that Andrew wasn't there.

"What do you mean he's not here?" I asked Seth, the assistant manager.

"He's with the lawyers," Seth replied, looking confused, his tone saying he thought I knew this already.

"The lawyers?"

"Well, yes." He suddenly looked uncomfortable.

"What lawyers?"

Seth didn't respond.

"What lawyers?" I repeated.

A muscle in Seth's jaw flinched. "I thought you…" He paused. "You need to talk to Andrew about this."

"About what?" I asked anxiously, my stomach churning. So something bad *was* going on at work, something worse than the affair. Why hadn't Andrew told me?

Seth held up both hands, the only response he gave me. Then he walked behind the hotel's front desk counter and spoke to a young clerk.

She was blond, just like in my dream.

I turned away. Noticed Kathryn, the pretty receptionist who was an exotic mix of African-American and Chinese. She grinned my way, but I couldn't reciprocate.

Had Andrew fucked her?

I turned again. Saw another pretty woman, this one dressed as a hotel maid. With her looks, why was she cleaning hotels?

Was Andrew fucking her on the side?

The thoughts going through my mind were making me crazy, and unable to deal with them, I all but ran toward the front door. Once outside, I leaned against a column and gulped in humid air.

Lawyers? What was going on? And why hadn't Andrew told me about it?

I dug my cell phone out of my purse and dialed his cell. It went straight to voice mail, meaning it was shut off.

"Andrew," I said after the tone beeped, "I'm at the hotel. I came to see you, but you aren't here. I heard that you're meeting with lawyers?" My statement turned into a question. "What's going on?"

As I hung up, I found I was worried. Worried about Andrew and if the issue he was dealing with was a serious one. It didn't matter that he'd hurt me: my protective feelings for him surfaced, and I hoped he was okay.

Two hours later, when my cell phone rang and I saw Andrew's name on my caller ID, I quickly pressed the talk button. "Hello?"

"Sophie. Hi."

He sounded calm, and that set my heart at ease. I asked, "What's going on?"

"Where are you?"

"I'm at home."

"Good," Andrew said. "Can I come see you?"

"What's happening?"

"I'll tell you everything when I see you, if that's okay."

"All right." My concern returned. Andrew might sound calm, but the fact that he didn't want to tell me what was happening on the phone meant that whatever was going on was serious. "Are you coming now?"

"Yes."

I hung up, and spent the next twenty minutes worrying. I was in the living room, the cat on my lap, and I stroked her as much for my comfort as hers. The moment the front door opened, Peaches leapt to the floor. I stood to face Andrew as he walked into the living room.

He looked worn-out. There were dark circles under his eyes, and a tired expression on his face.

"Andrew?"

He tossed his keys onto the end table beside the sofa before meeting my gaze. "Hello."

"Why were you meeting with lawyers?" I asked, getting to the point. I didn't want to be kept in suspense. "Is someone suing the hotel?"

"Sit, please." Andrew motioned to the sofa.

I didn't argue. I sat, and he sat on the sofa beside me. The light smell of his musky cologne wafted into my nose, and part of me ached to touch him. I longed for the familiarity of his lips on mine.

But his touch wouldn't be familiar anymore, would it? He had tainted what we had when he had fucked someone else.

"I want you to know," he began, "that the only reason I didn't mention this before is…" He paused, fiddled with his hands. "It was bad enough telling you about the affair. I felt it was best to wait, give you a chance to deal with that first."

My stomach twisted at the word *affair*. But I tried to push the awful feeling aside and concentrate on the here and now—the legal issue Andrew was facing. I'm sure that some women, learning their husbands had cheated, wouldn't care if they got hit by a bus, or if they were struck with terminal cancer.

Clearly, I wasn't one of those women.

"There's no other way to say this," Andrew went on. "Someone has threatened a lawsuit against me."

"A lawsuit! Oh, my God." I reached for his hands, took them in mine. It was a reflexive act, but I didn't pull away. "Why?"

Andrew hesitated, lowered his gaze, then raised his eyes to meet mine. "She's claiming sexual harassment."

I narrowed my eyes as I stared at him, not understanding. It took a full five seconds for his words to register. And when they did, I jerked my hands away as though I'd been scalded.

It was one thing for Andrew to have met a woman in a bar and fucked her, but someone he worked with…

"You jerk." It was the only thing I could think of to say.

"She's lying, Sophie. She's the one who came on to me."

I slowly stood. "You fucking jerk. What are we talking here— millions of dollars? Are we going to lose our home because you couldn't keep your hands off this woman?"

"It wasn't like that," Andrew said. "If anything, I should be able to charge her with sexual harassment."

I snorted.

Andrew got to his feet, standing in front of me. "She's lying."

"You think that's what matters here—that she's lying? What matters is that you put yourself in the position to jeopardize not just our marriage, but our assets. All because you had to fuck someone else."

For several moments, neither of us spoke. The only thing to be heard was our loud, frustrated breathing and the cat's concerned meows.

"So you do work with this woman," I said.

Andrew nodded.

"How much does she want?"

"She came up with the crazy figure of five million dollars."

"Are you serious?"

"She wanted me to leave you, I wouldn't, and I told her it was best she find another job," Andrew explained hurriedly. "That's when she claimed sexual harassment."

I shook my head, disgusted. "So we're going to lose everything."

"She hasn't sued—yet. She's threatening to."

"If you don't leave me," I said. A statement, not a question.

"I…I guess." Andrew threw his hands in the air. "I don't know what's going on in her warped mind."

I turned away from Andrew, rethinking my earlier position on how I'd feel if he got hit by a bus. A million thoughts going through my mind, I wandered toward the window that faced the backyard.

I looked out at our deck. Two years ago, we'd added a gazebo and a hot tub, but we hardly used either. We had everything we needed for romantic nights and weekends right here, and yet our romance had fallen by the wayside.

"Maybe you should," I began slowly. I turned. "Maybe you should go to her."

"No!" Andrew protested. "I don't want her!"

"If it will stop her from suing you…" I said the words, but I didn't really mean them.

Andrew rushed toward me. I didn't move. Not even as he placed both hands on my shoulders.

"I don't want her," he repeated. "Yeah, I screwed up. I learned my lesson the hardest way possible, but I'm going to make this right."

I said nothing. I felt only numb.

"I think I know how to make her go away. Make the problem go away. I got some good advice from my lawyers."

I said nothing.

"Say something, Sophie. Please."

"What do you want from me?"

"I want your forgiveness. I know it won't be today. Maybe not tomorrow. But I want to know that at some point in the future, we'll be back to normal."

"I don't know if that's possible."

Andrew nodded grimly as he lowered his hands from my shoulders.

"I hope she was worth it," I said softly.

My eyes blurring with tears, I pushed past Andrew to the kitchen. I opened a cupboard, pulled out the first mug I saw, which happened to be one we'd had specially made with our photo on it. Before I could place the mug on the counter, Andrew was there, taking it from my hands.

"I've never wanted anything more than I want your forgiveness," he said. "I know you're angry. And you have every right to be. But these past few days without you have been the worst days of my life. I still love you. And I don't want to lose you. I'll do whatever it takes to get you back. If that means we're not together for a few months, so be it, but I need to know I've got a reason to hope. Hell, if you want to have an affair to even the score, do it if that's what you need to do. Do it and then come back to me and let's move on."

"So now you want to pimp me out to someone else?" I asked, aghast at the suggestion.

"No! Of course not. But I hurt you. Maybe in a situation like this you need to hurt me back."

"You need to go now."

"I don't want to leave. Not like this."

"*Now.*"

Andrew stared at me, but my hard expression gave him no cause for hope. Sighing in frustration, he turned. He made the short walk to the hall table where he'd deposited his keys, scooped them up, then walked past me to the front door.

The moment the front door clicked shut, I hurled the mug against the fridge, shattering it into a thousand pieces.

5

I was on my second glass of wine when I called Marnie.

"Hello?" she said sweetly.

"It's only me, Sophie, not TRULYACUTIE."

"Hey, Soph."

"What are you doing tonight?"

"Nothing special."

"Good. Then we should go out. Somewhere hot and happening. Maybe even CityWalk at Universal Studios, where all the tourists go hoping to get laid."

"You all right?"

"But you'll have to pick me up, okay? Cuz I'm already drinking and a little fucked-up."

"Sophie—"

"Whenever you're ready." I hung up.

Forty minutes later, Marnie was at my door. "Hey, girl!" I trilled, and pulled her into a hug. "Ready to party?"

Breaking the hug, she took a step backward and eyed me with concern. "What the heck is going on?"

"You mean besides the news that Andrew's slut is suing him for five million dollars?"

Marnie stepped into the house and closed the door behind her. "Oh, my God."

"No, it's fine." I waved off her concern. "I've got it all figured out. Andrew can go live with her so she doesn't sue him for everything, and I can fuck someone else—with my husband's blessing, even."

"Okay, you're making no sense."

"Time's a-wasting." I wiggled my hips. "Let's go par-tay!"

Marnie took me by the hand and led me to the kitchen, where she deposited me on a chair at the table.

"What are you doing?" I protested.

"First of all, it's five-thirty, way too early to go partying. Secondly, you're drunk. And third, you need to back the fuck up and explain what you just said. Andrew is being sued?"

My false bravado crumbled, and I burst into tears. Of course, the wine I'd consumed helped my tears flow a little easier.

I told Marnie everything that Andrew had told me. She got a box of Kleenex off of the nearby counter and put it in front of me. I pulled out a wad, wiped my eyes and blew my nose.

"I'm sorry you have to go through all this shit," Marnie said.

"The good news is, he still loves me and still wants our marriage." I snorted in derision. "Lucky me."

Marnie rolled her eyes. "What is it with men? They can have affairs and we're supposed to be grateful when they decide they still want us?"

I blew my nose again.

"Can I get you anything?" Marnie asked. "And no, not more wine. How about coffee?"

"Okay." I nodded. "That'll sober me up until we go out later."

"You still want to go out?"

"Absolutely. I need to listen to music, dance. Drink some more." At the mention of alcohol, my stomach turned. "And eat something," I quickly said. "Something starchy, like bread or crackers. Popcorn! Do you mind making some?"

"Popcorn?" Marnie sounded surprised.

"It's in the second cupboard from the right."

"Okeydoke."

First, Marnie set about making a fresh pot of coffee. Then she put a bag of popcorn in the microwave and, three minutes later, she was pouring it into two bowls. She passed one to me and put the other one at her place on the table. The popcorn taken care of, she poured two cups of coffee.

"You want cream and sugar?" she asked.

I shook my head. "Right now, I need it black."

Carrying both mugs of steaming black coffee, Marnie rejoined me at the table.

"Thank you," I told her. "What would I do without you?"

"Lucky for you, you don't have to find out."

I sipped the coffee. It was strong. Perfect. "Take my mind off my problems—tell me about your date."

"Are you sure?"

"Of course I'm sure. Do you like TRULYACUTIE?"

"I do. I wasn't expecting anything, but there was a little spark. I think. At least on my part."

"Have you talked today?"

"No. But he said he'd call. Or e-mail. However—" She grinned, then reached across the table to give my hand a comforting squeeze. "I already turned off my cell phone, because tonight, you and I are hanging out."

I smiled softly as I squeezed her hand in return. I could always count on Marnie. I'd learned that in eighth grade when she'd let me copy her answers on a math quiz after I'd forgotten to study. The teacher had caught her angling her paper towards me and, as a result, flunked us both. Instead of being unhappy, Marnie had shrugged off the incident, saying, "If you can't help your friends, what good are you?"

That sealed the deal for me, and we'd been best friends ever since.

Marnie's expression suddenly grew wistful. "I know you still love Andrew. How can you not? Unfortunately, our hearts don't come with an on/off switch. But sweetie, you deserve better, and with what he's putting you through…I'd be seeing a divorce lawyer. Like yesterday."

I nodded, but I only half agreed. What Marnie said about me deserving better was true, I knew that. But she was also right about our hearts not having an on/off switch.

Life wasn't black and white. Love wasn't black and white. I didn't know if I'd ever stop loving Andrew. But just because I might always love him didn't mean we had to be together.

"You want to know what the icing on the cake is?" I asked after a moment. "Andrew told me that if I wanted to, I could have an affair to even the score."

Marnie stopped chewing her popcorn. "What?"

"How thoughtful of him, huh?"

"Right," Marnie said sarcastically.

"I don't know if he meant it," I went on. "He was likely just rambling. He seemed to be saying anything that might get me to tell him I'd forgive him."

We ate in silence for a while longer, and Marnie's eyes wandered. After a moment, her eyebrows rose. "I see you have a new wedding picture."

I followed her gaze and saw the painting I'd put up over my wedding portrait. "It was quicker than taking it down," I explained.

"And helpful if you bring a man home home." A beat passed. "Would you?"

"Would I screw some other guy to even the score?" I asked, my tone saying it was definitely something I would *not* consider.

Marnie dropped popcorn into her mouth and chewed. "Maybe you should."

"What?"

"Hear me out. And I'm not saying you should go fuck some other guy to even the score. But maybe it's a good idea to see what else is out there," she said tentatively. "You've been with Andrew for ten years. Twenty when you started dating, twenty-two when you married. Maybe, just maybe, he isn't the man you're supposed to be with for the rest of your life."

I didn't say anything. I wasn't sure I could contemplate moving on—at least not yet.

"Do you want him to move back in right now?"

"No."

"Do you think your marriage is going to be the same even if you do work things out?"

I shook my head. I couldn't imagine our marriage ever being the same. Not after this.

"I stayed in my marriage much longer than I should have, hoping Keith would stop cheating and realize that he loved me. At the time, I didn't think I could be happy without him. I was so stupid. The truth is, the day I let him go was the best day of my life. Have I found my knight in shining armor yet? Maybe not, but fuck, it's far better to be alone than to be with someone who doesn't respect you."

"With all due respect," I began slowly, "this is the first time Andrew has cheated."

Marnie gave me a look. I wasn't sure if it was pity or something else.

"That's what he said. And I...I believe him."

Marnie shrugged.

"You knew Keith was cheating on you. You always told me you felt it. You'd find phone numbers stuffed in his pockets, lipstick on his collar..."

"And some guys are smarter than Keith ever was."

"Marnie, that's not what I need to hear right now."

She held up both hands. "All right. Forget about Andrew and whether or not this was the first time he cheated. My whole point is that you need to start concentrating on *you*. On what *you* need, on what's good for *you*. What if what's good for you is fresh cock?" She wriggled her eyebrows.

"Marnie!" I slapped her hand, and she laughed. I laughed, too.

"First of all, dating someone else will be a good way to take your mind off Andrew. And who knows, you just might meet the man of your dreams while you're at it."

"Marnie—"

"And if not...it's been ten years and you've only had sex with one man."

"That's what happens when you're married."

"Tell that to guys," Marnie mumbled.

I made a face.

"Bottom line, if all you get out of this is another sexual experience...is that so bad? It might even help."

I stood. "Okay. Enough about my marriage."

"What are you doing?" Marnie asked as I started to walk out of the kitchen.

"Going to take two Advil before we head out for dinner. Because if I'm going to continue to drown my sorrows in alcohol, I'm going to need more than popcorn in my stomach."

Marnie smiled.

"And the last thing I want is a migraine if I might possibly meet the man of my dreams tonight."

Now Marnie laughed. "That's the spirit."

I continued to the bedroom. I didn't really plan on meeting anyone, but I was up for a fun evening of music and dancing.

There was no point spending the night alone in an empty house that would only remind me of Andrew.

6

As Marnie drove us to CityWalk, I couldn't help thinking about her words.

And Andrew's unorthodox suggestion.

Maybe my friend was right. Maybe I needed to see what else was out there, experience being with a new man before I decided what I'd do next. At the very least, I needed a diversion. Something to distract me from thoughts of Andrew cheating and the possible lawsuit his scorned lover might launch against him.

The more I mulled over the idea, the more it appealed to me. After all, I'd given Andrew no reason to cheat. I loved him. I did as much as I could to be the best wife possible. And we got along well, even if the passion of our earlier years had waned.

If he'd wanted to recharge that passion, he could have suggested something to me. Anything, really. It wasn't as if Andrew and I couldn't talk.

That's what made his cheating even harder to accept. That he wasn't the type of man I expected would betray me before talking to me about a problem.

"Do you think he isn't attracted to me anymore?" I suddenly asked.

Marnie glanced at me as if I were crazy. "What?"

"You know. Maybe he wanted me decked out in miniskirts and tank tops all the time or something."

"Now this is what bugs me. Women always end up blaming themselves when their man cheats. Trust me, I know." Marnie stopped at a light, then made a right turn. "You're beautiful, sexy, and if Andrew cheated, he's the one with the problem—not you. That's my whole point about seeing what else is out there. Another man—the kind who'd never betray you—might just sweep you off your feet."

"And I thought you were such a cynic," I teased.

"How many people are on the planet? Five billion? At least a few of those guys have to be decent and trustworthy. Oh—and hot as hell." Marnie grinned devilishly, as though that last qualification was the most important.

"Of course," Marnie continued, "if you decide just to look, that's perfectly fine. A little eye candy never hurt nobody."

"If nothing else, I'm going to have a good time tonight. You always make me laugh."

We decided on BB King's Blues Club, since we could kill two birds with one stone there—enjoy authentic Southern cuisine while listening to a live band.

I was dressed to the nines, in a short black skirt and low-cut red top that had heads turning as I stepped into the club. Marnie was wearing a leopard print dress that showed off her voluptuous curves. I'd been determined to head out and find a little action, but I halted, suddenly unsure.

"Hey," Marnie said in a low voice. "It's okay. You don't have to do anything you don't want to do." Knowing me as well as she did, she'd clearly picked up on my hesitation. "And there's no guilt if you *do* choose to go for what you want. If you meet someone you like, think of it as a freebie."

A freebie...it was an odd way to look at having an affair. And yet, Andrew had given me not only his blessing but his encouragement to go out and even the score.

"Right." I rolled my shoulders backward to work out some of the tension, then smiled when the hostess appeared and asked if we wanted a table or to sit at the bar.

"A table," Marnie said. "Close to the stage, if possible."

At seven-thirty, we were seated at a table near the stage. At eight, the band began to play. Flip Side, a group of three men in their thirties and one woman with long dreads of about the same age, started their set off with "The Thrill is Gone," B.B. King's duet with Tracy Chapman, which warmed the crowd. Then they played some classic B.B. King numbers, some Ray Charles, Ida Cox and other blues artists from the early twentieth century. By the time they rocked the house with some Jimi Hendrix rock 'n' roll blues, everyone was either dancing, clapping or toe tapping.

When the female singer announced that there would be an intermission before the next set, Marnie touched my hand. I looked her way. "Have you noticed a certain someone checking you out?" she asked.

"No," I replied, and began looking around. I caught the eye of an older gentleman, who winked at me. I returned my gaze to Marnie. "Who are you talking about?"

"You really have been out of the game too long," she said. "The drummer," she went on, in a tone that said the answer was obvious.

"The drummer?" I quickly looked toward the stage.

"Isn't he cute?"

I checked him out. He was thin, tall, and sported short dread-locks. "Yes, he's definitely cute. But not really my type."

Marnie gaped at me. "What are you talking about? He's hot."

"Yeah…just not my type."

"I don't think he'd agree," Marnie said in a singsong voice.

"You're seeing things," I told Marnie. "He didn't check me out once."

"He totally was," Marnie insisted. "You should go talk to him. I think he'd make a good booty call."

I glanced toward the stage. There was a flock of women swarming the band. I shook my head at the pitiable sight. All those women hoping to bed a musician, or maybe even find a sugar daddy.

That wasn't for me.

"Marnie, stop worrying about my sex life. I'm out having a good time. That's all that matters."

"Oh, no-no-no." She wagged a finger at me. "You're gonna meet someone."

Rolling my eyes, I laughed. "Sure, whatever you say."

My gaze wandered around the bar. There were some attractive men here, but most of them were with dates. I wasn't against the idea of meeting someone, if a guy here got me excited.

And maybe Marnie was right. I *had* married Andrew young. Until a few days ago, I'd never questioned that decision. But what if Andrew's affair was a sign that we'd drifted apart, that we weren't meant to live happily ever after?

What if there was someone else out there for me—the kind of man who would always appreciate me and never screw around?

I'd had friends in the past who'd been cheated on, and I always encouraged them to move on and find someone worthy of them. And yet, the thought of being without Andrew was very hard to contemplate.

But it was equally hard to think that I would simply accept what he'd done, forgive him and resume our life as it had been. Especially now. Would I be setting myself up for future heartache from him if I decided I wanted to save my marriage? Would he feel that if I'd forgiven him once, I would do so again…and again?

"I'm ready for another drink," Marnie announced, her words pulling me from my thoughts. "Want another margarita?"

"Definitely," I answered quickly. I'd certainly had enough already, but I didn't want to think about Andrew anymore. Booze would help me forget.

As Marnie glanced around in search of our waitress, I spotted the older gentleman I'd seen eyeing me before. This time, I noticed that he was with a friend.

Both he and his friend were grinning at me now. A wink from the shorter man, and they started walking our way.

"Warning," I said. "Creep alert."

"Where?"

"Don't look!" I said in an urgent whisper as Marnie started to turn her head. She abruptly halted. "Two guys who have to be in their sixties. Now they're heading this way. Shit."

"Just what I like," Marnie muttered. "Old men with hard-ons."

"They're definitely interested in us." I could see them getting closer through my peripheral vision. As they reached our table, I whispered, "Showtime."

"Hello, ladies," the shorter man said. He was probably five foot nine, with a medium brown complexion and a beer gut. He also seemed to have eyes only for me. "How about a dance?"

"Sorry," Marnie said sweetly. "We were just about to order dessert."

"We don't mind waiting," the other man said. He was darker skinned, taller, and quite handsome—but about thirty years too old for either of us. "We can show you a thing or two on the dance floor."

"I'm married," I pointed out. "Sorry."

"Thanks for the offer, though," Marnie said. She barely suppressed a smile as she added, "We're flattered."

"All right," the taller man conceded. "But if you change your mind..."

"We won't," Marnie told him.

The two men wandered off. Marnie made a face, then burst out laughing.

"In their defense, they did seem nice," I said. I'd assumed they'd be creeps because so often creeps approached me.

"Yeah, but you know they've got to be back at the nursing home by nine."

"Marnie!"

"I've got nothing against old people. Just old people who think I'm going to sleep with them. If I'm going to fuck someone, he's going to be young, hot and able to maintain an erection."

"Enough, Marnie." I shook my head. "Let's hit the dance floor."

Marnie and I worked our way to the dance floor in front of the stage. I noticed our two suitors talking to two women younger than Marnie and me. At least they took rejection well.

Marnie shook her hips to the rock 'n' roll beat. "Ooh, he's cute."

I didn't bother looking at the guy she was referring to. Marnie's eyes continued to bounce over the crowd. She was clearly on the prowl, but I suspected more for herself than for me.

No sooner were we shaking our butts on the dance floor to the latest Beyoncé hit than Marnie leaned close and whispered, "Oh, over there. He's pretty hot."

She pointed, and I followed the direction of her finger. I saw a guy who was probably twenty-two, with a decent build, and a very attractive face.

Seeing me, he smiled. And revealed a mouth full of gold teeth.

"Ew!" Marnie and I proclaimed at the same time.

"Okay, so he's a negative," Marnie said. "But there'll be someone else."

Halfway through the song, Marnie raised her eyebrows at me. I wondered what she was trying to tell me—until I felt someone's hand on my arm.

I glanced over my shoulder at the stranger, saw a teddy bear of a man with dark skin. Normally, I would have pulled away from him. Like I'd pulled away from the men in the Bahamas who'd wanted to dance with me. But this time, I didn't pull away.

I shook my butt against his groin, having some fun with teasing him. He grew hard in an instant, his cock now pressing against the top of my ass. Before, I would have been wary of this and backed off. But tonight, his erection turned me on, reminding me that I was a desirable woman.

Something Andrew had forgotten.

I got bolder, bending forward slightly while pushing my ass harder against him. He planted his hands on my hips and pulled me against his cock, and as we danced, our bodies moved like we were fucking with clothes on.

"Sweet Jesus," the man said.

Giggling, I turned to face him. He was grinning at me as though I were the sexiest woman in the world. The look lifted my spirits. Yes, I was beautiful and sexy and had a hell of a lot to offer.

We continued to dance close, but not too close this time, our hips pumping to the fast beat. At the end of the second song, I leaned forward and patted the man's arm in a friendly gesture. "Thanks for the dance," I said.

"You're gonna leave a brother hanging like that?"

I shrugged apologetically. "I'm married."

"Married?" He sounded surprised. "Damn, girl."

"I know," I said, a hint of self-chastising in my voice. "I guess I got carried away. But, yes, I am a married woman. Out having a little bit of fun."

"That's it?" His eyebrows lifted hopefully.

"Yes. That's it."

"All right." The man nodded his understanding. "Lucky man."

I turned around and saw Marnie, who was standing with two margaritas in hand. She must have gotten them while I'd been dancing.

"Having fun?" she asked, offering me a drink.

"Yes," I answered honestly. I sipped the new magarita. "And I made a decision about something," I found myself saying.

"Oh?"

"If I meet someone, I'm gonna go for it."

"Woo-hoo!" Marnie gave me a high five, and I had to quickly steady my glass so my drink didn't spill. "Does that mean you like that guy?"

"No. Not him. He's nice, but…he's more fun. I want someone who makes me hot with one look."

One dance, and I was in the mood to get lucky. One dance had reminded me that I was a beautiful woman with a lot to offer. A woman who didn't deserve to have her husband cheat on her.

Andrew had said I should even the score. Marnie said I should see if there was a better match out there for me.

Well, I would at least even the playing field. If I was ever going to forgive Andrew, I needed to do this.

And satisfy my own curiosity in the process.

I'd been with only one other man before Andrew, and the experience had been horrendous. Chad, my high school boyfriend. I'd been into him, but I wasn't in love. Partway during some heavy foreplay I told him I didn't think I could go through with having sex. He ignored me, got rougher, and took my virginity despite my cries to get off me.

My experience with Andrew had been totally different. He hadn't pressured me the way Chad had. Instead, he'd taken his time and waited until I was truly ready. If, while kissing, he sensed any hesitation on my part, he pulled away. I really loved that about him, and when I gave Andrew my heart and my body after eight months of dating, I knew that it would be forever.

The memory hurt, and I downed my drink. Then eyed the men in the crowd.

With Andrew having been my only positive sexual experience, I'd naturally been curious about what it might be like to be intimate with another man. Curious, but not tempted.

Until now.

Marnie flagged down a passing waitress with a tray of pink-colored shooters. She bought two.

"I don't know, Marnie."

"If we get too drunk, we'll call a cab." She offered me the shooter.

"Absolutely." I took the glass, and on the count of three, we both downed the shots.

I don't even know what the alcohol was, but it had a citrusy tang to it. It warmed my insides, and made my buzz come back with full force.

The sounds of Wyclef Jean filled the club, and my inhibitions gone, I threw my hands in the air and seductively moved my body.

"Girl, you are getting some serious attention," Marnie informed me. "You should see all the guys checking you out."

I glanced around coyly, noticed several eyes staring my way. But I didn't notice anyone who got my libido going, and I was starting to wonder if I would.

"That guy right there," Marnie said, pointing through the crowd of people to a man that was hard to miss. He was tall, and had muscles all over from what I could tell. He was dark skinned and handsome, but I didn't feel a spark of attraction as I stole a glance at him.

I shook my head. "No."

"You are being way too picky."

"It has to be the right guy," I said. It wasn't hard for a woman to find a man to fuck. All she had to do was ask. But I didn't want to bed just anyone. It had to be a guy who gave me butterflies in the pit of my stomach.

I continued dancing, gyrating my hips in a motion meant to seduce. I knew guys were watching me. Their blatant stares made me remember that, at my core, I was a sexy woman.

I made my hip movements even sexier. Thanks to the alcohol, I was feeling good. No pain, as they say.

When the beat picked up with an Usher tune, I gripped my skirt in both hands and shimmied my dress around my legs, showing off tempting amounts of skin. My eyes were closed, my head moving from side to side.

"Damn, girl," a male voice said, and I opened my eyes. "You're fittin' to give a brother a heart attack."

I smiled graciously at the man I'd danced with earlier. He brazenly licked his bottom lip as I kept dancing.

He leaned in close. "Your husband know you dance like this when he ain't around?"

I didn't answer, just shook my hips.

"You look like you want a little something something," the teddy bear whispered. "I can give you what you need."

I wondered if my desire for sex was painted on my forehead.

"I'm just here to have fun," I said, reiterating what I'd told the man earlier. From behind the man, I could see Marnie giving me two thumbs up.

"I can show you fun." He placed a hand on my waist.

"That's no way to speak to a married woman," I teased.

"What's your name?" he asked.

"Sophie. Yours?"

"Teddy."

No way. I started to laugh.

"What's so funny?" he asked.

"Just that…I was thinking you kind of look like a teddy bear, and here your name is Teddy." I shrugged when Teddy didn't crack a smile. "Maybe it's not that funny after all."

I soon realized why he hadn't smiled. Because he was seriously checking me out. The look Teddy gave me was smoldering. It traveled over my face, paused on my lips, then went lower, to my breasts. It screamed "I want to fuck you."

"You never step out on your man?" Teddy asked.

I smiled sweetly, hoping he'd take my rejection well. I was starting to get a tad worried, wondering if this guy wasn't the type who liked to hear *no*. "Like I said, I'm just here to dance and have a little fun."

"All right." Teddy shrugged, and I was relieved. Knowing he'd lost the fight, he wandered away.

As he disappeared into the crowd, I asked myself what was wrong with him? He was cute, had a nice body. Most women wouldn't kick him out of bed in the morning. So why was I rejecting him?

Maybe I was deluding myself. Perhaps I was all talk in terms of thinking I could have an affair, when in reality I wouldn't be able to go through with it.

Marnie leaned her head in close. "Seriously, Soph, what's wrong with him? He could have me in a bear hug all night long and I wouldn't complain. Not one bit."

"Maybe I should go."

"Don't be so hasty. The night is young. And don't forget, you're not looking for a new husband. Just someone to give you a night of endless orgasms."

As I started to laugh, I felt someone's eyes on me. As surely as if someone had reached out and touched me.

Slowly, I turned. Got a jolt when my eyes connected with his.

And in that instant, I knew.

He was the one.

7

As my eyes made contact with the sexy stranger's, the corners of his mouth lifted in the slightest of smiles. It wasn't a polite smile, but the kind that seemed to say *I want you.*

My heart fluttered as I returned his smile. Then I elbowed Marnie. "I think I'm in business. Over there. The guy with the dark hair hanging past his shoulders."

"Ooh, the one who looks a bit like Antonio Banderas? I didn't know you were into Spanish guys."

Now that Marnie mentioned it, yes, he did look a bit like Antonio Banderas, but with slightly darker skin. He looked black, but mixed with another race. Maybe white. Maybe Hispanic. All that mattered to me was that he was hot, and that he was the first guy I'd had a connection with tonight.

"I haven't been into any guy besides my husband," I pointed out.

"Whatever you do, don't mention the word 'husband' when that guy gets here. Cuz honey, with the way he's looking at you, you know he'll be here any second."

I met the man's gaze again. Even though he was about twenty feet away, I could see the lust simmering in his eyes.

Lust for me.

That reality turned me on.

I swallowed, knowing that I was feeling the same lust. This was the connection I'd been hoping to find. Something instantaneous, and electric.

And yet, this was foreign territory. I hadn't allowed myself to feel sexual attraction for another man in the past ten years.

The man started toward me, and my heart thundered in my chest. The very fact that I hadn't been with another man in ten years suddenly got to me, making me nervous. Would my heart really let me go through with this, even though my brain said I should?

"Shit, Marnie. He's heading over here. What do I say? Maybe having an affair is really a crazy idea."

"You say hi," Marnie told me, and gave me a little shove.

I stumbled slightly into the man's path, feeling like an idiot as I did so. I shot an annoyed look over my shoulder at Marnie, who gave me a false apologetic look.

Then I drew in a breath and turned back to the man.

"Hello," he said. He had some sort of accent. Maybe Marnie was right and he was Spanish.

"Hi," I responded. "How are you tonight?" *Duh!* Couldn't I have thought of something more intriguing to say?

He chuckled softly. "I'm well. And you?"

"Oh, I'm feeling pretty good." Okay, I had to stop drinking. I sounded like an idiot.

The man's eyes roamed over me from head to toe, and I got the feeling that no matter how foolish I sounded, he wasn't going anywhere.

"You are very beautiful," he said simply. But his eyes said he wanted to have me for dessert.

"Thank you."

"May I buy you another drink?"

"Oh, no." I waved off the suggestion. "I think I've had enough."

"You're sure?"

"Well, maybe one more wouldn't hurt," I said, backtracking. My nerves had me babbling. That, and the realization that if I was actually going to have an affair, I could use some more liquid courage.

"Strawberry margarita?" he asked.

"How did you know that?"

"I noticed," he replied, making me wonder if he'd been watching me for longer than I'd realized, or if he'd simply made a lucky guess.

"I'll be right back," he said, and started for the bar.

I watched him go, butterflies dancing up a storm in my stomach. He was sexy, no doubt about it. He also had a mysterious quality about him. Something that was a little dark.

And a lot tempting.

"Girl, if you don't like him," Marnie said into my ear.

"I do," I responded. "He looks like exactly what I need. Very different from Andrew." Which was important. I didn't want to fuck a guy who would have me thinking about my husband. I wanted someone different. A guy who didn't wear a suit and tie every day. A guy who looked like he had a bit of a bad boy in him.

That was the man who wore a devilish grin as he approached me carrying two frosty drinks. He wore black jeans and a white shirt that was unbuttoned to the mid part of his chest. He had no chest hair that I could see, but perhaps closer to his navel…

"One drink for you," he said, handing one to me. "And one for your friend."

"Why thank you," Marnie said, accepting the drink.

"Yes, thank you," I echoed. And it was nice of him to buy a drink for Marnie. It was a small thing, but the last time I'd been out with Marnie and Andrew, Andrew had asked Marnie for cash before heading to the bar to buy her drink. I'd been embarrassed that he couldn't fork out the cash to buy a drink for my friend.

Andrew could be very frugal—and not just where Marnie was concerned. He said it was because we were saving for a family. I understood the argument but missed the romantic gestures of our early days. He no longer did spontaneous romantic things like send me flowers on occasion or surprise me with my favorite perfume.

"What's your name?" the man asked.

"Sophie," I replied. "Yours?"

"Pietro. But you can call me Peter."

"Pietro? What is that?"

"Italian," he responded.

"Aww. I guess that means you're Italian." *Brilliant deduction, Sophie.* I sipped the margarita, though I clearly didn't need it.

He nodded. "And you are stunning. I'm sorry if I can't stop staring at you. I've simply never met a woman more beautiful."

I'd been married for eight years, and out of the game, as Marnie had said. But I still knew a line when I heard one. And yet, my vagina throbbed at the compliment nonetheless. It was the way he was looking at me that had me believing everything he said. His eyes had an intensity that was both unnerving and thrilling. I had the feeling that he could look inside my mind and see everything I was thinking.

Everything I wanted.

"To be exact, I am part African, part Italian."

"And part hot," I blurted out, then laughed at my uncharacteristic boldness.

He reached for my hand. I let him hold it. "You're not shy, are you?"

"What I am is a little drunk." I swayed slightly, proving my point. "Say something to me in Italian. Anything."

"*Tu guardi bella.*"

"That sounds nice," I said, impressed. "What does it mean?"

"It means you look beautiful."

Peter's eyes were steadfast on mine. The heat in his gaze literally warmed my skin.

"Are you married?" he asked.

My eyes narrowed as I looked up at Peter. "Why would you ask that?"

He ran the pad of his thumb over the base of my bare ring finger. "You used to wear a ring there. Am I right?"

I laughed nervously. "Are you psychic?"

"No. I'm interested."

Peter got to the point in a way I liked—a lot. I sipped some of my drink. "Thank you for the drink."

"You said that already."

"I did, didn't I?"

Peter leaned his lips close to my ear, so close they almost touched my skin. "Did he hurt you—your husband?"

Was he particularly astute, or did every betrayed woman out on the town act the way I was, to the point where it was a cliché?

"Did he?" Peter repeated.

I wasn't sure what to say. I didn't want a commitment with this man. Only a night of delicious sex. "Yes, he hurt me," I said, answering honestly. "But I'm out tonight because I want to forget all about that."

"I can help you forget."

From any other man, I would consider this conversation extremely forward. But perhaps Peter had known just by looking at me that I would welcome his advances.

That I needed him to make the first move.

"Yes," I agreed. "I suppose you can."

During our conversation, we'd been mildly moving our bodies to the music. Now, Peter wrapped his arms around me and pulled me close. Though a fast song was playing, he gyrated his hips against mine—slowly. His erection left nothing to the imagination.

I matched his movements, my own slow and seductive. I wasn't thinking, only feeling, and this felt right.

Balancing the drink in my hand, I turned so that my ass was now against Peter's cock. I shook my ass against him, and grinned when a primal groan escaped his throat.

My drink was in the way. I took a few steps to a nearby table and plopped it down. Then I danced my way back to Peter, my hands in the air, my hips moving left to right.

He met me, and together we danced, this time keeping up with the fast rhythm. His fingers moved up and down my arms, leaving delicious sensations in their wake. He stroked my face, dipped his mouth close to mine. Pulled his face away without kissing me.

So the man was a tease.

I stroked his chest through his shirt, then with the tip of one finger dared to touch his exposed skin. I let my other hand wander lower, and Peter's eyes widened in both surprise and expectation. I pulled my hand away before it reached his groin.

Peter laughed, slipped his hands around my waist. "I want to take you home."

"I want you to take me home," I replied.

Everything was easy between us. Easy and electric. I'd even for-gotten all about Marnie while flirting with Peter on the dance floor. I glanced around, but didn't see her.

The band was back onstage, preparing for their next set. "This is a good time to leave," Peter said.

"I'm just looking for my friend," I said. "Will you excuse me for a minute?"

Peter nodded. "Of course."

I looked around the club but didn't see Marnie anywhere. I found myself strolling toward the restrooms.

It was crowded inside, but I spotted Marnie immediately. She was in front of a mirror at the far end of the restroom.

I made my way over to her, and her face lit up when she saw me. "Hey, girl!"

"Everything okay?" I asked.

She planted a hand on a hip. "Girl, you missed the drama."

My eyes widened in alarm. "What happened?"

"Some asshole made a play for me. You remember the guy with the gold teeth?"

"What did he do?"

Marnie applied face powder. "Stuck his hand down my top."

"What?" I asked, outraged.

"It's okay. I told him if he ever touched me again, I'd break all his fingers one by one."

I smiled. My friend had balls bigger than most guys'.

"Then Walt and Denny came over and gave the guy a talking-to. Told him he needed to learn to respect women."

"Hold up," I said. "Walt and Denny?"

Marnie rested her hip against the sink as she faced me. "The two older guys who were checking us out."

"Wait a minute—the ones you were making fun of for being old? Now you're on a first-name basis with them?"

Marnie produced her lipstick from her purse. "Actually, they're very sweet. And Denny—the taller one—is quite something on the dance floor. We're having a good time."

I shook my head, but I was grinning.

"A *platonic* time, of course," Marnie stressed. "Walt and Denny are nothing like the hottie who's all over you." Marnie paused, pressed her lips together to even out her lipstick. "It looks like everything is going very well with him."

"He said he wants to take me home."

"When are you leaving?"

I hesitated. In the heat of the moment, I'd been ready to leave with Peter. But now that I was talking with Marnie, I was suddenly having doubts.

"Maybe I shouldn't," I said. "I don't have a car, which means I'd have to leave with him...and is that smart?"

"You're considering fucking him but you don't want to leave with him?"

"Not so loud, please," I whispered, glancing around. The other women were either applying makeup or hanging around chatting. Women's restrooms were about so much more than using the toilets.

"You don't think he's a creep, do you?"

"No," I answered easily. "But you know, I haven't done this, like ever. I want to be smart."

Marnie nodded. "Okay, the way I see it, you have a couple options. One—there's the Hard Rock Hotel across the way. You can spend the night there. Or, I can drive you to this guy's place. Just make sure to casually slip in that your friend is a cop. That should do the trick."

"I like the hotel idea." This was only going to be a one-night stand, not the start of forever. We could fuck each other, then leave in the morning and never have to see each other again.

"You have money for a cab?" Marnie asked.

"Yes, I've got cash." I always had a good amount of money in my wallet. Andrew had drummed into my head the necessity of having cash on hand in case of an emergency.

Marnie put her makeup back into her purse and snapped it shut. "I'll drive you."

"Are you sure?"

"I had a couple tall glasses of water and now my buzz is gone. I'm good to go."

"What about Walt and Denny?" I asked.

Marnie laughed. "I think they'll be fine without me."

We exited the bathroom. I glanced around, but didn't see Peter anywhere. I frowned. "I don't see him."

"He's got to be around somewhere," Marnie said.

"You know what—let's just go."

"What?"

"He's not here…maybe that's a sign."

"But he could be in the rest—"

"I've made up my mind." I wrapped my fingers around Marnie's forearm and steered her toward the club's exit. Now that Peter was nowhere to be found, I was taking the chicken's way out.

"Oh, all right." Marnie sounded disappointed.

"I thought I was ready, but…" My voice trailed off. But what? Why was I running?

The answer came to me in the next instant. I was running because I was afraid of the intense reaction I was having to Peter. How easily a man who wasn't my husband turned me on and made me want to get naked.

A man who was a stranger.

When we stepped outside, the air was warm and moist, but far more refreshing than the sweat-filled air in the club. My head swayed a little, reminding me that I'd had too much to drink. Marnie offered me her arm, and we began to walk.

We strolled past the various clubs along CityWalk, passing giggling groups of young women in skimpy clothes. Their night was just beginning, while I was headed home.

Sexually frustrated.

"Sophie!"

Marnie stopped abruptly. Her face lit up. "Did you hear that?"

I did, and my stomach jumped. Slowly, I turned, secretly excited that Peter had followed me out.

But when I saw who'd called me, my stomach jumped again— this time from fear.

8

"Oh, my God," I muttered, dread rushing through my body. I suddenly got the sense that something terrible was about to happen, the way I had the night everything had gone so horribly wrong with Chad.

The night he'd taken my virginity against my protests.

"What?" Marnie asked.

"That's not Peter. It's the guy from the bar. The buff guy who was hitting on me."

"No big deal," Marnie said.

"I told him I wasn't interested," I said, turning around. "I told him I was married. So why's he following me out of the bar?"

I didn't give Marnie a chance to answer, and instead began walking briskly, taking her along with me.

"Maybe he's a little drunk," Marnie said. "You know guys with liquid courage. I'm sure he's harmless."

"He's reminding me of Chad."

"Chad?" Marnie asked, sounding shocked.

"Yes, damn it! Chad." Every fiber in my being was saying that this guy was trouble. That I'd taken my flirting with him too far and now I was going to pay for it.

"Sophie!" He sounded closer.

I let go of Marnie's arm and started to run. More of a jog, really, considering my high heels.

"He's not Chad," Marnie said. "Don't freak out."

Marnie didn't understand. She hadn't been raped. I had, and the same instincts I'd ignored that night were telling me to run like hell now.

Suddenly, Teddy was in front of me. I jolted to a stop. Before I could turn, he grabbed me by my upper arms.

"Sophie," he said, slightly out of breath. "Why the hell you running away?"

"I told you, I'm *married*," I said, stressing the word as I shrugged out of his touch. "Will you please just leave me alone?"

"I only want to talk to you."

"What part of 'leave me alone' don't you understand?" Marnie asked. I guess she finally realized this guy was more of a pest than I needed to deal with, even if his plan wasn't to rape me.

"I'm not talking to you," Teddy said to Marnie. Then he turned back to me. "I want to get to know you. Maybe take you for a drink. I'll take things slow." He bit down on his bottom lip as lust pooled in his eyes. "Damn, you're beautiful."

I didn't say anything. I stood, paralyzed, Teddy's words making me remember the night with Chad. How it had started out as a date with someone I liked, but ended with emotional trauma I wasn't sure I'd ever lose.

"Go home, buddy," Marnie told Teddy. "Sleep it off."

"You're not really married, are you?" Teddy asked me.

"All right," Marnie said. "Enough. We're leaving." She took hold of my arm and started to move.

But Teddy grabbed my elbow, yanking me backward with so much force that I actually cried out.

"So what the fuck was that in the club?" Teddy demanded, clearly feeling I owed him an explanation. "Were you just being a cock tease? That it? Get a guy hard, then leave him hanging?"

Marnie stepped between us. "Now you've crossed a line. Get the fuck out of here, asshole."

Teddy gave Marnie a shove, knocking her to the ground.

"Marnie!" I screamed, just as Teddy grabbed my arm and yanked me against his hard chest. But just as quickly he let me go, his eyes bulging in surprise a moment before he whipped his head around.

In an instant, I saw why.

Peter.

Peter had grabbed Teddy by the collar and jerked him off me. He glowered at Teddy, asking, "Why are you bothering the lady?"

Even though my heart was pounding, I couldn't help smiling. And being grateful that Peter had come looking for me.

"Who the hell are you?" Teddy asked.

"The person who will be your nightmare if you touch Sophie again." Peter rammed both of his hands into Teddy's chest, and he stumbled backward, nearly falling.

Teddy's hateful eyes landed on me, then he turned to Peter. "You want her? Fine. A woman like that—she's nothing but trouble. Fucking cock tease!"

Marnie, fuming, came to stand by my side. Her hands were balled into fists and I suspected she wanted to kick Teddy's ass for touching her. "Touch me again—no, say another word—and you'll live to regret it."

I smiled at her, thankful for her guts. I wished I had half of her bravado.

Peter stared Teddy down, emphasizing Marnie's threat. Teddy tried to look tough, but I saw a hint of defeat in his dark eyes. Peter was at least six foot two, a good two inches taller than Teddy. Even though Teddy had more weight on him, there was no mistaking the very serious look on Peter's face that said not to mess with him. Teddy clearly got the message, and began backing up.

But his eyes were on me, menacing. An unspoken threat.

Then the jerk turned around and marched back toward the club.

With Teddy gone, Peter slipped his arms around my waist. I was surprised at how much comfort his touch gave me, considering I'd only met him tonight.

"Who was that guy?" Peter asked.

"Someone I met in the club. I guess he was hoping to take me home."

"Asshole," Marnie quipped. "A guy wants you but you don't want him, he turns into a prick."

I glanced at my friend, shooting her an appreciative look. Marnie never failed to come to my defense. The night everything had happened with Chad, she'd wanted to rip his eyes out—literally. I hadn't wanted to tell anyone, but she'd gone to the dean of our university on my behalf, and while Chad hadn't been arrested, he'd been questioned and reprimanded.

"Peter, this is my best friend, Marnie. I didn't get to introduce you in the club."

"Hello," Marnie and Peter said in unison.

Peter returned his attention to me. He looked a little confused as he said, "You left without me."

I glanced down, embarrassed.

"Were you planning to come back?" Peter went on.

I didn't know what to say, so I said nothing. But I did feel foolish for having run out on him.

Marnie cleared her throat. "Sophie?"

I turned to look at her.

"I'm gonna be going now, okay? Are you coming with me, or..."

Peter's fingers tightened on my waist, a silent plea. I gazed into his eyes, and knew I was going nowhere but with him.

"Or," I replied with a smile.

The edges of Marnie's lips curled. "Call me when you get where you're going. And Peter, so you know—my boyfriend's a cop."

"Don't worry, I'm going to treat your friend very well."

Marnie smirked. "I'll bet." She mimed putting a phone to her ear and said again, "Call me."

She started off.

"Wait," Peter said, and Marnie turned. Peter fished out his wallet and produced thirty dollars. "Here—for a taxi."

Marnie narrowed her eyes in confusion.

"If you get to your car and realize that you're not okay to drive, call a taxi."

"Don't worry, I won't drive if I can't. I'd sleep it off in the car if necessary. And I've got cash."

"Take it," Peter told her, and pressed the money into her palm. "This way, I won't feel guilty for taking your friend away from you tonight."

Marnie shrugged. "All right. But you still have to call me, Sophie."

"Of course," Peter and I said at the same time.

As Marnie strolled away, I once again thought of how different Peter was from Andrew. Andrew would never, *ever* give Marnie thirty bucks for a cab.

I liked that Peter wasn't frugal when it came to his cash.

Peter said, "Looks like it's just you and me."

I met his gaze. "It looks that way."

"So. What do we do now?"

I glanced over my shoulder in the direction of the Hard Rock Hotel, but didn't mouth my suggestion.

Peter followed my line of sight. "Are you sure that's what you want?"

I licked my bottom lip, stalling for time. Wondering if I would go through with making my fantasy a reality.

Heat radiated from Peter as he stared at me. Excitement warmed every inch of my body. I wondered what it was about this man that made me so hot with a single look.

"I know I want you," I said.

He trailed the pad of his thumb along my bottom lip. "Are you sure?"

"Yes," I answered, my hesitation gone.

I was attracted to this man, and I was going to go for what I wanted, no guilt.

He ran his thumb across my bottom lip again. I wanted to open my mouth and lave my tongue over his thumb, give him an idea of what I would do to his penis later.

"I don't live far from here," he said. "My place is comfortable. I've got a big bed…. We don't have to go to a hotel."

I was trusting this man enough to get naked with him, so it didn't really matter where we ended up in bed. After a night of hopefully fantastic sex, I'd be on my merry way. Simple as that. Without him knowing where I lived, there'd be no future contact unless *I* wanted to see him again.

I placed my hand on his chest, and could feel his heart beating beneath my palm. "All right, then," I said. "Take me to your place."

Smiling, Peter took my hand. It was warm, and a little moist. I wondered if he was nervous, or if he routinely took women home.

Again, it didn't matter. I wasn't concerned with commitment—just sex.

And evening the score, as Andrew had so eloquently instructed me to do.

Peter lived in a sprawling apartment complex on Orange Blossom Trail, just down the road from the Florida Mall. With very few exceptions, unless an apartment was on the beach in Florida, it wasn't a high-rise. Instead, apartment complexes consisted of several low-rise buildings, two to three stories high, with probably four to six units per building.

Though it was dark, I could see that Peter's apartment complex was very attractive, with lots of bushes and colorful flowers and pristine lawns. The buildings themselves were peach in color with orange or red California shingles. That I'd be better able to see during the day.

Peter pulled into a parking spot in front of a building that had a large number 9 emblazoned at its highest point over the stairwell. He killed the engine, then looked at me.

"Do you have condoms?" I found myself asking.

A slow grin spread on his face. "Yes."

"I know I should have asked before...." I didn't finish my statement, figuring there was no point. I was still tipsy from the alcohol I'd consumed, and from this point on, I'd be better off concentrating on extracurricular activities as opposed to talking.

A gentleman, Peter opened my car door for me and offered me his hand to help me get out. It made me think of Andrew, how he didn't do that for me anymore.

Again, he held my hand and walked with me. I liked that. This building had two levels, and Peter lived on the second one. At the top of the stairs, he went to the first door on the left.

That was when he let go of my hand to go about opening the door. Something made me turn, look over my shoulder.

I saw no one.

What was I concerned about—that someone Andrew knew would bear witness to me going into another man's home? It wasn't like I didn't have my husband's permission to fuck someone else.

My thoughts fled my brain as Peter enveloped me in his arms and pulled me into his place. He gave the door a shove to close it, then covered my lips with his.

I started, surprised at the sudden action. But a moment later, I melted into the kiss. Peter wasn't shy, or hesitant. His tongue entered my mouth hungrily and tangled with mine. He kissed me with the kind of passion that said he'd wanted to do that all night long.

Heat spread through my body, and my vagina began to throb.

Peter broke the kiss and took a step backward. The air touched my moist lips, making them feel cool where a moment ago they'd been warm.

"Would you like a drink?" Peter asked me.

"No. I'm fine." I'd definitely had enough for the night.

"You don't mind if I have one, do you?"

"Of course not."

My permission granted, Peter started off for the kitchen. My eyes swept over his place, checking out the abstract paintings on the wall. The place wasn't what I'd expected. It was very neat, and unlike what I'd expected of a bachelor, he had a sense of style and color. The walls were white, but the leather sofa and armchair were a warm beige. The carpet was cream colored and I couldn't see even one mark on it.

"You have a nice place," I commented, Peter out of earshot.

The next instant, he rounded the corner from the kitchen, a Coors Light in hand. My stomach fluttered as I saw him again. He really was attractive. More than attractive—he oozed sex appeal.

He tipped the bottle to his lips and sipped, and for some reason I found myself wondering how his tongue might feel on my pussy...

The thought jarring me, I sat on his sofa. He eased himself down beside me. He took another quick pull of his beer, and before he even moved the tip of the bottle from his mouth, he curled his fingers around my neck and pulled me close.

The moment his lips met mine, it was as though I'd been touched by a live wire. A jolt of searing heat shot through me. My lips parted on a moan, and Peter gently captured the tip of my tongue with his teeth. He suckled my tongue, my bottom lip. My entire body was alive with an intense sexual desire I hadn't felt in a very long time.

I slipped my fingers into his hair, took fistfuls of it and gently tugged. Peter broke the kiss and I moaned in disappointment, wondering if he'd mistakenly gotten the idea that I'd wanted him to stop.

He eased his face away from mine and stretched his arm out to put his beer bottle on the glass coffee table. Then he returned to me, using both hands to caress my jaw and neck. I could hear his ragged breathing as the tips of his fingers slowly trailed over my skin. He touched me reverently, as though I were a priceless piece of art.

I'd never felt more beautiful.

"How would you like me to please you?" Peter asked, his tone husky.

"You are pleasing me."

Peter moved one hand down the length of my neck to the area between my breasts. I held my breath, wondering if he would pull my top down and expose me.

Wanting him to.

"What is it that you love the most?" he asked.

His hand moved lower, to my belly, where he pulled the hem of my blouse out of the way. The pale brown skin on his hand was a touch darker than the pale brown skin on my stomach. He skimmed my stomach with his fingers in a rhythmic motion. I sucked in a breath.

"I want to please you in every way imaginable."

I'd been out of the dating game for a while, but I doubted that Peter was the typical guy who picked up a woman for sex. Guys tended to be out for number one, a woman's pleasure secondary in their minds. And yet here was Peter, concerned with my pleasure first and foremost.

"What is it your husband didn't do that you'd like me to try?"

My stomach twisted. "No, please. Don't mention him. I don't want to think about my ex."

Peter didn't say anything, just moved his hands lower, resting them on the outside of my skirt. "You're nervous," he said.

"Yes," I agreed.

"You haven't been with another man in a very long time."

"I want to be with you."

His hand moved over the top of my thighs. "I can tell by the way you've pressed your legs tightly together that you enjoy someone playing with your pussy. A lot."

I couldn't help it. I moaned.

"So I'm right." Peter inched a hand under my skirt while using his upper body to ease me backward on the sofa. "But why do I think that your pussy is starved for affection?"

"What makes you say that?" I asked, wondering if this man could somehow read my mind.

"It's the way you won't spread your legs for me…and yet, I see the desire in your eyes." He placed one hand on my belly. "I feel it in your breathing."

I glanced at his hand on my red shirt, noticed how quickly it rose and fell. Peter was right.

And I was right about him. He was no ordinary man.

"Relax your legs, *bella.*"

I did, and he easily parted them. He moved a hand up my thigh, slowly, as though savoring every touch of my skin. When he reached my pussy, he moaned his pleasure, then stroked his thumb over my clitoris through my panties.

"Do you like that?" Peter asked.

I exhaled a shaky breath. "Yes…"

Back and forth he stroked me. Stroked me until I was panting. Then he moved my panties aside and touched me skin to skin.

My eyes fluttered shut as raw sexual desire shot through me.

"Yes," Peter said. "That's it."

My moans grew louder, and my body began to tense. As though sensing I could come any moment, Peter stopped stroking me, but let his fingers rest on my pussy.

"Do you know what I love about a woman's clit?" He stroked me again, and I shuddered. "I love how it gets erect, just like a penis. I love the way it trembles slightly when a woman is really aroused. Right now, your clit is hard and it's trembling." Peter pressed his nose to my neck and inhaled deeply. "Tell me what you want me to do."

I took fistfuls of his shirt in my hands. "Fuck me."

"I think you want something else." He slipped one finger into my vagina, and I groaned wantonly. "My fingers?" he asked. "My tongue? Tell me."

"Just fuck me. Please…"

"There's no need to rush. We have all night." His thumb and finger were working faster now, making me breathless.

"I need you to fuck me," I begged. "I need it. Right now."

"It—or me?"

My eyes met Peter's. I didn't understand the question. "You," I told him, and gyrated my hips against his hand so there'd be no doubt. Slowly, he started playing with my pussy again. I closed my eyes. "Yes, yes. Yes, that's it. Make me forget…"

Peter's fingers stopped moving. "What did you say?"

My chest heaving, my eyes popped open. "Huh?"

"You said 'Make me forget.' Do you mean forget your husband?"

Had I said that?

"I want you to want *me*," Peter stressed.

"I do." I raised my head and kissed his jaw. "Of course I do."

Peter eased away from me, unconvinced. "I think what you want most is to forget about how your husband hurt you."

I stared at Peter, confused.

"I think that for you, any man will do," he went on.

"What? No. No, that's not true." I snaked my arms around his neck. "The moment I saw you, I knew it had to be you. I'm here because I want you."

Peter placed his hands on my arms, but not in a way that said he was going to succumb to my touch. "I like you, Sophie. And I don't want you to think of me as a mistake tomorrow morning."

I framed his face. "Why are you saying that?" I asked. "I won't think that."

Peter turned his lips into one of my palms and kissed it. "You know where I live."

My heart rate accelerated. "Are you sending me away?"

"If you wake up in the morning and decide that you still want me, you can return."

Disappointed, I groaned. Every part of my body was throbbing with carnal need. "Please don't do this."

Peter kissed my palm again, then the inside of my wrist. "You." Another kiss. "Know." Another kiss. "Where." Another kiss. "I live." Now Peter moved his lips from my wrist to my mouth and gave me a tender kiss. "If you want me."

"Please…"

Peter silenced me with his lips. He gave me a deep, hungry kiss that said he didn't want our night together to end. And yet, he broke the kiss, stood, and walked to the phone near the armchair.

"What are you doing?"

"Calling you a taxi. I'll pay the fare, of course."

"No, please don't. You can give me a ride home if you want."

"If I give you a ride, I'll want to touch you. And I don't want to touch you until you are ready." He punched in some digits. "And this way, I won't know where you live, so if you want to see me again, the decision is yours."

Before I could respond, Peter began speaking into the phone. He requested a taxi at his address, then replaced the receiver.

He came back to the sofa and sat beside me. Taking my hands in his, he pressed his lips to my cheek. "Did your husband cheat on you?" he asked softly.

I nodded.

"He is a fool," Peter said.

I said nothing but nodded again.

"May I use your bathroom?"

With a nod of his head, he indicated a door behind the sofa on the right. "It's right there."

I stood and made my way to the bathroom. One glance in the mirror had me frowning. My eyes were red and slightly dazed. I looked like a drunk.

No wonder Peter hadn't wanted to fuck me. Whether because he thought I was hung up on my husband, or because he felt I wasn't sober enough to do the act, he was a gentleman.

For which I could only give him credit.

When I exited the bathroom, I saw Peter standing at the door. The taxi driver was already here.

I wanted to tell him to send the driver away, reassure him that I wanted to be with him tonight, but I didn't. If Peter didn't want me to stay, I wouldn't beg him.

"I've given the driver enough to cover the fare," Peter said.

I realized he was making sure the driver wouldn't try to charge me, as well. Nodding, I stepped outside. The driver continued on, but I hesitated at the door. "You're a strange man," I said to Peter. "You get me all hot and bothered—"

He kissed me again, and I whimpered when he pulled away. "You know where I live."

With that, he stepped back into his apartment, blew me a kiss and closed the door.

9

"What do you mean *nothing happened?*" Marnie exclaimed through the phone line, so loudly I had to pull the receiver from my ear for a moment.

I brought the phone back to my ear. "Not exactly nothing," I corrected. "We got to first base, but after that, I struck out."

"I don't get it."

"Trust me, no one was more confused than I was," I told her. Still in my pj's, I was sitting cross-legged on my sofa, a cup of black coffee on the end table beside me. Peaches was lying on her bed near the patio doors, getting some mid-morning sun.

"How did the two of you go from being unable to keep your hands off each other on the dance floor to not fucking?"

I lifted my mug of coffee and sipped some before answering. This was my third cup, and still my head throbbed. I'd already taken two pain relievers, but the way I was feeling, I would need a couple more. I hadn't had a hangover like this in a long time.

"I guess I said the wrong thing," I admitted.

"What on earth did you say? Hell, what *could* you say that would turn a guy off?"

"I was drunk, and I apparently said something like 'make me forget.' Peter took that to mean I wasn't really into *him*—only into using him to escape my problem."

"What guy in his right mind turns down sex, no matter the motive?" Marnie sounded positively bewildered.

I shrugged. "That's what I've been thinking about all night. He's not like any guy I've ever met, that's for sure."

"Tell me about it."

"On one hand, I can't blame him. I was so drunk, I'm surprised he took me home in the first place. By the way, remind me to *never* drink that much again." As if on cue, my head throbbed.

"Oh, well," Marnie said. "There are other guys. You'll find someone else."

"No." I waved off the suggestion, even though she couldn't see my hand motion. "I'm putting my affair plans on hold."

"Why?"

"Because. Maybe Peter was right. Maybe I really wasn't ready. Maybe I shouldn't be rushing into screwing some other guy just because Andrew cheated."

"That's exactly what you need," Marnie countered, as if she were an authority on the matter.

"With all due respect, Marnie, this is my life. This isn't about you and Keith."

"Ouch."

I regretted my words immediately, even if I believed that Marnie's opinion on what I should do was influenced by her own past. She had stayed with a cheater, forgiven him time after time, only for him to ultimately leave her. She'd done everything possible to hang on to him and their relationship, but nothing had worked.

"I didn't mean that," I said, my tone softer. "Trust me, I know that you care. And maybe you're one hundred percent right. It's just…I need to figure out for myself what I'm going to do."

And, quite frankly, I was still intrigued by Peter. I wasn't nearly as frustrated as I'd let on with Marnie, because the truth was, I respected Peter for sending me home. Ninety-nine percent of other guys would have fucked me, no questions asked.

"I understand," Marnie said. "You know I'm not telling you what to do."

"I know that," I told her, then drank more coffee. "And guess what?" I said after a moment. "I can't find my bracelet. I remember having it on in Peter's car, so it must have fallen off at his place while we were making out on his sofa. Think I ought to go back and get it?"

"The platinum and emerald bracelet Andrew got you for your first anniversary?"

"Yeah, that's the one."

"Girl, your marriage might be in trouble—"

"I know," I said, frowning. "I have to go back for it. Even if it is from Andrew, I love that piece. Not to mention that it's expensive."

"Maybe there's hope for you and Peter yet." Marnie's voice rose on a hopeful note. "In fact, maybe you left it there deliberately, even if you don't realize it."

I didn't get a chance to respond, because my phone beeped, indicating there was a call on my other line. "Marnie, let me call you later. I've got another call coming in."

"All right, Soph. Later."

I pressed the flash button to click me over to the other line. "Hello?"

There was a pause, then, "Sophie."

Pain shot through my stomach at the sound of Andrew's voice. "Andrew." I swallowed, wondering if it would always be like this from now on—pain instead of pleasure where my husband was concerned. "What do you want?"

"I miss you."

My stomach clenched at the simple statement. "I...I can't do this. It's too hard—"

"I know you need more time," Andrew hurriedly said. "I just wanted to hear your voice, Sophie."

The sound of my name on his lips was bittersweet. This wasn't the way it was supposed to be.

"I also wanted you to know that I'm trying to work things out for us. On my end."

"What does that mean?" I asked, then wished I hadn't. I didn't want to be having this conversation right now.

"With—you know. I've got a couple options I'm considering to make the problem go away."

My stomach lurched again. I felt sick. "I—I can't hear this right now."

"Okay—"

"No, it's not okay, Andrew. You messed everything up."

"I know that, and I'm—"

I hung up.

My hands were shaking as I reached for my mug of coffee and downed the lukewarm liquid. It curdled inside my stomach, and I thought I might retch.

"Damn you, Andrew," I muttered.

As I sat on the sofa thinking about his words, anger quickly replaced my feeling of unease. *The problem,* Andrew had said. *You know,* he'd said. The thing was, I didn't know. Other than telling me he'd had an affair, Andrew hadn't even mentioned the other woman's name.

He claimed he wanted our marriage, but in order for anything to work, he had to be completely honest with me.

I shot to my feet and went to the bathroom. I turned on the faucets in the shower, adjusted the temperature, then got out of my oversize T-shirt and thong. I stepped into the shower and let the warm water splash over my face. Keeping my head under the steady stream of water, I held my breath until my lungs started to burn before jerking my head backward and gulping in air.

Tears fell from my eyes, even though I didn't want them to. Peter had been right about one thing. I *had* needed a distraction last night. I still did. Because every time I thought about Andrew, I didn't know if I could go on.

Think about Peter...

I forced the image of Peter's sexy smile into my brain. I thought about the way his dark eyes had fixated on me, letting me know in no uncertain terms that he wanted me.

I squirted some body wash into my hands, then smoothed my palms over my breasts. They were heavy and full, my nipples high. My breasts were beautiful. I knew that. I stroked my nipples, and they hardened. Then I ran my palms down my flat belly, let them rest there. A sorrowful moan caught in my throat as I thought of something. Andrew and I had been trying to get pregnant for a few months now.

And yet he'd screwed another woman.

Had he taken a shower with her, tweaked her nipples into hardened peaks? Had he slipped soapy hands between her folds and massaged her until she'd come?

I pounded a fist on the shower wall. The images of what Andrew might have done with this woman were going to drive me crazy. I'd dreamed about him and this faceless woman, and the way he'd possibly touched her. Now I was thinking about it in the shower.

I would never get past this, not until I had answers.

I'd gone to see Andrew at work yesterday, and he hadn't been there. When he'd come to talk to me at home, the news about the possible lawsuit had made me forget about why I'd gone to see him originally.

To ask him exactly what he'd done with the woman he'd been screwing. How he'd touched her, how she'd touched him. If he'd fucked her in our bed.

And the bigger issue—just how emotionally involved the two of them had gotten.

Though I didn't want to go back to Andrew's workplace, I would. Because I needed answers. The kind that had to come face-to-face. Looking into Andrew's eyes, I could tell if he was lying.

I certainly didn't want him coming back here to have this chat. Being in our home would be far too distressing for me.

I needed some emotional distance.

At least, I hoped distance would help me deal with the truth I needed to hear.

When Andrew saw me in the hotel lobby, his face lit up as it had on so many occasions in the past. It broke my heart, seeing his smile. Because something was instantly clear. The future would never be the way the past had been. Even if we got to the point where we were a happy couple again, our future would always be marred by the memory of what he'd done.

Would I ever be able to forgive him? I wasn't sure I could. But the way Andrew's smile tugged on my heartstrings also made it clear that it wouldn't be easy to cut the ties if the time came to live without him.

Andrew rounded the front desk and started toward me. The joy in his eyes said he thought I was here for a happier reason. And I don't know why, but it pissed me off.

Yes, I did know why. It pissed me off that he could screw another woman, and that only a few days after that revelation, he thought I was here to tell him I forgave him. What else could account for that look on his face?

As he reached me, Andrew put a hand on my arm. "Hello, Sophie."

My emotions were all over the place. From sad to angry, love to hate. "Tell me what you did with her," I demanded.

"What?"

"You talk about 'the problem,' as though it's some random thing that came into our lives. But it wasn't. You had an affair!"

Andrew's eyes volleyed around the lobby. He was clearly worried that people might be hearing me.

I didn't care.

"Tell me what you did." I squeezed my eyes shut as my head throbbed, but after a moment I continued. "Tell me what you did with that woman."

Andrew gently guided me toward the far corner of the lobby, away from the front desk.

"It matters," I said. "I didn't think I'd want to hear the details, but now...I need to know. You need to tell me."

"What happened with her was just sex," Andrew whispered, then glanced around again.

"What kind of sex?"

"I don't see how this will help."

"Did she suck your cock? Did you eat her pussy? Did you fuck her in a bed, on the grass, in the backseat of a car?" I couldn't keep the anger from my voice, and I knew that anyone within earshot would have definitely heard me.

Andrew grabbed me by the arm and whisked me through the lobby. He didn't stop walking until he reached the first door we came upon, the handicapped restroom. He ushered me inside.

"What are you doing?" Andrew demanded the moment he shut the door.

"You say you still want me? Then you damn well better answer my questions!"

Andrew dragged a hand over his head in frustration. "You can't come into my place of work and cause a scene like this."

I gave Andrew a hard shove, and he staggered backward, landing against a tiled wall. His eyes widened. I don't know if he was afraid, or surprised.

"Fuck you," I snapped. "I hate you, you hear me? I hate you."

I started for the door, wrapped my fingers around the brass knob.

"Sophie, please. Don't leave."

There was a desperate note to Andrew's voice and, despite myself, I didn't yank the door open and run away. Instead I sighed, my eyelids fluttering shut. My heart was heavy as I contemplated what to do.

"Fine," Andrew said. "You want to know, I'll tell you. But I don't see how this will help anything."

I turned. "Maybe it won't help. Maybe it will make me crazier. But if I'm ever going to move forward, I need to know exactly what happened between you two."

I waited for Andrew to say something, but he didn't. His chest rose with each heavy breath. He looked pained, like this was difficult for him. But it was far more difficult for me.

"Ask me what you want to know."

"All right. What's her name?"

A beat. Then, "Isabel."

Isabel. My stomach twisted. "I'll bet she's beautiful."

Andrew said nothing.

"Is she beautiful?" I asked.

"Yes, she's beautiful. But that doesn't mean anything."

"Who came on to whom?" Andrew had already told me she had come on to him, but I wanted to see if he said the same thing again, or changed his story.

"She hit on me."

"And you were so flattered, you couldn't help dropping your pants." I snorted.

"It wasn't like that."

"What—she put a gun to your head and forced you to fuck her?"

Andrew said nothing.

"What did you do together?" I forged on. "Did she suck your cock?"

Andrew said nothing.

"Son of a bitch, answer the question." But I could already see luscious lips locked around my husband's hard shaft, and the image made my stomach turn.

Beautiful Isabel would have luscious lips.

"Yes, she did. Jesus, Sophie—"

"And you of course went down on her."

Andrew groaned. Dragged a hand over his face.

Hot tears immediately filled my eyes, and a cry escaped my throat. I'd wanted to get through this talk being angry—anger was better than crying. But knowing my husband had done things with another woman that he hadn't done with me was too much for me to handle.

"Sophie, please." Andrew took my hand in his. "I told you no good would come of this."

I jerked away from his touch. I wanted to scream every disgusting name at him I could think of. Instead, I managed a barely audible "Why?"

"Because I was stupid," Andrew said. "Hell, I don't know."

"Yes, you do know." My anger returned with a vengeance. "You know exactly why you put some other woman's pussy in your mouth and not mine." Andrew had always said he didn't really care for oral sex—neither giving nor receiving. I hadn't pushed the issue, as everything else about our lovemaking had been extremely satisfying. Yes, our lovemaking had become a bit routine, but we'd still pleased each other.

Or so I'd thought.

"What did she taste like?" I asked.

Andrew's eyes bulged. He hadn't expected that question. "Come on, Sophie. You already know I fucked up."

I glowered at him. "Did you ever."

"Okay, wrong choice of words. The point is, I don't want her. You're the one I love."

"Did you like her pussy?"

Andrew looked dumbfounded.

"Is it pretty?" I enunciated my words. "The kind of pussy you couldn't wait to put your fingers in and play with? The kind you couldn't resist licking and sucking?"

"What has gotten into you? Since when do you talk like this?"

"What—I can't talk like this because I'm your wife? Is that why you wanted to keep sex simple in the bedroom? Are you one of those guys who can't completely let go with his wife, but if you're with some whore, the sky's the limit?"

Anger was flowing through my veins like electric energy, causing my hands to shake. I waited for Andrew to answer, but he wasn't speaking.

I went on. "You say she came on to you, but you couldn't wait to touch her, could you? You couldn't wait to get her naked. You loved fucking her." My voice was rising. "You loved the way your cock felt inside her. Didn't you? *Didn't you?*"

"Yes!" The word seemed to have escaped Andrew against his will, because his eyes widened, then he glanced down, uncomfortable. "It was sex, Sophie. Of course I enjoyed it. But like I said—"

"Good. Then you can go right on fucking her. At least that way, she won't sue you." I meant my words. I was sick of Andrew. I could no longer stand the sight of him.

I was about to turn, but he grabbed me by both my shoulders and forcefully pulled me to him. "I don't want her. I know you won't understand what I'm about to say, but having sex with her proved to me that you're the only one I want. A person can get sex anywhere. But we make love, Sophie. There's a difference. A huge one."

"Really."

"Yes, really."

Anger fueling my actions, I took Andrew's hand and placed it on my breast. "You still want me?"

"Of course."

I squeezed his hand over my breast, but I didn't do it lovingly. I wasn't sure what I was doing, really. Something else in me had taken control.

"Do you still like touching me?" I asked.

"Of course." Andrew's breathing changed, got heavier.

Hastily, I yanked my skirt up with my free hand, then dragged

Andrew's hand to my pussy. I honestly didn't know what I was doing, but I couldn't stop myself.

Holding his hand over my vagina, I asked, "Do you want to make love to me right now, Andrew?"

He groaned softly. He was getting turned-on. Good. I had the bastard right where I wanted him.

"I do." His breathing was ragged now, ripe with lust. "Oh, Sophie…"

I let him kiss my neck. Let him slip his fingers into my panties and stroke me. In a strange way, I was turned-on, but nothing about what I felt was loving. It was all fueled by my rage. Part of me hated my husband for what he'd done to me. And yet, another part of me wanted him to strip me naked and fuck me to prove not only that he still loved me, but that he still wanted me sexually.

That he found me as desirable as he'd found Isabel.

But knowing he'd touched another woman this intimately…that he'd sucked her pussy. There was no way I could go through with fucking him, not right now. Maybe not ever. I was about to bring him back down to earth, let him know that my desire for him hadn't been genuine.

I kissed his cheek, then whispered in his ear, "Is this how you touched Isabel?"

Andrew's fingers stopped cold.

"What's the matter, sweetheart?" I asked, my voice extra syrupy.

The vein in his jaw flinched as he took a step backward and I grinned, satisfied with his discomfort. But I wasn't really satisfied, not in my soul.

"How many times did you screw her?" I asked. "One? Two?" I searched his eyes for an answer. "Twenty? Fifty?"

Andrew looked away.

As the seconds of silence ticked by, my stomach dropped.

"Oh, my God. She wasn't just some fling. Your relationship was serious." I gripped my stomach. Andrew had said that Isabel had wanted him to leave me for her, but I'd let myself believe that the woman had been delusional, that her feelings for Andrew had been one-sided. But maybe he'd had feelings for her, too, and I was the one deluding myself, wanting to believe that Andrew had only been physically attracted to someone else. What if his connection to Isabel was greater than that?

"No wonder she wants to sue you. Were you going to leave me for her?"

"No! Of course not."

My head grew light. I turned away from my bastard of a husband, wondering if I would actually throw up. I drew in several deep breaths, tried to keep myself under control.

"Is she here now? Your Isabel? I've never met her, so she must be new. Where does she work—in guest services?" When Andrew didn't respond, I moved to the door. "I guess I'll just have to find out."

Andrew grabbed me, forcefully this time. "Do not go out there and look for Isabel."

"Why not? Because you want to protect her? Protect her from your wife?"

"That's not why."

"Tell me the truth, Andrew." I'd been trying to maintain control, or at least hold on to my anger, but I could feel that control slipping through my fingers. "Were you going to leave me for her?"

When Andrew didn't immediately answer, I finally lost control of my emotions. I began to cry. Huge, quavering sobs. This time, when Andrew wrapped me in his arms, I didn't have the strength to pull away.

"I was never going to leave you," he insisted. "Never. But she wanted me to."

"Lucky for her, she might end up with you yet," I managed.

Andrew kissed my temple. "I don't want her."

Several seconds passed, and my sobs faded into whimpers. "But what if I don't want you anymore? What if I can't ever forgive you for what you've done?"

Andrew sighed wearily and eased his head back to look at my face. "We've been together a long time, Sophie. And yeah, maybe I did get bored. Well, not so much bored as curious. I know it's no excuse. I know nothing I say will make this any easier. But I am sorry, Sophie. I was weak." Andrew paused. "But I mean it when I say that my…my affair…made me realize how much I love you and want the life I have with you."

"Don't you dare act like you did us a favor," I quipped, my anger returning. I was riding an emotional roller coaster, and I wanted to get off. Escape the madness.

"I'm not. I'm not saying that. Look, I'm not stupid. I know it won't be easy for you to forgive me. It's why I said that maybe… maybe you ought to have your own affair. You know?"

I said nothing.

"Maybe other guys would say I'm nuts for suggesting that, but I've been thinking a lot about it, and I do believe that if we're going to go forward, one of us shouldn't have something to hold over the other's head. I'm not saying I like the idea of you being with another man, but if that's what it'll take for us to be together, then I deserve nothing less. One of my buddies told me his wife did that after he cheated, and they were able to get past everything."

"Someone told you that?"

"Yeah."

"Who?" I asked, skeptical.

"Seth."

"Seth," I repeated, disgusted. Were no men faithful anymore?

"He said it worked for his marriage," Andrew said softly.

"What if I told you I already met someone?" I jutted my chin out, defiant.

Andrew's eyes narrowed doubtfully. "When?"

"It doesn't matter when."

"Well." I watched Andrew's Adam's apple rise and fall as he swallowed. "I meant what I said. You do what you need to do—then come back to me."

As simple as that. All I had to do was fuck someone else and that would solve all our problems.

"What if I told you that not only did I meet someone else," I continued slowly, "but that I'm starting to fall for him?"

Something flickered in Andrew's eyes—a quick flash of jealousy. "Is that true?"

"You don't get to make the rules, Andrew. Be careful what you wish for—you just might get it."

Then, knowing that Andrew had to be wondering if I was serious or messing with him, I headed out of the handicapped bathroom and didn't glance backward.

Let the bastard get a taste of his own bitter medicine.

10

I was all set to head to Peter's house that evening, all set to get my revenge. But I refrained. What he'd said had suddenly registered. If I fucked him, I didn't want it to be about Andrew. Yes, Andrew would be the cause of my affair, but I didn't want to fuck Peter purely out of spite for my husband. When I went to bed with Peter, it would be because I had made the decision that I wanted to have sex with *him*.

Maybe I was simply stalling for time, but my argument made sense to me. I needed to sleep on my desire for a night or two, see if I still woke up thinking about bedding a new man.

I didn't tell Marnie what had transpired with Andrew in the hotel bathroom. I knew I wasn't going to be able to completely put the affair out of my mind, but the more I talked about it, the worse I felt.

For my sanity, I needed to think about something else.

Or *someone* else.

Someone like Peter, who, with just one look, had made me remember that I was a desirable woman.

On Saturday morning, I was still angry, sad and confused about

Andrew, but I also hadn't stopped thinking about the time I'd spent with Peter.

I was certain now. I wanted to see him again. Wanted to get naked with him and finish what we'd started earlier in the week.

Tonight, I was going to get what I wanted.

I didn't think about whether or not Peter would even be home when I went to see him. Didn't consider that he might be in bed with another woman. I drove across town to his apartment complex nonetheless, hoping for the best.

I wanted to look irresistible, so I put on a formfitting white top with a low V-neck and matching skirt that I'd bought while in the Bahamas with Marnie. Together, both items could pass as a dress. I'd originally planned to wear the outfit for Andrew, maybe surprise him at work with it on and hope it sparked his lust for me. Now, I would put the dress to good use with Peter.

I had no problem getting to his place. I remembered exactly where he lived. There was no security gate to enter the property, so once I was at the apartment complex, I was good to go.

"Building number nine," I muttered softly, glancing around. There were at least ten buildings from what I could tell, and they all looked alike. I drove to the left, and when I saw the buildings with low numbers, I realized I had gone the wrong way. I doubled back, and within a couple minutes, I was pulling into a space outside of Peter's apartment.

I saw a light on in his place, and I hoped that meant he was home.

Exiting my car, I headed upstairs. My high-heeled white sandals clicked against the concrete as I ascended the steps. They were the kind of shoes that screamed *fuck me!*

That and the fact that it was after ten o'clock and I was wearing a skirt I'd had to shoehorn myself into.

I raised my hand to the door but didn't knock. Instead, I rested my knuckles on the wood and gathered myself.

I wanted this. I was sure of that. It's the reason I was here. Especially at this hour. But what if Peter wasn't home? Or worse—inside with someone else?

If he was, so be it. Drawing in a deep breath, I eased my hand back, preparing to knock. But before I could, the door swung open and Peter appeared.

His dark eyes widened slightly. He was surprised. But was he happy, or disappointed?

He didn't speak—just stared. I could smell the alluring scent of his musky cologne. Dressed in black jeans and a close-fitting black T-shirt, he looked as though he was heading out for a night on the town.

I cleared my throat. "Hi."

"Hello." His eyes moved over my face, then lower, to the cleavage I was so obviously showing off.

"I didn't think I would see you again," Peter said, the hint of his Italian accent sexy as hell.

"I, uh…I think my bracelet must have fallen off here the other night."

"Yes, I found it on my sofa." He paused. "Is that why you're here—to collect your bracelet?"

I shifted my weight from one stiletto to the other. "Yes."

"Then let me get it for you."

Peter stepped backward, then turned.

"Wait." I snagged his wrist before he was out of reach. "That's not the only reason I'm here."

"No?" One of his eyebrows rose as he faced me again.

"No." I shook my head. "I'm here because…because I want you.

I haven't been able to stop thinking about you since you made me leave that night."

Peter's lips spread in a slow grin.

"Unless, of course, you're heading out."

"I was, but now that you're here..." His voice was ripe with implication. "Come in."

He stepped backward and, as I was still holding his wrist, I moved with him.

"I bought something for just this occasion," Peter announced as he led me to the living room and sat me on his sofa.

"But you didn't know I was coming back."

"I was hopeful."

I curled a leg onto the sofa. "What did you buy?"

"A special Italian wine," he told me. I was sitting, and he was standing, but still holding my hand. It was nice.

"Okay..."

"Actually, it's an Italian sparkling wine, and it's very nice. Prosecco. Have you ever tried it?"

"No."

"It's light and refreshing, a little sweet. Perfect for a hot day." He trailed his finger along my palm. "Or a hot night."

Peter raised my hand to his mouth and kissed the inside of my wrist, something I realized I liked very much. Then he released my hand and headed to the kitchen.

Licking my lips, I watched him go. The way his shoulder blades moved beneath his shirt gave the impression of power, much like a stealthy jaguar.

"Would you like to try the Prosecco?" he asked, opening a cupboard that housed wineglasses.

"I'd love to try it." My stomach fluttered, and I took a

moment to breathe in and out slowly. I was really here, really going to do this.

I was both nervous and excited.

About a minute later, Peter returned to the living room. He had two champagne flutes in his hands, one of which he held out to me.

"Thank you." I took the flute and sipped the beverage. It had overtones of citrus and melon and was both delicious and refreshing. "Mmm, delicious."

Peter took a sip as well, his eyes never leaving my face. He wasn't afraid of intimacy, I realized. I liked that about him.

I liked him, period.

"Forgive me," Peter said, sitting beside me. "I should have offered a toast. To…new experiences."

"To new experiences," I echoed, and we both drank to that. I didn't stop drinking until I'd finished off what was in my glass. Not because I wanted to get drunk—I'd learned my lesson a few nights earlier—but because I was ready to get down to business.

The glass still in my hand, I quickly leaned forward and placed my mouth on Peter's.

He stiffened slightly, indicating his surprise rather than reluctance. I moved my mouth over his, skimming his skin at first, then softly kissing him, urging his lips into submission.

With a groan, Peter parted his lips and began to kiss me back with total abandon. Curling his fingers around my head, he held me to him as his tongue delved into my mouth. It was hot and wet and had the flavor of Prosecco. It tasted better on his tongue than it had straight from my glass, and I opened my mouth further, needing more of him.

"Slow down," Peter rasped, but I didn't listen. Instead, I moved forward, forcing his body backward on the sofa. "Wait," he said. "My drink."

I stopped then, and let him place his champagne flute on the coffee table. He did the same with mine, and before he could fully turn back to me, I was already kissing his jawline and running my hands down his chest.

"Let me please you first," Peter offered.

"You are pleasing me." I reached for the button on his jeans and tried to work it loose. "I want you inside me. I *need* you inside me—right now. I've thought about nothing but getting you naked ever since that night."

My lips found Peter's again, and I kissed him. A deep, wet kiss that had both of us moaning in pleasure. Unable to get his jeans undone, I lowered my hand to his penis. I grinned as I felt the evidence of his desire for me straining against the fabric.

"So big, so hard," I whispered in his ear. "I love it."

No sooner were the words out of my mouth than I was suddenly on my back. Peter had reversed our positions with ease and strength. He'd wrapped his arm around my waist, lifted me as he raised his body, then swiftly laid me on my back. Now, he was between my thighs, his powerful cock pressed against my pussy.

"You want it hard and fast?" he asked, pushing my blouse up. I was wearing no bra, and my breasts spilled free.

"God, yes."

He covered both of my naked breasts with his hands and began to squeeze the full mounds. Not gently, but hungrily. In a way that said he understood I wanted it rough.

He pushed both of my breasts together, grazed his teeth over one nipple. My body shuddered as desire shot through me.

"And what about this?" Peter grazed my other nipple. "Do you want me to play with your breasts?"

Before I could answer, he drew one nipple deep into his mouth and suckled me. Hard. Hard enough that I felt prickles of pain.

"Yes." I exhaled heavily. "Like that. Just like that."

I wanted wild sex. I wanted nothing like what I'd shared with Andrew. Sex with my husband had been slow and tender.

Meaningful.

And he'd still fucked someone else.

I stopped thinking about Andrew as Peter sucked my other nipple with the same fervor he had the first. He ground his cock against me the entire time, causing the sweetest sensations to shoot through my pussy and spread to the rest of my body. Soon, I was digging my fingers into Peter's hair and moaning shamelessly.

"Do you like that?"

"Yes—hell, yes. But I need this." Slipping a hand between our bodies, I put my hand over his cock and squeezed. I wasn't gentle either, letting him know that I was ready for him to be merciless with me.

Peter moved his lips from my nipple and sucked a fleshy part of my breast. He sucked, bit, pulled, sucked even harder. As though he was trying to brand me with his mark. I didn't think I'd like the pain that stung my skin—it was so foreign to me—but not only did I like it, it turned me on.

Peter stood abruptly and made fast work of undoing his jeans. I bunched my skirt around my waist, slipped my panties off, then eased my butt back onto the sofa.

"No." Peter shook his head. "Take everything off. I want you naked."

My vagina pulsed at the brazen words. He wanted me naked. Wanted me completely.

I understood now what Marnie had meant when she talked about the thrill of being with someone new. The living room was lit, and being completely naked in a lit room left a person much more vulnerable than being naked in a dark room. And yet instead of feeling nervous, I felt a delicious thrill.

Slowly, I stood. My eyes never left Peter's as I pulled my blouse over my head and shimmied my skirt over my hips.

"Your turn," I said, now fully naked.

Peter's eyes drank in the sight of my naked pussy, a wicked grin curling on his mouth as he kicked his jeans free. He was wearing black briefs, and my gaze locked on the sight of his cock straining against the cotton fabric.

Finally, he lowered his briefs, and I actually gasped when his cock sprang free. It was large in every way. Nice girth, nice length. Larger than Andrew's. The kind of cock that countless dildos had been designed to look just like.

Peter moved toward me slowly, like a cat getting ready to pounce on its prey. Unlike prey, I didn't run.

Peter encircled me with his arms, pressing the palms of his hands to the small of my back. My nipples brushing against his hairless chest, and I stared up at him and he down at me. His cock was twitching around in my vaginal area, as though instinctively seeking entry to the place it craved the most.

Peter splayed his hands over my ass, pulling me close with a hard thrust. He dug his fingers into my flesh and pressed my pussy against his cock.

Easing up on my toes, I wrapped a hand around his penis and stroked the tip of it against my clit.

"That should be my tongue caressing you there," Peter said. "Like this." He lowered his face to mine and gently flicked his tongue over the top of my lip. Up and down. Left and right. Then a soft suckle.

My knees buckled, imagining just how sweet it would be to have him tease my clit the way he was describing.

"I love the way your body responds to mine," Peter murmured. "It turns me on."

"I am so turned-on right now…."

Easing his head back to stare at me, he dipped a finger into my folds, then raised it to his mouth and slowly tasted my essence.

The erotic sight made me shudder. My vagina pulsed wildly. "Oh, my God, I need you inside me," I said, my voice raspy. "Did I tell you how much I've thought about this for the past few days?"

"Let me please you first," Peter said. "*Bella*—you taste so sweet."

If he kept talking like that, I might just come before he was even inside me. I stroked him again. "I'm already ready to come. I need your cock."

"You think you will only come once tonight? I promise, you will come more than that."

His warm breath tickled my ear, and made my body shudder again. I had no doubt that he would make me come, perhaps countless times.

I closed my fingers around his shaft and pumped him. "First, this. I'm impatient."

Peter cupped one of my breasts, causing heat to course through my veins. "All right, sweetheart. Your wish is my command."

11

I wanted to adjust my body and slip his cock into me, but common sense wouldn't let me. I wanted to fuck him—desperately—but I couldn't do so without protection.

I took a tentative step backward, hoping Peter would react well to what I said next. I knew some guys could forget all reason when in the throes of passion, but if he didn't want to use a condom, then we couldn't have sex. "I'm not on the Pill," I said softly. "So we need to use a condom. I brought some."

"I have some in the bedroom." He gave me a soft kiss on the lips. "I'll be right back."

I watched Peter walk away. Really, I checked out his naked butt. It was muscular and firm, just like the rest of him. I didn't think I could ever tire of looking at him.

As I waited for him to return, I settled on the sofa. I ran the tips of my fingers over my hard, swollen nipples. They were tingling from how hard Peter had sucked them.

When Peter walked back into the living room, his attention fell to my fingers fondling my breasts, and he grinned widely. "You are such a vision."

He had the condom on, ready. I extended one hand toward him and purred, "Come to me."

He did. Lowering himself onto the sofa, he braced his arms on either side of me to keep his upper body raised above mine. I draped one leg over his ass and ran my tongue along the underside of his jaw. I tasted a hint of salt on his skin, felt a bit of stubble. Mixed with the scent of his cologne was the faint smell of Irish Spring soap.

His cock finding my pussy, I only had a moment to ponder that this was really going to happen, that another man was about to fuck me when Peter entered me with a strong, fast thrust. Crying out, I dug my fingers into his shoulders. I hadn't been prepared for the sensations I would feel as he filled me, how delectable another man's cock would feel inside my pussy. My God, he was so large, so impressive. With every stroke, his cock strained against my inner walls, making me feel the utmost bliss.

"*Bella...*" he murmured. "Oh, my God..."

I almost didn't recognize the sounds of rapture coming from my mouth. They were loud, forceful, uninhibited. As Peter drove his cock into me, I moaned until I was breathless.

He was more than I'd expected, and yet, I couldn't get enough of him. I snaked my other leg around his waist and locked my ankles together.

Peter withdrew almost completely, then entered me again with another hard thrust. My eyes rolling backward, I dug my nails deeper into his skin. With each stroke, he reached a spot deeper and deeper inside me. With each stroke, he moved faster and faster, bringing me closer to coming.

"Is that hard enough for you?" Peter asked, ending the question on a powerful thrust.

I screamed.

A groan rumbled in Peter's chest, almost like that of a lion, and he pushed himself completely inside me and burrowed himself there. He ground himself against me, moving his cock around inside me without withdrawing.

I thrashed my head about, pressed my fingers harder against his skin.

Peter picked up the pace.

My breathing accelerated, coming in quick raspy gasps. I didn't want to let go, not yet, but the pleasure was too intense. With Peter's cock inside me, and the friction on my clit…

"Look at me," he said. He kissed my forehead. "Look at me, *bella*."

I forced my eyes open, met Peter's smoky gaze.

"I can feel your orgasm building," he said. He withdrew, then thrust into me again, but this time slowly. "I want to look in your eyes as you come."

I didn't say anything. I couldn't manage words, only passionate cries. But I kept my eyes locked on Peter's, letting him know I would do as he asked. I don't know why I wasn't shy with him, why I was giving a stranger my body completely, but it felt right. There was a level of intimacy and comfort between us that I didn't understand, but I took that as a sign that I was right where I was supposed to be.

"Are you going to come?" Peter asked between thrusts. He was moving slower now, but hitting my spot with every delicious stroke.

My head was getting light, my body growing more taut. I drew in a breath, tried to summon the energy to speak. "Almost," I said weakly. "Almost there…"

"How about now?"

As soon as the question left Peter's lips, he picked up his pace until he reached bionic speed. I couldn't think anymore, only feel blinding ecstasy.

Peter lowered his head to suckle one of my breasts—hard—and suddenly I was coming, a powerful orgasm ripping through me. It felt as if my body had been pulled back in a giant slingshot and released into orgasmic orbit. I shuddered from head to toe, my moan loud, long and feral.

Peter moved his mouth from my breast to my lips, and he ravaged my mouth the way he'd just ravaged my pussy. Only when my moans began to subside and my body stopped twitching did he pull his lips from mine and look into my eyes.

And he smiled.

My body flush and sated, I grinned back at Peter. Then, giggling, I turned away.

"Why are you blushing?" he asked.

Not facing him, I shook my head. I had to press my lips together to silence my laughing. It seemed inappropriate after having a whopper of an orgasm.

"Come on," Peter urged. "Tell me."

"Because." Inhaling a deep breath, I faced him. "Because I didn't know…I didn't think…"

"Didn't think what?"

"That sex with you would be this amazing," I answered, and raised my hand to his face. I stroked his jaw. "But you didn't come."

"The night is long," he replied.

"How do you want me?" I asked.

"Just as you are." Easing backward, Peter withdrew. My eyes narrowed in confusion then widened with understanding as he settled his face between my thighs.

"What are you doing?"

"Making you come again."

I pushed my body up onto my elbows. "But what about you? You just gave me one helluva orgasm. It's your turn."

"When I have you in my mouth and your body is trembling from my tongue, that gives me just as much pleasure as coming."

His words made my body quiver again. How different he was from Andrew. For Andrew, oral sex had been a chore. But for Peter, it seemed as much about my pleasure as his.

"You are beautiful," he said. "Look how your clit is already trembling, and I haven't even touched you yet."

I blew out an unsteady breath. It was weird to be talking to a man whose face was perched between my thighs. And yet it was downright erotic.

Peter ran his finger along my folds, groaning as he did. I could see his eyes darkening with lust, and I was riveted by how much he enjoyed simply looking at me.

I watched him slowly part his lips. Lower his head. Extend his tongue. My clit throbbed with anticipation even before he made contact with my skin.

And when he did, it was as though I'd been hit with an electric current. My body jerked, my back arched, and I balled my hands into fists.

"Relax, *bella*," he said.

I didn't know if I could. The sensation spiraling through me was intense, delicious, and the first touch of his tongue almost pushed me right into another orgasm. I steadied my breathing, regained control as Peter pleasured me in the most intimate of ways.

Then I started thinking.

I found myself wondering how long it would take for me to

come this time, and if Peter would grow tired of eating my pussy. Maybe I *couldn't* come again, because at the moment, my clit was hypersensitive.

Peter twirled the tip of his tongue over me, then suckled me gently. Moaning, I closed my eyes and waited for my orgasm to build.

"Relax," Peter murmured again.

"I don't know if I can," I admitted. I wasn't used to coming like this, and I didn't know if I could let go in this way with a man I was fucking for the first time. I could count on one hand the number of times Andrew had made me come with his tongue, and I'd always felt guilty afterward, as though I'd taken too long to come. Once, Andrew had said as much, and after that I'd never asked him for oral sex again.

"You don't enjoy this?" Peter asked.

"I do." I exhaled loudly as he suckled me again. "I just…"

"You're not used to this," Peter said, a statement. "Your husband didn't like to please you in this way."

The comment stunned me. How did he know? In so many ways, Peter seemed to know me, and yet we'd met only days before.

I looked stunned but didn't respond.

"It's okay," Peter said softly, making eye contact with me. I'm certain he took my silence as confirmation of his statement. Slowly, he slipped a finger inside me, then two. "You don't have to be afraid with me. When I am pleasing you, there is no clock. My pleasure comes from giving you as much pleasure as you need."

I believed him. Totally. Peter would probably spend two hours sucking and licking me if that's what I needed to get off.

But I didn't want that right now. What I wanted was for him to come. Maybe I wasn't ready for the level of intimacy it would require for me to come in his mouth. The mental barriers I'd put up with Andrew weren't going to come down so easily.

Easing my body to a sitting position, I reached for Peter. He gave me his hand. "What will please me right now is if you come."

I sensed he was a little disappointed, but he didn't argue. Instead, he came up to meet me. I kissed him, tasting my essence on his lips. This was foreign to me, but did it ever give me an erotic charge.

As our tongues tangled in a heated kiss, I used my upper body strength to push Peter backward. When he was flat on his back, I straddled him.

"I want to ride you," I whispered. "And this time, I want to watch you come."

Peter framed my face, thrust his tongue into my mouth again. He sucked on my tongue, giving my mouth no mercy. The man knew how to kiss, knew how to please.

He wrapped an arm around my waist, and before I knew it, we were both on the floor. He was still on his back, my legs still astride his waist. My mouth still fused with his.

Easing my hips up, I was the one who reached for his cock this time and guided him into me. But while I'd guided, he took command, startling me with a deep, hard thrust. I threw my head backward, a rapturous cry tearing from my throat.

The man was a machine. Hard and strong and fast and relentless. Even from beneath me, he jutted his hips up to thrust inside me at a speed my brain couldn't fathom. Then, his cock nestled even deeper inside me than when I'd been on my back, he planted his hands on my hips and began rocking me back and forth over his cock. The friction on my clit, coupled with the way he felt inside me, had another orgasm quickly building.

"Oh, my God, oh, my God." I was trying to breath steadily, stay in control, but I couldn't. Nothing had prepared me for Peter's stamina and skill. Within seconds, I was screaming as a powerful orgasm tore through me again.

"Look at me," Peter said.

Weak and whimpering, my eyes met his. He stroked my face, pushed deep inside me, then made some sort of animalistic sound as his body began to twitch.

Locking his fingers around my head, he pulled my face to his and kissed me like a man starved as his semen spilled into the condom. Only when we were both absolutely breathless did we pull apart and gasp in air.

His cock still inside me, I rested my head against his shoulder and tried to catch my breath.

I was beyond satisfied, and yet I knew there would be more to come.

Peter had said that the night was young and I would come many times.

I knew without doubt that he was a man of his word.

12

The next morning, I felt like I'd put my body through a wrestling match, then a marathon, and yet I couldn't stop smiling. My body throbbed in places I didn't know it could throb, and I was even bruised in a few spots. The upper part of my right arm had a purplish mark, as did my right breast. My nipples were swollen and still tingled from Peter's fervent suckling.

The man was incredible. Absolutely unbelievable. After fucking on the sofa, we moved to the bedroom where we spent three more hours trying out different positions.

Every position had been so amazing that I couldn't pick a favorite with Peter. I only knew that I wanted to try them all again.

And again.

I glanced at the bedside clock. It was ten-eighteen. How on earth was I even up at this hour after the energy I'd expended the night before? I hadn't gotten home until four in the morning, and quite frankly, I should be in a coma for the next few hours until my body's energy had been replenished.

And yet I couldn't sleep.

I threw off the covers and swung my feet over the side of the bed. As I did, I suddenly had a memory of how unabashedly I'd screamed as I came the second time, and I started giggling. Oh, God. Peter's neighbors must have heard me. I was surprised that no one had called the police.

I'd already showered at his place—the kind of shower that had led to a quick and satisfying fuck beneath warm water—so I got up from the bed and went right to the kitchen. I needed a cup of amaretto-flavored coffee.

Probably a whole pot.

I poured the ground beans into the filter to make the coffee extra strong, then, with it brewing, I lifted the wall phone in the kitchen and dialed Marnie's number. I couldn't wait to tell her about how incredible my night had been.

She answered on the second ring. "Hey, Sophie."

"Hey, girl," I replied. "What are you doing?"

"Being lazy. I'm still in my pj's, watching *Sex and the City*."

On second thought, I decided that I'd rather tell her about my night in person. Heck, I just wanted the company. It was still a bit unsettling to be in this house alone. "Turn off the television and get your ass over here," I said. "I've got something far juicier to tell you than what you'll see on *Montel*."

"Ooh. I like the sound of that. I'm on my way."

I was finishing a second cup of coffee when my doorbell rang. Marnie had made fast work of getting over here. I placed my mug on the kitchen table and ran to answer the door.

The moment I opened the door and saw Marnie, I couldn't stop from breaking out in a grin.

"You slut," she said playfully. "You did it, didn't you?"

In reply, I help up my left hand, displaying the bracelet that was once again on my wrist.

Now Marnie squealed. I grabbed her by the arm and pulled her into the house.

"I can tell by that smile on your face that you had a fabulous time. I want to hear every detail."

I didn't answer, just waltzed into the kitchen.

"Wait a minute," Marnie said, her tone aghast. "Are you *limping?*"

Now in front of the coffeepot, I braced my hands on the counter and whirled to face her. "I'm hurting in so many places, I wonder if I shouldn't check myself into the hospital."

Again, Marnie squealed.

"Coffee?" I asked casually. "I know I need another cup."

"You have any Baileys to add to it?" she joked. "I have a feeling I'll need a drink as I listen to what you have to say."

"I do have Baileys if you want it."

Marnie shook her head. "I'll take it black. And tell me what happened already."

"When we're both sitting."

Impatient, Marnie thrummed her fingers on the counter as I poured coffee for both of us. The moment we sank onto the sofa in my living room, I knew she'd had enough of the waiting game.

"Okay," she said, her eyes wide. "Tell me *everything.*"

"Oh, my goodness, where do I start?"

"Where it gets good," Marnie answered instantly. Then she shook her head. "No, no. I'm not that depraved. Start at the beginning."

"That *is* where it gets good," I told her, raising one eyebrow.

"What are you saying—you walked in the door and started fucking him immediately?"

"Pretty much."

Marnie's eyes grew as wide as her grin.

"That's not exactly true. We said hello, he offered me something to drink…"

"I'm sure he was the perfect gentleman. How long, how hard, how many times did you come?"

"I told you I'm hurting all over. I'm throbbing in places I didn't even know *could* throb. As for how many times I came—it was so many, I couldn't even begin to tell you. Seriously, the guy is like a machine. No, no. He's like the Energizer Bunny. He keeps going and going…"

"And you keep coming and coming. Girl!" Marnie spit out a laugh, then her eyes narrowed on my mouth. "Are your lips swollen?"

Slowly, I ran a finger along my bottom lip. It was one of the parts of my body that was throbbing. "That's not the only part that's swollen."

"Oh, my God. Okay, I think I'll have that Baileys now."

"You serious?"

"You're damn right I am."

I went to the fridge, retrieved the bottle of Baileys, and poured some into both our mugs.

"Seriously," I said as I settled back on the sofa, "it went on for like five hours. I think it could have lasted longer, but I told Peter I needed to get some sleep."

"Talk about an amazing booty call."

"Amazing doesn't even begin to describe it."

"I know I shouldn't ask this," Marnie said. "But what the hell, I'm going to. How does Peter compare to Andrew?"

"No comparison," I said, perhaps too quickly. "Don't get me wrong—Andrew knows how to please me. But with Peter, the sex was animalistic. Not tender, but mind numbing. It's exactly what

I needed in an affair. Something far different than what I experienced with Andrew."

"Sounds like you got that and then some."

I didn't bother to mention the other key difference between Andrew and Peter—how much Peter loved playing with my pussy. I guess I didn't want to mention that I'd been unable to come that way, when for the first time in my life, a guy had truly enjoyed going down on me.

"Are you going to see him again?" Marnie asked.

I shrugged, then sipped more of my coffee. The amaretto and Baileys made it extra flavorful. "I don't have his number. He doesn't have mine."

"You forgot to get the four-one-one?"

"I didn't forget."

Marnie looked at me as if I was crazy. "A booty call like that, I'd have him on speed dial."

"We'll see."

"You'll see? I know you want to see him again. I can tell by the look on your face. And if a guy had me coming countless times, I'd be calling him every night."

"A guy like that can be addictive," I pointed out. "You said yourself you forgave Keith so many times because the sex was so great. And in the end, you were heartbroken."

"First of all, Keith was my husband. I married him because I loved him, not just for the sex. Second, you're not in love with Peter. It's all about the sex, which makes things a lot less complicated."

"Maybe. But I don't want to get in too deep with him...you know."

"No, I don't know."

"Because of Andrew," I explained.

"Because of Andrew?" Marnie repeated, her tone full of shock.

"Right now, we're not together, and I'm not ready to be with him. But who knows, maybe after some time, we'll work things out. I don't want to be too involved with some other guy if Andrew and I are going to end up back together."

Marnie snorted. "I wouldn't worry about Andrew if I were you."

Marnie's obvious disdain for my husband made me plummet from my high over Peter. "Why do you suddenly seem like you can't stand Andrew?"

"Uh, maybe because he fucked around on you. And maybe because of the fact that his girlfriend might sue him and you could lose everything."

"I know that," I said. I didn't need Marnie to throw the painful facts in my face. "But, at least he had the decency to tell me about it. Unlike *Keith*."

A beat passed. Then Marnie asked, "Do you really believe that Andrew told you about his affair for any other reason than because the bitch was threatening to sue him?"

Marnie's words gave me pause. So much so that I couldn't answer her question.

"I know you think this is just about Keith for me, that I can't get over how he hurt me and I'm somehow projecting that onto Andrew."

I said nothing.

"Trust me, I'm not," Marnie went on.

"You think this is easy for me?" I asked her. "I don't know what the right thing to do is. It's hard enough trying to come to terms with Andrew's betrayal, and the fact that my heart still loves him. I need you to be a friend, and support me no matter what. And if you can't be objective about Andrew, then let's just not talk about him. Okay?"

Several moments passed. I broke the silence. "Here I was,

reliving my incredible night with Peter—and now I'm feeling like shit again."

"There's something I haven't told you," Marnie said, the words spilling quickly from her lips.

"What?"

I looked at her, but Marnie didn't meet my eyes. And that's when an eerie feeling started to spread through my body. I don't know why.

"What, Marnie?" I repeated, a little anxiously. "What is it you haven't told me?"

"I want you to ask yourself a question. Do you think this is the first time Andrew's screwed around on you?"

"Why are you—" I stopped cold, my mouth falling open as I stared at her. The thought going through my mind…

Marnie finally met my gaze, really looked at me, and took a deep breath before speaking. "Andrew came on to me once. About five years ago."

The words were like a knife slicing through my chest. I gasped. "No."

"First of all, you know I would never betray you. So don't even think it got beyond that. And in his defense, he was drunk, which is why I wrote the incident off and didn't mention it to you."

"He came on to you?" My voice was shaky.

Marnie nodded. "That's why I'm wondering…was this the first time?"

I wanted to be strong in the face of what Marnie had said, but I couldn't. Hot tears streamed down my face. "You think he's been cheating on me all these years?"

"I don't know," Marnie said softly. "Honestly, I wouldn't think him the type, but— Oh, sweetie." She brushed away my tears. "Maybe I shouldn't have said anything. It was a long time ago, and he never did anything like that again. I don't know why I said anything."

"No, I'm glad you told me." I got to my feet.

"Me and my big mouth," Marnie mumbled. "Leave it to me to take the focus off of Peter and bring you down."

I waved off her concern, feigning a nonchalance I didn't feel. "No, you should have told me. I wish you'd mentioned it before. Maybe you're right. Maybe I am deluding myself into thinking Andrew and I can resolve things."

"I didn't say that—"

I forced a yawn. "God, I'm exhausted. I should go back to bed."

Marnie stood. "Shit, you're mad at me."

I hugged her to prove that I wasn't. "No, I'm not."

I wasn't mad at her. I was mad at myself.

Mad at myself for being so naïve.

13

I saved myself the trip to Andrew's workplace. I didn't think I could stomach the sight of him. But once Marnie was gone I called him, because I had to know.

"Andrew Gibson," I said, when a friendly female voice answered the hotel's phone.

"One moment."

One moment turned into more than a minute. By the time Andrew came on the line, I'd convinced myself that he'd been sneaking in a few moments of illicit pleasure instead of doing his job.

"Andrew Gibson," he said.

"What were you doing—fucking your whore in one of the empty rooms? Or maybe the handicapped bathroom?" I hated myself for being so childish, but I couldn't stop my words.

"Of course not." He paused. "Sophie, I'm at work."

"I know where you are," I snapped. "I dialed the number."

"You can't call me at work to fight with me, okay? I've got a job to do here. If you want to see me later, you can yell at me in private all you want."

"Did you fuck my friend?" I asked, getting right to the point.

There was a pause then a confused "What?"

"Marnie said you hit on her."

"What?"

"Did you or did you not fuck her?"

"I have no clue what she's talking about."

"That's a yes or no answer."

"No! No, of course I didn't."

"But you did hit on her," I pressed on.

"No," Andrew said, but his voice seemed to waver. Or was I imagining that?

"Oh, so now *she's* the liar—as opposed to the man I *know* has fucked around on me?"

"Jesus, Sophie, will you stop the swearing?" Andrew spoke in a frustrated whisper.

"Maybe when you stop lying!"

"I'm not lying. I don't know what your friend is talking about. Yes, I had an affair. With one woman. I've never hit on Marnie, and God knows I've never slept with her." Andrew sighed. "If I have to tell you a million times, I will. I'm sorry, Sophie. And I still love you."

"Fuck you," I said, and slammed down the phone.

Less than a minute later, the telephone rang.

I figured it was Andrew, so I didn't answer it.

I spent the better part of the afternoon at the Florida Mall. It wasn't the first time I'd resorted to retail therapy when I was in a funk, though I'd usually have Marnie tag along. This time, I wanted to be by myself, since I knew I'd be terrible company.

I was well aware that Peter's apartment wasn't too far from the mall, and while I browsed the huge department stores, I contemplated driving to his place.

But I wouldn't, not in my mood. This was a time for me to be alone with my thoughts.

And my thoughts were grim. I couldn't stop thinking about what Marnie had said about Andrew. How, exactly, had he come on to her? Had he whispered something crude in her ear? Had he squeezed her ass? Had he cornered her in a bathroom and asked for a quickie?

In my wildest dreams, I couldn't imagine Andrew asking for a quickie. Then again, I never would have thought he'd have an affair.

But I did know that he could be a little frisky when he got drunk, which wasn't very often. Maybe he'd jokingly slapped Marnie's ass, and she'd taken him seriously.

And maybe I was pathetically grasping at straws.

How did I really know that Andrew wasn't the type to jump at pussy when the opportunity arose? He could have had me completely fooled, and, like Marnie had said, only confessed his infidelity because his mistress was threatening to sue him.

The thought made my stomach queasy, and I tried to put Andrew out of my mouth altogether. I focused my attention on trying on dresses, shorts, shoes, sunglasses.

I bought a pair of sandals, a straw hat, and a new bathing suit at JCPenney. At Sears, I bought a new pale peach towel set and an expensive coffeemaker I'd been eyeing before, the kind that allowed you to make cappuccinos and espressos. I didn't need any of this stuff, but shopping helped pass the time.

I made a trip to my white Honda Civic to put all my purchases in the trunk. Then I went to Barnes & Noble, hoping I'd find a gory murder mystery that would take my mind off love. Instead, the first book I saw when I entered the store was *How to Cope with Being Newly Single*. Turning my head, my eyes locked on *He's Just Not That Into You*.

So much for retail therapy. I turned and fled the bookstore.

I forced myself to think about Peter, which wasn't hard, considering my body still vividly remembered his touch. I remembered the primal sound that had rumbled in his chest when he'd had his face between my thighs. I remembered how easily our bodies had connected, as though we'd been lovers before.

I needed to see him again. I needed more of that animalistic passion and toe-tingling sex.

Even the score, Andrew had said. I would do that and then some.

That thought in mind, I went back into the mall and headed straight for Victoria's Secret, which I had passed earlier. But when I got there and saw the mannequins in the window wearing lacy bras and panties, I kept walking.

I didn't want pretty and sexy. I wanted naughty.

So I went to Frederick's of Hollywood, where I bought the kind of bra and panty set that Andrew would have been shocked to see me wear. See-through, with puffy balls over the nipples and at the sides of the thong. I would wear it tonight when I went to see Peter, maybe with only a trench coat over top.

The thought made my ravaged pussy throb.

If Peter and I went at it at the same pace we had the night before, by the next morning, I might just have to seek medical attention, as I'd joked with Marnie.

I was counting on it.

At home, I went right to the bedroom where I dropped all my purchases onto the bed. The red message light on the bedside phone was flashing.

I went to the phone and punched in the code to retrieve the messages. The first was from Andrew. He sighed before speaking, having the nerve to sound frustrated. "Sophie, I know you're there." A beat. "Okay, I guess you're not going to pick up. Listen, you have to believe me when I say that I don't know what Marnie is talking about. I really don't. Hell, I'm not even attracted to her. I love you, Sophie. And as pissed off as you get, I won't stop. Please remember that."

The next message was also from Andrew. "Sophie, I really want to talk to you. Call me back, please. I'm here till five. After that, you can reach me on my cell phone."

I heard Marnie's voice after that. "Hey, Sophie. Just calling to check up on you. Look, forget what I said about Andrew. It was a long time ago, and he was likely too drunk to know what he was doing. Whatever you decide to do, know that I'm here to support you one hundred percent. I'm sorry it didn't seem that way."

Contrary to what she thought, I wasn't mad at her. I would call Marnie back, but not yet. I wasn't in the mood to talk about anything that had to do with Andrew. It was too painful.

Instead, I tried on my lingerie. At the store, I'd only tried on the bra to make sure it fit, but now I put on the thong as well. Wearing the two racy items, I paraded in front of my dresser mirror.

Perfect, I thought. I looked good. More than good. I looked tempting.

How would Peter react if I appeared at his door wearing a light jacket and opened it to expose this naughty lingerie? For the first time since Marnie's shocking news earlier, I actually giggled. I bet Peter would mutter something in Italian, then pull me into his apartment and have me naked in five seconds flat.

There was no reason I had to wait until night to pay him a visit. As the saying goes, there was no time like the present.

I had just the right jacket. The light coat was black and made of cotton, and had a belt that tied around the waist. And while the jacket reached me mid-thigh—certainly longer than the minis and short-shorts young women sported in Florida—I felt as though everyone who saw me would know I was dressed only in lingerie under my coat.

I exited my house and tried to hurry to my car without anyone seeing me, but no such luck. Mr. Warner, my elderly neighbor who lived across the street, was in his driveway. He raised his hand and waved enthusiastically. Was I mistaken, or was he smiling a bit more brightly than usual?

I returned his wave and hustled into my car. I officially lived in Kissimmee, home of Mickey Mouse, and it took me twenty minutes to drive into Orlando proper where Peter lived. Seeing the apartment complex during daylight, I noticed for the first time the vibrant green grass and colorful hibiscus. The fountain at the entrance to the property was more impressive at night, only because it lit up. The property was beautiful, but that was Florida for you. With warm temperatures all year round, lawns were always well maintained and gardens always lush.

I pulled up in front of building number nine and killed my car's engine. I gazed up at his second-floor window, which had a view of the parking lot. I hoped he would sense me and look out.

He didn't.

Waiting until I saw no one around, I got out of my Honda Civic and climbed the steps to the second floor. I would have to alter my plan somewhat. With it being daylight, I wouldn't flash Peter until I was in his apartment and the door firmly closed.

I raised my knuckles to his door and knocked. Then waited. After several seconds, I knocked again.

No answer.

I frowned, disappointed. How stupid could I have been? I hadn't even considered that he might not be home when I got here. It was barely after five. No doubt, the man had a job. He was likely still at work.

I don't know what I expected, but when, at four in the morning, I'd had to pry his greedy hands off of me, I certainly hadn't figured that he'd had to get up and go to work for nine.

I glanced around, looking for his vehicle. There were three black SUVs in the parking lot.

Of course, he just might be out. Shopping or something.

Or in another woman's bed.

Making my way back to my car, I thought about the fact that I knew nothing about Peter other than his cock size and that he was great in bed. I didn't know what he did for a living. I didn't know if he made his own pasta. I didn't know if he had any brothers or sisters.

He was a stranger.

And yet, I'd given him my body without any inhibitions.

And that was perfectly fine. I wasn't trying to build a personal connection with him. My time with Peter was about one thing.

Sex.

When I was two feet away from my car, I heard footfalls and turned. A young man, early twenties, was walking on the sidewalk about ten feet away from me. His eyes went directly to my torso, as though he had X-ray vision and knew exactly what I had on beneath my coat.

I opened my car door and pressed the coat to my butt before

climbing inside. I didn't want to reveal any more of my body than I already was.

I decided to wait on Peter, because I certainly didn't want to go back to my place. Not yet. But after ten minutes, I accepted the fact that I had no idea when he would be getting home, and I couldn't stay in the parking lot all evening.

I opened my glove box and scrounged around until I found a piece of paper and a pen. Best to write him a note, and if he wanted to, he could contact me when he got home.

Peter, I came by to see you, but you
weren't home. Call me. 407-555-0987.
Sophie

I made the way back to his apartment, where I slipped the note under his door. "Don't keep me waiting," I said softly.

14

At home, I made dinner and waited for Peter to call.

And waited.

When the clock struck ten, I came to the conclusion that Peter had already moved on to a new fuck buddy, or was the type of guy who didn't want to bed a woman more than once. He certainly could have his share of women, and for all I knew, he did.

That thought depressed me a little, and I decided to call Marnie. I didn't want a new day to dawn with her believing I was mad at her for what she'd told me earlier. One thing I didn't doubt—Marnie was my best friend, and she would never do anything to hurt me.

Marnie picked up on the third ring. "Hello?"

"Hey, hon. It's me."

"Sophie."

"I just wanted you to know that I'm not mad at you, okay?"

"Good." She sounded relieved, as if she'd been waiting to hear me say this all day. "Like I said, Andrew might have been so drunk, he didn't know what he was saying."

So Andrew's come-on had been verbal. I hesitated, tempted to ask exactly what Andrew had said. But I didn't. It didn't really matter. What mattered was the fact that he had cheated on me, confessed to that, and that was the issue I needed to deal with.

"The bottom line is that I have to be careful," I said. "I need to figure out if I can really trust Andrew to be a faithful husband from here on in. *If* I decide to take him back."

"And just to set the record straight, that's exactly what I hope. If you guys can work this out and have a happy marriage…more power to you."

"I know you want what's best for me," I said, a faint smile forming on my lips.

"I do, Soph. You're the best friend I've got. You're closer to me than my own sister."

"I know that. And you're the sister I never had."

The call-waiting beep sounded in my ear, preventing either of us from getting too sappy. "Marnie, hold on a sec." I glanced at the phone's display and saw the name P. Bacchio.

Italian. *Peter.*

"Marnie, I think that's Peter calling on the other line."

"Oh, okay. Night, sweetie."

I clicked over to the other line, paused for a moment to wipe the grin off my face, then said, "Hello?"

"You came to see me."

I curled my legs beneath me on the sofa. "Yes. Yes, I did. But you weren't home."

"I was working."

"Until now?" I asked.

"Until half an hour ago, yes."

"What do you do?"

"Why don't you come see me and I'll tell you?"

I grinned from ear to ear. It was an offer I couldn't refuse. I didn't care if Peter had been making a buck, or if he'd been in bed with a harem of women. We were only fucking.

"Right now?" I asked.

"Works for me."

"Then I'll see you soon."

I went as I was, in a simple sundress, as opposed to changing into the sexy getup I'd worn to his place earlier. Changing would have taken more time, and I wanted to see Peter already.

En route to his place, I found myself feeling nervous. How would Peter react to me this time? Would it be with the same level of passion as before? The second time around, would we connect with the same intense electricity?

The question was answered when I got to his door. As soon as he saw me, his face lit up and his eyes darkened with lust.

I felt a jolt of raw heat—especially when I realized that Peter was wearing only a towel.

"Hello," he said.

"Hi." I maintained eye contact with him, acting as though I hadn't seen his naked chest and the beads of water glistening on his skin. The man oozed pure sex. Already, my libido was in overdrive.

"It's okay to look," Peter said, clearly picking up on the fact that I was deliberately not ogling him. "Okay to touch."

I cracked a smile. "I figured it's better that I wait until I'm inside your apartment."

"Whenever you want me, I'm yours."

God, but the man was irresistible. He stepped backward, and I walked into the apartment, letting my eyes fall lower to his impressive chest and six-pack abs. Obviously, he worked out to keep his body in such amazing shape.

I didn't need a psychic to tell me he'd done his fair share of working out on women. With his stamina and strength, it was no wonder he had such great abs and quite likely the world's greatest ass.

I reached for Peter as I stepped into the apartment, but he moved backward before my fingers were able to graze his skin. I moved forward again. He moved away from me again. A teasing smile danced on his lips as he continued to take slow steps backward, as though he enjoyed being just out of my reach.

"You know how sexy you are, don't you?"

"I know how sexy *you* are," he replied, but he didn't stop moving. He rounded the sofa, and the glint in his eye told me he wanted me to chase him.

"I get it," I said. "You want me to prove that I want you."

Peter winked at me. I lurched. He ran.

I paused to consider my next move. Then I took a few steps, stopping in front of the sofa. Peter matched my steps until he was directly opposite me behind it. I kicked off my shoes, because the low-heeled sandals would only hinder me.

And then I sprinted around the sofa. Peter sprinted as well. His towel flapped with each of his strides, but stayed in place.

I stopped behind the sofa. He grinned at me from the other side. "I imagine you are not used to being the cat," he said. "Only the mouse."

"Don't you worry about me," I told him, feeling competitive. "I can catch a mouse or two."

And then I charged. It didn't look like he'd expected me to run when I did, and he had to move extra quickly before I reached him. I chased him for two laps around the sofa before I finally stopped.

Perhaps I should cheat.

I gave chase again, and this time, when I was behind the sofa and Peter in front, I dove over the back. My fingers skimmed his legs as I landed on the cushions, and he laughed.

When I got to my feet, I saw that he wasn't standing directly behind the sofa, as I'd expected, but about halfway between the sofa and his bedroom door. I was slightly winded but tried not to let it show.

Slowly, Peter loosened the towel from around his waist. Revealed himself to me completely. Even though his penis wasn't erect, it was still impressive.

He balled the towel and tossed it toward me. It landed on the floor behind the sofa. "How badly do you want me?" he asked.

He didn't give me a chance to answer, just ran toward his bedroom. I ran after him. The lights were off in the room, so I paused when I crossed the threshold, trying to see where he was.

In the moment I realized he wasn't on the bed, a shadow lunged at me from behind the door. Though I knew it had to be Peter, I screamed and instinctively turned away. Then giggled as his arms came around me from behind.

My giggles turned into moans as he pressed his lips to my neck and began flicking his hot tongue over my skin. While his tongue worked magic, he took my hands in his. Raised my hands high in the air and walked with me like that until I was at a wall.

His tongue dipping into my ear, he guided the palms of my hands to the wall. I pressed them flat, my moaning growing louder as the sensations of pleasure became more intense. Peter moved my hair out of the way and planted a slow, wet kiss on the back of my neck.

Then both his hands and mouth moved lower. His fingers stroked my back, his tongue my spine. My dress was in the way as his mouth ventured lower, but I felt the heat of his lips nonetheless.

Suddenly, I felt nothing. Not his fingers. Not his lips. It was odd to feel nothing when you couldn't see and know what was coming next. Seconds ticked by, and my heart began to beat faster as I wondered exactly what Peter would do.

Then his hands were on my thighs, pulling my dress up to my waist. My dress went up, my thong went down, and Peter sank his teeth into my ass.

He groaned. I gasped.

His teeth pulled at my skin. His tongue flicked over it. He sucked it hard, and I knew he was going to give me a hickey on my ass like he'd done on my breast.

I flinched when I felt his fingers on my pussy. Then groaned when his fingers began to stroke my clit. They fondled me, dipped inside me, wiggled around and stretched me.

Peter withdrew his fingers, and I could hear the soft sounds of his tongue lapping at my essence.

The sound made my pussy throb.

Bringing my hands down from the wall, I turned around. Peter was on his knees, one finger still in his mouth. He really did love to eat pussy. I bent to meet him and trailed my tongue along his strong jawline. His mouth sought and found mine, and we necked as fervently as a couple of teenage kids in the backseat of a parent's car.

As we kissed, Peter lowered himself onto the carpeted floor. I held my dress up and tried to straddle him, but my thong being partway down my legs prevented that. Realizing my predicament, Peter wrapped his fingers around the side of my thong and snapped the fabric.

Then he urgently curled his hands around my ass and pulled me downward while he kissed me.

His cock rested beneath my pussy, and I savored the feeling. I wanted nothing more than to have him enter me. But I managed to whisper "condom," knowing we couldn't risk sex without one.

Peter groaned, sounding a little disappointed. I slid off of him. He rose and went to his night table, where he fumbled around until he found a condom. Moonlight spilled into the room through the partially open blinds, allowing me to see his imposing erection. I touched my clit, finding it hard the way Peter had described that first night.

I couldn't wait to feel his cock inside me again.

While Peter hastily opened the condom wrapper and began to roll it on, I started to take off my dress.

"No," he said. "Leave it on."

My hands stilled. "Okay."

The condom in place, he moved toward me and got down on his knees to meet me. As he held my gaze, he lightly trailed his fingers over the spaghetti straps of my sundress. Then he dipped his fingers beneath the material and drew it down.

He pulled on the halter part of my dress, which was made mostly of elastic, freeing my breasts. Moaning as if he'd discovered the world's greatest treasure, he lowered his head to one breast and began to suckle me.

Unlike the night before, when he'd suckled me hard, this time he did it gently. He suckled, twirled his tongue around my nipple, then gently grazed my hardened peak with his teeth.

He did the same to the other breast, sucking exquisitely until the delicious vibrations tingling my skin had me panting. He was stroking the pad of his thumb over my other nipple, heightening my pleasure.

My clit was pulsing wildly. "Fuck me," I rasped. "Please, fuck me now."

With a primal-sounding grunt, Peter flipped me onto my back and landed between my thighs. The move was surprisingly gentle. I eased my legs back, Peter adjusted his position, and then he was inside me.

Pure sexual bliss shot through me. This was the absolute best moment during sex, that first moment when a cock plunged inside your pussy. Even though I'd had Peter for hours the night before, the moment he entered me again I knew that this time would be a new, thrilling experience.

"Hard and fast?" he asked, his breath warm on my ear. "Or nice and slow?"

I kissed his neck. I wasn't sure my vagina could withstand the same kind of energetic fucking tonight. "Nice and slow."

The moan that escaped his throat sounded like one of appreciation, and locking his arms behind my knees, he burrowed himself deep inside me. Burrowed and stayed there. Kissed me. Then pulled back slowly, thrust slowly.

My entire body filled with sensation. Even if Peter didn't move, I bet I could come like this. Just having him inside me made my body feel amazingly incredible.

"Yes, *bella,*" Peter said, and planted his lips on mine. We kissed the entire time his cock was inside me. Our tongues tangled as he moved his cock with slow skill.

This was intimate sex. Slow and sweet and personal.

So when my orgasm seized me with the strength of a category five hurricane, I didn't expect it. Not given the pace we'd been maintaining. It spiraled from my center and spread to the tips of my fingers and tips of my toes, the depth of the pleasure indescribable.

I tried to tear my lips away as I gasped, but Peter kept his mouth on mine. He continued to kiss me as I moaned, swallowing my cries as if to make them a part of him.

Only when my orgasm subsided did Peter free my lips. I turned my head to the side and gulped in a deep breath.

"I love how you tremble in my arms. I love the taste of passion on your lips."

I met Peter's gaze, thinking that there was something special about him. He had his own brand of passion that was entirely addictive. Andrew never talked to me this way, but I liked it.

Liked it a lot.

"Did you come?" I asked.

"Your satisfaction is what is paramount to me," he said simply.

"I know, but..."

"Don't worry. We have all night."

Peter eased his cock out of me and moved beside me. He covered one breast with his palm as he kissed me again.

I closed my eyes, unable to prevent my body's surrender. And as Peter slipped his hand between my thighs, made me come again with only a few skilled strokes while he kissed me, I wondered if I would ever be able to get enough of him.

15

I stayed with Peter that night, woke up to find his arms wrapped around me as we lay spoon-style. My pussy was raw and slightly sore, and yet I knew that if Peter woke up and pulled me on top of him, I would be helpless to resist him.

He was as decadent as chocolate, and as tempting.

"What are you thinking about?" he asked, and I was surprised at the question. Surprised he was awake.

"You," I answered honestly. His hand was resting on my stomach, and I placed my hand on top of his.

"I'm glad you stayed with me all night. I like waking up with you in my arms."

Something tugged at my heart. Once again, I had the feeling that he was special. I wasn't exactly sure what was happening between us, but I was happy to know that it wasn't simply the wham-bam-thank-you-ma'am kind of fucking. I thought I was capable of that, thought I'd wanted that, but I now knew that if Peter hadn't wanted to see me again after that first night, I would have felt used on some level—even though we'd been strangers.

It wasn't that I wanted to walk off into the sunset with him, but I didn't want our exquisite encounters to end just yet.

Not until I'd had my fill.

"Are you going to work today?" he asked.

"No." I paused. "I'm a teacher, so I have the summer off."

His hand tightened on my stomach, as though the news pleased him. As if he figured we could now spend the next six weeks in this bed.

That thought was extremely appealing....

"What about you?" I asked. "You said you were going to tell me about your job when I got here, but then we...we got distracted."

He brushed my hair aside and planted a soft kiss on the back of my neck. My clit throbbed in response.

My God, you'd think I hadn't spent the better part of the night having orgasm after orgasm. What was it about Peter that made his every touch on my skin so utterly delectable?

"Are you trying to distract me again?" I asked, my eyes fluttering shut. "Stalling for time so you don't have to answer the question?"

"I make corporate videos, infomercials that air on late-night TV. Things like that."

I turned in his arms to face him. "You make videos?"

"Well, I don't really make them. But I shoot them. I'm a videographer."

"Wow," I said, unable to hide how impressed I was.

"It's a job," he said.

"It sounds fun."

"Actually, it can be tedious. One day, maybe I'll make some movies. Who knows?"

"What have you worked on?"

"Nothing you would know. Boring corporate videos for various companies. An infomercial for Ford—you might have seen that on late-night television. Testimonials about how wonderful the Ford Focus is, and how easy to get financing."

I hadn't seen that, but it didn't matter. "I'm impressed."

"Why?"

"I don't know."

"Because you think it's a glamorous job?"

I shrugged. "Well, I guess you could say I have an appreciation for creative things. A long time ago, I even thought I might be an actress."

"You can still be one. You're beautiful."

"No, not anymore."

"Of course you are still beautiful."

"That's not what I mean. I'm saying I can't be an actress anymore. My time for that has passed."

"Why would you say that? If you have a dream, you should go after it."

"I'm too old now," I said.

"How old are you? Twenty-three?"

I laughed. "Yeah, right. I'm thirty."

"Thirty!" Peter gave me a soft kiss on the lips. "You don't look a day over twenty-three. The camera only cares how old you look, not your real age."

"Maybe," I said. "But my life has changed. That's no longer my dream now." I didn't want to say that once I'd gotten married, I'd put my dreams on the back burner. "I'm happy teaching, so it's not like I'm missing out on anything. And when I want to be creative, I paint."

Now Peter was the one who looked impressed. "So you *are* an artist."

"I wouldn't go that far, but I like painting."

"Have you had a showing?"

"A showing?" My eyes bulged in surprise. "Hardly. I'm not that good."

"Will you let me see your work?"

"You're not serious."

"Of course I am."

"Why?"

"Because I am."

"It's not like I'm any good or anything."

A beat passed. Then Peter asked, "Your husband was not interested in your painting?"

"Oh, no," I responded easily. "Not at all. Well, he didn't hate me painting, but he saw it as a hobby. Nothing more."

"And you see it as something more." It was a statement, not a question.

I hadn't thought about my dreams for such a long time, I'd put them behind me. But there was a time when I thought I'd pursue something creative, either painting or acting. Instead, I'd gone into teaching, a far more stable career.

"Like I said," I went on. "I enjoy painting, but I'm no professional."

We fell into silence, Peter seeming to realize I didn't want him pushing the issue.

My eyes wandered past him to a five-by-seven photo on his night table in a silver frame. A pretty black woman and dark-haired white man were sitting side by side, their cheeks pressed together. Huge smiles were on both of their faces.

"Are those your parents?" I asked.

Peter turned his head, followed my line of sight. "Yes."

"What a beautiful couple," I said wistfully, thinking of my own parents. Had my parents ever looked that enamored with each other? "They look happy."

"They were. They were very happy."

"Were?" I asked.

Peter nodded. "Yes. They died."

I gasped. "Oh, Peter. I'm so sorry."

"It's not your fault," he said. "And I'm at peace about it. They died together, the way they would have wanted."

I stroked Peter's face. "It was tragic?"

"They died in a house fire. I believe my father tried to save my mother, and died for his efforts."

I stroked Peter's face again, conveying in my touch my concern for him. "I'm so sorry."

"They were inseparable in life, and they're together in death."

"I guess that's a nice way to look at it," I said softly.

"What about your parents?"

The mention of my own parents stirred bitterness in my gut. "My father died. Car accident. But they were never as happy as your parents look in that photo." I left out the fact that my mother had left my father for another man, and that he'd died brokenhearted. "My mother is remarried and lives in California."

"Do you have brothers and sisters?"

"I have a brother. He's older than I am. Eleven years ago, he was on vacation in England and met a woman. He moved there for her and they've been happily married ever since. You? Do you have brothers and sisters?"

"Three brothers, two sisters. All older."

"Wow."

"They live in Italy, near Rome. I lived there too, until eight years ago."

"What brought you to America?"

"I met someone online, and went to visit her. I stayed two months. We broke up, but I fell in love with Orlando and wanted to stay." Peter paused. "I also wanted a new start. It was the year after my parents died, and it was hard for me to stay in Italy after that."

"Of course," I said.

"Let's talk about something else," he suggested.

I nodded. I couldn't blame him for not wanting to talk about family anymore, given that he'd lost both his parents so tragically.

"How many boyfriends did you have before you got married?" Peter asked me.

"That's quite a change of subject."

"You don't want to tell me?"

"I have no problem telling you," I said. "Only one. Well, two— but one of them I married."

Peter's eyebrows rose. "Have you only been intimate with two men?"

"These days, I suppose that's hard to believe. But yes. Until you. You're the third."

Peter smiled, seeming to like my answer. "How do I compare?"

"Peter!"

"Seriously, *bella*. I want to know."

"Well, the first one? There is no comparison. I shouldn't even call that a sexual experience," I said sourly. "That—" I didn't finish my statement, instead exhaling sharply.

"What happened?" Peter asked.

I didn't respond.

"*Bella?*" The pitch of Peter's voice rose with alarm.

I still said nothing, but my mind went back to that awful night.

"Look at me, *bella*."

Only then did I realize that I'd closed my eyes. I opened them, and saw that Peter was looking at me with concern.

"What did he do to you?" he asked.

I sighed. Then I said, "He raped me."

"What?" Fire flashed in Peter's eyes, and he pulled me closer, his arm tightening around me protectively. "My God. When? Who was this man? Was he charged?"

"He was a boyfriend—sort of. And no, he wasn't charged. It was a long time ago. Eleven years ago when I was in college."

Peter was angry; I could tell by his heavy breathing. And despite the unpleasant memory of what Chad had done, it made me feel good to know that Peter cared.

"I was dating him at the time. He wanted to have sex, and I thought I did, too. Then I changed my mind and told him no, but he wouldn't stop." I recited the facts casually, without any emotion. I had to keep up a wall when I thought about that night with Chad. Otherwise, I might fall apart.

"*Bella,* I'm sorry you had to experience that."

"I'm fine," I said. "It could have been worse."

But how much worse could it have been? I had lived with the memory for eleven years, sometimes having horrible nightmares. With Andrew, I'd been content with comfortable sex, never caring to explore anything too intense. Sometimes even when making love to Andrew, I'd think of Chad and have to stop. Andrew had always been thoughtful of my feelings, and he never pressured me at all.

But now that I'd gotten involved with Peter, I had learned something about myself. I understood now that I'd been holding back sexually with Andrew, perhaps not willing to completely trust a man because of what Chad had done. I had only felt safe with comfortable, tender sex, never exploring my wild side. Andrew's affair had freed me in a sense, and now I was discovering the depths of my sexual satisfaction in a way I would never have considered in the past.

And I was no longer afraid to ask for what I wanted.

"Your ex-husband hurt you," Peter said. "Your first boyfriend hurt you. But *bella,* I will never hurt you. I will love you the way you deserve to be loved."

Peter's words made me feel warm inside.

"I wish I could kill this man who raped you," Peter said, then kissed my temple. "He had no right to hurt you the way he did."

"He'll go to hell," I said, not wanting to think about Chad anymore. "I believe that."

Peter gently kissed my forehead. "Now it will be harder for me to go on my trip and leave you here."

I narrowed my eyes as I stared at him. "What? You're leaving?"

"Yes. Will you miss me?"

"Where are you going?"

"I have to go to Key West for four days."

"Key West…" My heart thundered. "What's in Key West?"

"Work. I'm shooting a promotional video for the Sheraton Hotel."

"Oh." I frowned.

"Don't be sad." Peter slipped his thumb beneath my chin and lifted my face so I could meet his eyes. "I'll be back in four days, *bella.* On Tuesday."

"How am I supposed to survive without you for four days?" Tuesday seemed like a lifetime from now. I'd hoped to spend most of this weekend in Peter's bed, but now that wouldn't happen.

Peter laughed softly. "I don't leave for the airport until this evening. You can spend most of the day with me if you like."

I slipped one of my legs over his while placing a hand on his cock. "I can?"

"Of course. In fact..."

In an instant, Peter repositioned himself between my legs. He spread my thighs, exposing my pussy. Lust shot through me immediately. And when Peter kissed my nub, my vagina grew instantly wet.

He licked me, suckled me, dipped two fingers into my pussy. "I'm going to give you something to remember me by every day that I'm gone."

"Peter," I mewled. "Oh, baby." My breathing picked up speed, and so did his tongue. "No one has ever made me feel as good as you do. No one..." My voice trailed off as delicious pressure built in my pussy. I closed my eyes and savored the sweet feel of Peter's tongue.

Minutes later, I was screaming his name as I came.

By four o'clock that afternoon, after stopping for a quick bite and a large coffee, I was home and already missing Peter. Peaches was glad to see me, and the first thing I did was go to the kitchen to refill her bowl with food. However, I found it full. There was also a fresh bowl of water.

Andrew had been here?

I whirled around, half-expecting to find him inside, although his car wasn't in the driveway. That's when I noticed a note on the kitchen table.

I lifted it and read.

Sophie, I came by early to get some things. I was hoping to catch you at home. Sorry I missed you. I hope you're okay. Call me when you're ready to talk.
Love, Andrew

I crumpled the note and walked to the trash can. But I hesitated before I tossed it and, instead, unfolded the note and read it again. Then I crumbled it again and threw it away.

I wasn't ready to deal with Andrew yet, and I didn't like the idea of him coming here unannounced. *I came by early,* he'd written. How early? Did he realize I hadn't been here last night?

It didn't matter if he did. He'd been the one to give me his blessing to screw another man. But still, I found myself wondering what he was thinking…and how he might have reacted to the thought that I was in another man's bed.

If he knew how many orgasms Peter had given me, would he regret having had an affair?

"Stop thinking about Andrew," I told myself, but I knew that was easier said than done. How could I stop thinking about the man I'd been married to for eight years?

My feet began moving, and the next thing I knew, I was lifting the phone's receiver. I wanted to hear Peter's voice, a man who was making me feel good instead of bad.

Maybe I'd even offer to go to Key West with him, promise I wouldn't get in the way of his work.

Peter, however, didn't pick up. *Hell, he must at the airport already,* I thought, frowning.

Should I pack a suitcase and hit the road? Driving to Key West from Orlando would take several hours, but it wasn't impossible. With good traffic, I could be there by midnight.

Immediately, I frowned. I couldn't go to Key West. Sure, I could possibly track Peter down there. He'd mentioned the Sheraton, and someone there would have to know something. But if I showed up unannounced like that—when he was there to work—he'd think I was a stalker.

No, I would stay home.

But I had a feeling I'd be bringing myself to orgasm quite a lot over the next four days.

16

All I could think about was Peter for the next few days. He had called me every night, usually after ten, and it was nice. Every time the phone rang, I got butterflies in my stomach, anticipating hearing his voice on the other line.

It made me realize just how much I'd come to care for him in such a short time. Yes, I liked the sex. Okay, I *loved* the sex. But it was more than that. I enjoyed spending time with him. I enjoyed the way being with him and hearing his voice boosted my spirits.

Even though he was in Key West, his whispered naughty words into the phone line at night turned me on as much as his touch. Something about the way he spoke to me made me truly believe I was the most beautiful woman in the world.

It was great to know that a guy was so into me.

The contrast between Peter and Andrew was glaring. Andrew and I certainly had decent sex, but nothing like what I was experiencing with Peter. Peter enjoyed getting me off on the phone, something Andrew had never done, not even once. Andrew was safe, predictable.

Peter was exciting, wild.

The fact that I hadn't been able to stop thinking about Peter while he was gone helped me make a decision about something. Not a major decision, but a minor one. I didn't want to stay in the house and look at Andrew's stuff anymore. I didn't want to see his clothes in the closet, his cologne in the bathroom. I knew I couldn't simply erase him from my life by putting his things away, but nonetheless, I didn't want the constant reminder of him around.

So I called Marnie and asked if she'd help me pack up Andrew's things into boxes. For now, I could store them in the garage.

"You want to pack up Andrew's things?" Marnie asked.

"Yeah. I think it's something I need to do."

"What does that mean?" Marnie asked. "Are you—"

"Making this a permanent split?" I offered. "Not necessarily. But, I kind of feel like I need to explore what I'm feeling for Peter. I can't stop thinking about him. I don't know, I just…" My voice trailed off. I wasn't sure what I was feeling.

"Hey, if you need me to help you pack up Andrew's things, I'm there. And if you want my help unpacking them as well, I'll help you do that too. But tonight's not good for me—"

"That's okay. We can get an early start tomorrow."

"I'll be there," Marnie said.

I hung up the phone and replaced the receiver, feeling as though I'd made the right decision.

After midnight, when the phone rang, I immediately bolted upright. I twisted my body to see the caller ID.

Private Name.

I smiled. That had to be Peter calling from his cell. I muted the television and snatched up the receiver.

"Hello?"

"Sophie, hi."

My body froze. That wasn't Peter.

"Andrew," I said, a little breathless from the surprise.

"I hope I didn't wake you."

Was Andrew drunk? His words sounded a little slurred, but wherever he was was noisy. Perhaps a bar?

"I miss you, babe. I don't think you realize how much I miss you."

Yes, he had to be drunk. "Where are you?" I asked. "A bar?"

"I want to come over. Can I see you tonight?"

"What?" Panic shot through me. "You—you can't come over."

"Is someone else there? Is that where you were the other night, with *him?*"

"You're drunk, Andrew. Do not come over here. And do not get into a car."

"You'd care if I got killed?" Andrew said, all the words practically blending into one.

"You're talking nonsense."

"Someone else there?" Andrew went on. "Is that where you were the other night—in someone else's bed?"

I didn't know what I should say, especially with Andrew being drunk. "Where are you?" I asked.

"Bahama Breeze. I'm listening to the live reggae band and re-membering our honeymoon in Ja-mai-ca." He feigned a Jamaican accent.

Bahama Breeze was on International Drive, not too far from where Andrew worked. I found myself throwing off the covers. Even though I didn't want to see him, I couldn't stay here and let him possibly get behind the wheel while drunk. That would be out of character for Andrew, but he definitely didn't sound like himself.

"Are you by yourself?" I asked.

"No. Dave's here."

Relief washed over me. That was good news. "Let me talk to him, please."

"Holdonasec."

There was some shuffling and, moments later, Dave came on the line. "Hello?"

"Hi, Dave. It's Sophie."

"How're you doing, Soph?"

"I'm all right," I said. He didn't sound inebriated, but still I asked, "Are you drunk?"

"Naw. I had one beer, but I've been drinking soda ever since."

"So you're able to drive?" I went on, to be sure.

"Yeah, yeah. I'm good. But I've got to say, Andrew's really hurting over you."

I didn't respond as I got back under the covers.

"He loves you, Sophie. He really does."

I waited a moment, then said, "He's got a funny way of showing it."

"He's sorry. You've got to believe him, Sophie. He's going crazy without you."

It felt as though a heavy weight was pressing against my chest. I didn't want to be having this conversation. And I certainly didn't want to be guilted into forgiving Andrew. I was going to deal with this in my own time, and forgive him when I was good and ready. *If* I was ever ready.

"I'm glad you're there for him," I said to Dave. "And I'm going back to bed now."

I clicked the talk button to end the call.

Less than a minute later, it rang again. Frustrated, I pressed the talk button and began without preamble, "Andrew, stop drinking and go home. And stop calling me."

"Who's Andrew?"

That wasn't what I'd expected, and I was momentarily speechless. Then I said, "Peter?"

"Who else calls you at this time of the night?"

"Hey, you." I smiled. "I was wondering if you were going to call tonight."

"It was a long day, and the crew went out afterward, or I would have called earlier. So, who's Andrew?"

"My husband," I answered. "You remember I told you I was married."

"I thought you were divorced," Peter said, and I could hear both surprise and disappointment in his tone.

"I'm separated," I clarified.

"Didn't you tell me you were divorced?"

"No. Actually, we didn't we really talk about it. But we're not together, if that's what you're thinking."

"Why did he call you?"

I sighed. "Because he's out, drinking. I guess he's sorry for what he did. But you know what, I don't want to talk about Andrew. I want talk about you. I miss you," I added in a sexy whisper.

"I miss you, too. Like crazy."

"Oh, yeah?" I asked, the stirring of desire rumbling in my belly.

"You cannot imagine how much."

"Oh, I think I have some idea. I can't wait to see you, touch you... When will you be back?"

"Tomorrow. Around eight."

"In the morning?" I asked hopefully.

Peter chuckled softly. "You really do miss me."

"Of course."

"Good. Because I want you at my place as soon as I get there, which should be around eight in the evening. I'll call you from the airport and you can head to my place to meet me."

"I will," I assured him. I lowered my voice and whispered, "I need you, and so does my body."

"Are you wet right now? Just from hearing my voice?"

"I'm turned-on."

"But are you wet?"

"Maybe. A little."

"Find out."

I giggled. "You mean…"

"Yes. Touch yourself."

I giggled again.

"Please, *bella,*" Peter said, his voice raspy. "I need to know."

"Okay," I said. I slipped my hand into my panties. Dipped my finger into my folds. "Mmm. Yes, I'm wet."

Peter's deep groan rumbled through the phone line, and the sound sent a jolt of desire straight to my clit. "Are you wearing panties?"

"Yes."

"Take them off."

"Really?" I glanced around the room. The cat was on her bed near the door, staring at me curiously.

"Please, *bella.* I need you to take them off. Take them off and touch yourself."

I didn't need Peter to ask again. I lowered the phone and slipped my panties down my thighs.

"Okay," I said when I picked the receiver up again. "I took them off."

"Are you wearing anything else?"

"A black negligee…but it's pulled up around my waist."

"Beautiful." Peter groaned again, and now I could hear the sound of him stroking his cock. "I can picture you, on your back with your legs spread slightly, showing me your pussy. I wish I could taste you right now."

I swallowed. "This is only going to make me more crazy."

"Play with your beautiful pussy. I want to hear you come."

Again, I looked at the cat, but she'd lowered her head and closed her eyes. Good. I switched the phone to my left ear so I could touch myself with my right hand.

"Are you touching your pussy?" Peter asked.

"Yes…" I ran a finger over my clit in slow circles.

"Do you know how much I love to touch you? How much I love the way your clit gets hard when you are turned-on? Play with it until you come."

"I am…" The pressure was building. I closed my eyes, remembering his touch.

"But what I love most is when your pussy is in my mouth. The sounds you make when my tongue is flicking over your clitoris. How your breathing changes…"

His voice was stoking my internal flame as much as the memory of his physical touch. "Oh, my goodness, Peter."

"Are you going to come?" I could hear his strokes, faster now.

"Almost…I'm almost there."

"That's the first thing I'm going to do tomorrow. Make love to your pussy with my mouth. Push my tongue so far inside you—"

I exploded, screaming Peter's name as I did. I rode the wave of pleasure, pushing my fingers deep inside my pussy the way Peter had described doing with his tongue.

"I'm coming, baby!" Peter yelled, then groaned long and hard with his own release.

My orgasm left me breathless, the same way Peter sounded. As his own breathing returned to normal, I smiled into the receiver. "That was amazing," I purred. "And you weren't even here with me."

"Imagine what it will be tomorrow night."

Imagine was all I could do. I dreamed about being with Peter, and in every scenario, we were fucking.

On his bed. In his bathtub. On the sofa.

Even on the balcony.

"What is it about him that is so damn irresistible?" I asked myself when I woke up in the morning, hardly rested at all. I'd been too wired and anxious to sleep deeply.

And yet, I was smiling.

Smiling because I would see Peter soon.

I did wonder how Andrew was doing, but only briefly. When I thought about Andrew, it only brought me down, while thinking about Peter excited me and made me forget the pain of Andrew's betrayal.

The phone rang when I was in the kitchen making coffee, and I quickly snatched the receiver off its base on the wall. "Hello?"

"My, oh, my, don't you sound excited. Who were you expecting?"

The sound of Marnie's voice yanked my thoughts away from Peter. "Hey, Marnie," I said. "What's up?"

"What's up? I thought you wanted me to come over this morning."

For a moment, I was confused. Then I remembered that she'd promised to come over and help me pack Andrew's things. "Right, right. Sure, you can come over."

"Is someone there with you?" she asked, almost in a singsong tone.

"No. It's just me and Peaches. So, whenever you're ready."

"You still want to do this?" she asked.

"I'm only putting his stuff in the garage," I said. "Not burning it." Time would tell what would happen between me and Andrew, but right now, I was totally focused on Peter.

And on reacquainting myself with his cock later tonight.

"So yeah," I went on. "I still want to do this."

"I'm just going to jump into the shower and I'll be right over."

"Great."

With Peter still out of town, this was the best time to pack up Andrew's things. Because once he was back, I wouldn't be spending much time at home.

17

Marnie arrived within the hour, carrying two cups of coffee from Starbucks. "Two grande Caramel Macchiatos," she announced.

"You're the best," I told her, taking one.

"Aren't you going to ask me why I'm on my third cup of coffee today?"

"This is your third cup of coffee?"

Marnie sipped her Starbucks brew and raised one eyebrow. "Mmm-hmm."

I knew that tone. "Marnie!" I exclaimed. "Did you and TRULYACUTIE—"

"Spend most of the night fucking?" Her face lit up in a huge smile. "You bet we did."

"You dirty girl," I teased. Marnie just laughed.

"So things are working out with him," I went on.

"He's not crazy, at least not as far as I can tell. He's actually very funny."

"And the sex was good?"

"The sex was *hot*."

I sipped my own coffee. "Nice."

"His name is Robert, by the way. Not Rob, not Bob. And definitely not Bobby."

"So when do I get to meet him?" I asked.

"Whenever," Marnie said. "Maybe even tonight. Hey—you and Peter can go out with me and Robert. Make it a double date. Maybe we can find a drive-in theater where we can neck in the backseat and miss most of the movie."

I was way beyond necking in the backseat, and what Peter and I would be doing later certainly had to be done in private.

"Well, tonight's no good," I said. "Peter gets back into town tonight, and no offense, but I want to keep him all to myself. But I like the idea of us all going out sometime. Maybe dancing."

I was feeling as carefree as the teenagers I'd read about in books and seen in movies—the only things on my mind were having a good time and having lots of sex. I hadn't been that kind of teen in reality, and maybe that's what I liked so much about Peter—that with him I was experiencing the kind of sex I'd never had.

I may as well enjoy my free time with him before school started again. Maybe even beyond that...

"Speaking of things working out," Marnie said, "you really seem to like Peter."

"I do," I said wistfully. "On one level, I'm not sure what we really have in common. Would he have been the kind of guy I'd talk to in college? Not really. I've always gone for the safe guy, the stable guy, and Peter definitely has a sort of wild streak to him. But on another level, do we ever connect when it comes to sexual chemistry! When we're together, he makes me forget that anything else exists. That anything else matters."

"I'm glad you're having a good time," Marnie said.

I led her to the bedroom, where we went into the closet. I'd gotten some boxes together before she arrived, so they were ready for our task.

"You can start with Andrew's shoes," I said.

"That's a lot of shoes," Marnie commented. "You don't think he'll need them?"

"He hasn't come back for them yet. And if he does, they'll be conveniently packed for him." I bent to pick up a black dress shoe and tossed it to Marnie. She caught it. "Pack them all," I told her. "I'll start with his clothes."

Marnie placed the one shoe in the box, then got onto her butt and positioned herself near the rack of Andrew's shoes. "Speaking of Andrew—have you heard from him?"

"He called last night," I said.

"Oh?"

"It wasn't pretty," I told her, pulling one of Andrew's neatly pressed T-shirts off a hanger. "He was drunk, and out with Dave. He called after midnight and rambled on about how he missed me and stuff."

"What did you say?"

I packed the shirt into the box, then took another one off the hanger, and continued that routine while I spoke. "Nothing, really. Except try to find out if he was there alone and might get behind the wheel. That's when he told me Dave was there. So Dave comes on the line, and he starts going on about how much Andrew loves me, that he made a mistake, yada yada yada."

I was surprised that I was relaying the facts casually, without feeling anxiety in my gut. Maybe I was actually moving beyond the hurt, or at least compartmentalizing it.

"It's weird," I went on. "I haven't been thinking about Andrew at all. All I've been able to think about this past weekend has been Peter and when I'll see him again." I paused and rested my hands on top of the box, which was almost full. "Remember in the Bahamas, when you were with Soriano, and you said you'd never felt that kind of sexual connection even with your ex?"

"Of course."

"Now I get it. Because I feel the same way about Peter. I don't remember *ever* feeling like this with Andrew. This kind of all-consuming passion where every single part of you can't wait to see a man again. I know my relationship with Peter is still new, but every time he touches me..." Just thinking about his touch was stimulating me. "Marnie, every time feels like the first time. Is it because it's new? Maybe. But again, when it was new with Andrew, it never was as intense as this."

"That's because Andrew doesn't like going down on you."

"Marnie!"

"It's true," she said. "From what you told me about Peter's tongue, it's no wonder you're hooked on the guy. You know how girls often fall for their first sexual partner?"

"I've heard. My case was different, of course."

"I know." Marnie's face first softened in sympathy, then hardened in anger. "I still wish I'd cut off Chad's balls for what he did to you."

I waved away the comment, mostly because I didn't want to allow myself to remember what had happened that night. Unfortunately, I'd learned firsthand that a stranger didn't have to grab you from the bushes and force himself on you for your life to change forever. Someone who was supposed to love you could hurt you in ways you'd never imagine.

Like Andrew had.

For the most part, I was able to keep the pain of the rape

locked away. No good would come from dwelling on it. But occasionally, the memory got to me. I supposed that from time to time it always would.

"Sophie?"

My head whipped upward. "Huh?"

Marnie's expression was full of concern. "Are you okay?"

"Let's not talk about Chad," I said. "Continue with the point you were making. You were saying that women often form attachments to the guys who are their first."

"Right. Well," Marnie began slowly, "you're experiencing great oral sex for the first time with Peter. That's bound to have you a little attached."

"Maybe that's part of it," I agreed. "But even if he didn't like doing that—and he *does*—I would still be drawn to him. It's like our bodies speak their own language. Know what I mean?"

"Yeah," Marnie said dreamily. "That's how I'm feeling about TRULYACUTIE—well, Robert. At least after the first night. Time will tell if the sex gets stale."

Marnie continued speaking, telling me about the dinner Robert had cooked for her last night, and how impressed she was with guys who could cook, but I hardly paid attention. My mind was on Peter, and the fact that I couldn't wait to see him. I wished he was here right now, that we were both naked and in his bed.

Sex might get stale with some people, but I had the feeling that Peter and I would never face that problem.

Hours later, all of Andrew's clothes, shoes and toiletries were in boxes and stored in the garage. The place looked very different, and a little weird without Andrew's stuff in plain sight.

It's only in the garage, I reminded myself. *Easy access, if necessary.*

But as far as I was concerned, the boxes would be staying in the garage for a long time.

I hadn't heard from him today, but assumed that Dave had gotten Andrew back to the hotel without incident.

I put him out of my mind and thought of my upcoming reunion with Peter. As the hours passed, I grew more excited. And more anxious. I couldn't wait to see him again, but the minutes seemed to be dragging by with agonizing slowness.

At six-thirty, after eating a bowl of cream-of-broccoli soup, I started to get ready. I showered and washed my hair. I smoothed a coconut-scented cream over my skin.

And then I got dressed.

Well, *undressed* was a better description. Because I got into the skimpy bra and underwear I'd bought at Frederick's of Hollywood.

I used more makeup than I normally did, with dark eyeliner and a smoky shadow, and two coats of lash-enhancing mascara. By the time I'd put on my glossy red lipstick, I looked like I could have been a pinup girl in a racy calendar.

I checked out my reflection in my dresser mirror and grinned devilishly at my sex-kitten transformation. "Oh, yeah. Peter, you're not going to be able to resist me."

The phone rang. I sprinted across the bedroom to snatch up the receiver.

"Hello?" I said breathlessly.

"I just got to my apartment."

Peter's voice. I smiled. "I'm on my way, baby."

I hung up the phone and within five minutes, had a sexy pair of black heels and my coat on. I opted for a higher-heeled strappy shoe this time as opposed to the lower-heeled slingbacks I'd worn with the outfit the first time.

This pair was much, much sexier.

Well, sluttier.

Oh, yeah, Peter and I would have some serious fun tonight.

18

Ready for a night of illicit fun, I left my house. Twenty-two minutes later, I was parked outside Peter's apartment. Unlike the first time I'd worn this outfit to surprise him, I didn't head to his door uneasily, but strutted there with confidence, knowing that within moments, I would be giving Peter one wicked surprise.

He opened the door before my knuckles hit the wood, his face lighting up when he saw me. Then desire darkened his gaze as his eyes settled on my coat.

"Interesting outfit," he commented.

"I was feeling a little chilly," I lied.

"I can help warm you up." He curled his fingers around the collar of my coat and pulled me inside.

He kissed me, and every part of my body grew instantly hot. I reached between us to loosen the tie on my coat, so Peter could see what I had on underneath, but Peter's hands came over mine.

"No," he said.

"You're going to like what I'm wearing underneath this," I told him. "Promise."

"I'm sure I will. Which is why I cannot allow myself to be tempted." He ran his hands down my arms and took a step backward, leaving me confused. "Are you hungry?"

"Starving," I replied, sinking my teeth into my bottom lip, leaving no question as to what I wanted to feast on. As much as Peter enjoyed oral sex, he clearly preferred giving as opposed to receiving, and wasn't particularly interested in me sucking his cock.

But I wanted to feel the same measure of power he must feel over me when he had me quivering against his tongue.

"I'm starving too." As he spoke, he took another step backward, and now I narrowed my eyes as I stared at him. "They didn't feed me on the plane, and I was running late so I didn't eat at the airport. Why don't we go out for a bite to eat?"

"You're joking."

"Don't be disappointed. I assure you, I will ravish your body— but to do that, I first need some food. For energy." He trailed a finger down the front of my coat. "Good things come to those who wait."

"Why don't we just order a pizza?" I suggested. "You don't realize what I have on under my coat."

A smile danced on his lips. "I think I have a pretty good idea. And that will be the best part. Me looking at you as we eat, knowing what I'll be having for dessert."

My eyes widened. "You're not trying to say…I mean, you don't actually want to go to a restaurant? I thought you'd go through a McDonald's drive-through or something."

His finger went from the tie on my coat to the base of my neck. Every time his skin touched mine, I felt an electrical charge.

"*Bella,* I would not take you to McDonald's."

"Then what do you have in mind?" I asked, suddenly uncomfortable. "Because if you want to go somewhere nice, I can go home and change."

Slowly, Peter shook his head. "This is exactly how I want you. Just let me put on my shoes."

I wasn't convinced about going out—not while I looked like a stripper—but I followed Peter to his doorway nonetheless. He slipped into a pair of black flip-flops. There he was, wearing blue jeans, a T-shirt and flip-flops, and I was dressed in a coat, high heels, and practically nothing underneath. We couldn't have been more mismatched if we'd planned it. One look at us and people would have to wonder if I was a prostitute Peter had hired for the evening.

"Think of this as an adventure, *bella,*" Peter said, taking my hand. "A naughty adventure."

Suddenly, I was no longer apprehensive, but turned-on. Excited. Hand in hand, we walked to Peter's car, and I no longer cared that we looked mismatched.

We were a perfect fit in the only way that mattered to me.

Peter clearly walked on the wild side, a side I wasn't familiar with. I sensed he was the kind of guy who didn't care what others thought and who played by his own rules.

I liked that about him. Found it intriguing. Andrew was so strait-laced that he was predictable—with the exception of his affair, which I'd never seen coming.

Or maybe Andrew was the type who liked to play by the rules because he cared what people thought, and therefore wanted to create the illusion of being the good guy. Which is why his affair had blindsided me so.

But Peter…there was something wickedly sexy about his intensity. Something wickedly sexy in his simple touches that conveyed so much desire. I loved the way he always made eye contact with me. The way his lust for me was obvious in his gaze.

I'd meant what I'd said to Marnie—even when love had been new with Andrew, I never remembered feeling like this. I'd felt safe, yes. Deep affection, yes.

But not this burning, uncontrollable passion.

"What are you thinking about?" Peter asked, his question pulling me from my thoughts. I saw that we were at his gold Lincoln Navigator.

"You," I replied simply.

He gave me a brief but wet kiss, then opened the passenger-side door for me. Moments later, we were both inside. Peter took my hand and brought it to his lap.

It was nice, the way he always wanted to be touching me.

"So," he began. "Where would you like to go?"

"I don't know. Surprise me."

"How about The Venetian Room?"

The Venetian Room was a fine-dining establishment. "You must be kidding."

"Why not?"

I chuckled uneasily. "You're not dressed for that. And neither am I." *Especially not me.* "Besides, I thought you said you were hungry. It'll take two hours to get through all their courses."

Peter leveled a charming smile on me. "I'm kidding. But how about Bahama Breeze?"

"No." Not after Andrew had been there last night. Besides, it was far too close to where Andrew worked. We might be separated, but I didn't want to run into him by chance.

"How about Denny's?" I suggested. "The one on Orange Avenue isn't too far from here. I don't know about you, but I can have breakfast any time of the day. It'll be fast enough, tasty."

"Grand Slam?" Peter asked.

"I tend to go for pancakes smothered in strawberries and syrup."

"Strawberries and syrup. Hmm." As he said the words, Peter moved my hand farther up his leg, until I was touching his groin. He was hard.

I looked at him. "Are you sure you want to go out? I'll be happy with a Big Mac and fries."

Peter's lips curling playfully, he drove out of his parking spot. "A naughty adventure, remember? Let's enjoy it."

As we approached the restaurant's door, I glanced around nervously. And it wasn't just because I was wearing hardly anything. I suddenly realized that I might see someone I knew. A parent of a student in my class. Or worse, a colleague of Andrew's who would report back to him about my being out with another man, and dressed like a stripper, no less. I'd been excited by Peter's talk about a naughty adventure, but now I wondered if this was a bad idea.

Peter tightened his arm around my waist, and as desire took hold, some of my concern ebbed away. Why did I care if someone Andrew knew saw us and told him about it? Surely everyone knew that Andrew had screwed someone else by now. Why the hell was I concerned that word might get back to him that I was seen with another man?

Besides, Andrew and I were separated, and whatever I did was no one's business.

"You all right?" Peter asked me.

"Fine," I replied. "And hungry."

We made our way into the restaurant. The lights were so bright I felt like a spotlight was on me. The curious and disapproving eyes of a middle-aged couple on their way out locked on me, and I shifted from foot to foot, uncomfortable. Even the hostess eyed me from head to toe with a probing gaze, as though she could see exactly what I had on underneath my coat.

"You're nervous, *bella*," Peter whispered.

I looked his way and shrugged slightly.

"You are in good hands. Trust me."

"Table for two?" the hostess asked. Her jaw smacked as she loudly chewed gum, something I'm sure she wasn't supposed to be doing while on the job. And right then I had a lightbulb moment. She could size me up all she wanted—her opinion didn't matter.

"Yes," Peter replied. "In a corner somewhere if possible, away from everyone. My girlfriend and I enjoy our privacy."

The hostess studied us for a moment, as if the "girlfriend" comment baffled her. She blew a bubble, then sucked the gob of pink gum back into her mouth. I expected her to start pulling on it with her fingers, that's how annoying she was.

"Sure. Table for two, for you and your girlfriend."

I leveled a "don't mess with me" look at her, and she flashed a syrupy smile before turning to head onto the restaurant floor.

I glanced at Peter, hoping he'd be annoyed by this girl's attitude or at least her gum-smacking—enough to change his mind about eating here. But instead, he followed the hostess without so much as a disapproving look. Thankfully, the restaurant wasn't all that crowded, and an entire section to the far left was completely unoccupied.

"How about right here?" Peter asked.

"No one's working that section," the gum-chewer said.

Peter ignored the hostess and took a seat at a booth. "Tell whoever takes care of us that we'll make it worth her while."

He fished a twenty out of his wallet and passed it to the hostess, whose attitude warmed considerably. She smiled genuinely. "Oh, certainly. I'll take care of that for you."

The hostess trotted off gleefully, and I rolled my eyes. I said to Peter, "She thinks I'm a hooker."

In response, Peter extended his hand to me. "She only wishes she could be as sexy as you. Come."

I hesitated, acting a little perturbed. Though Peter was right. I didn't care what the hostess thought.

"Come," Peter repeated.

I took his proffered hand and slid into the booth beside him. As soon as I was sitting, he drew me to him and kissed me deeply.

Far more deeply than people should kiss in public.

The kiss lasted no more than five seconds, but when I pulled away, I quickly looked across the restaurant to see if anyone had been watching.

"Sophie, are you ashamed of the passion we feel?"

I turned back to Peter. "No. No, I'm not ashamed. I just…wish we had more privacy."

"Get up," Peter said.

"Hmm?"

"Actually, you can just slide across my lap."

Before I could ask what he was talking about, he took me by the waist and pulled me onto his lap. He groaned softly as my ass settled over him, but the next moment, he urged me to his right, and I landed on the soft seat of the booth.

"What are—"

"Now, you are on the side away from the rest of the room. My body is blocking yours." He paused. Kissed my cheek. "We have more privacy."

I got what he was saying, and warmth spread through me. "What exactly do you have in mind?" I asked.

"Nothing you won't enjoy."

"Peter…"

He placed his hand on my lap, brushed his fingers against the skin on my thigh.

And even here, in a Denny's restaurant with bright lights, I found my body yielding to temptation.

"Did you miss this?" Peter asked, his eyes locked on mine. He was gently stroking my skin.

"You know I did."

His fingers went beneath my jacket, stretching the short distance to reach my pussy. Then he pulled his hand away when we both noticed a waitress walking toward our table.

I ordered pancakes with whipped cream and strawberries, and Peter ordered a Denny's Grand Slam breakfast. We both ordered orange juice as well.

The moment the waitress was gone, Peter slipped his hand between my legs again, this time not stopping until his fingers stroked my panties.

"Lace," he said, sounding intrigued. "Black?"

"You'll see."

He moaned softly. "I wish I could see right now."

"*That* will have to wait for later."

"At least I can touch." His fingers fiddled with the lace on my panties, pushing the fabric aside so he could touch my skin. "Oh, yes," he whispered hotly in my ear. "Touching is the best part."

I shuddered from the pleasure.

"Open your legs for me," Peter said.

I glanced across the restaurant. The closest person was probably thirty feet away, and had his back to me. Anyone who looked this way wouldn't be able to tell what Peter was doing unless they were brazen enough to stare, and I didn't think that was likely.

"Peter…"

"Open your legs, *bella*."

I couldn't deny him. Didn't want to. I opened my legs a little, giving him more access. He stroked me with abandon, and I had to bite down on my bottom lip to keep my moan inside.

When he slipped a finger inside me, I instinctively pressed my legs together because of where we were, but that only heightened the pleasure.

"Peter," I rasped. "Every time you touch me…oh, shit. I see the waitress coming."

With a groan, Peter pulled his hand from my pussy. "I'm not sure we can stay."

"You think she saw us?" I whispered in alarm.

"No." Peter pressed his lips to my ear. "I'm not sure I can stand another moment of being here when I need to get you naked. Immediately."

Giggling, I pulled my head away from his lips just as the waitress arrived with our drinks. Peter thanked her, then kissed my cheek when she was gone.

"It was your idea to go to a restaurant to eat," I told him. "I wanted to go to a drive-through."

"What was I thinking?"

He put his hand between my legs, touched me again, and I also touched him. Found him rock hard. And then we started kissing.

I was powerless to stop this inappropriate public display of affection. I was a slave to my desire.

I expected someone to yell, *Get a room!* No one did, but I wouldn't be surprised if that's what some were thinking. And I certainly wouldn't blame them. Peter and I couldn't keep our hands off each other. Being in a public restaurant right now was not the place for us.

And yet…

And yet, our being here was heightening our mutual desire for one another. It was like a foreplay session with lots of teasing.

The waitress arrived with the food a short time later, and the first thing Peter did was dip his finger into the whipped cream on my pancakes and offer me a taste. I opened my mouth, and he slipped his finger inside. I sucked the whipped cream off slowly.

He repeated the action, this time putting the finger into his own mouth. "Not as sweet as you," he announced once he'd swallowed. "But this whipped cream is giving me an idea. If only I could get you naked right now, we could have some delicious fun."

My clit pulsed. If Peter wanted to get under the table and eat my pussy, would I be able to stop him?

I pushed the scandalous thought from my mind. Of course, neither of us would get that out of control, but the thought aroused me even more.

Peter scooped up more whipped cream, and this time put it on my nose. Then he licked it off slowly.

"Imagine my tongue on other parts of your body…parts that will be much more appreciative."

"The more you talk and don't eat, the longer it will take for us to get out of here."

Sighing, Peter turned his attention to his food, and we both wolfed down our meals. We didn't care about the taste; after all, we weren't eating meals prepared by a gourmet chef. But I suspected that even if we had been, we'd have eaten for sustenance rather than enjoyment, as long as it meant we could get naked faster.

We barely made it to Peter's car before we were in each other's arms in the parking lot, hotly kissing as though there weren't cars and people passing by on the busy avenue.

In my brain, I knew this. And yet, I didn't care.

Peter pulled his lips from mine, then took my hand and jogged with me to the back of the restaurant.

"What are you doing?" I asked.

In response, he placed my hand on his cock so that I could feel how hard he was. "I can't wait until we get back to my place. Can you?"

He meant that literally; I could tell by the look in his eyes.

He wanted to fuck outside? Yes, it was dark behind the restaurant, but anyone could come out at any time.

Pulling me into his arms, Peter made fast work of slipping his hands under my coat to cover my ass. "Am I the only one who cannot wait?"

"No," I answered honestly. "But—but what if someone comes out here? Sees us?"

He turned me around, making me face the wall. "I know." His warm breath tickled my neck. "But some of the excitement comes from the risk." He brushed his lips over my skin. "Of knowing that I want you so badly I have to have you, even though someone might witness us together." He pushed my coat up, and groaned when he saw my ass. "This is all you're wearing underneath your coat? It's almost nothing."

"I also have on a bra," I pointed out.

"I need to fuck you," Peter said. "Right here."

My legs shook. I wanted that too. But... "What about your car?"

"Right here. Please." He ran his fingers along my folds. "My God, you're dripping wet."

All reason fled my brain. "Fuck me, Peter. I can't wait."

I heard the quick rustling of his pants, felt one arm lock around my waist. Then I gasped as he entered me with a hard, desperate thrust.

He thrust in and out, in and out. Hard and fast and relentless. I braced my hands against the cool wall, tried to keep my cries locked in my throat.

Peter kissed my neck, suckled my skin, and played with my pussy while he fucked me.

Within seconds, I was coming. Hard. Peter gripped my hips and drove his cock into my pussy, and his loud groan told me he'd just come, too.

There was no time to luxuriate in orgasmic bliss, not when someone could walk by at any moment. I turned, pulling my coat down as I did. Peter was doing up his pants.

Our urgent need for sex satisfied, reality was sinking into my brain. "You came inside me," I said.

Peter met my eyes. "I know. I—I wanted to pull out."

"I'm not on the Pill." I ran a hand over my face. I didn't feel like my body was ovulating, but still.

"Are you unhappy, *bella?*"

Was I? I was a little worried, yes. But I was likely being paranoid.

"I wouldn't mind if you had my baby," Peter said softly, stroking my face.

"You wouldn't?"

"No."

I said nothing, but once again told myself that I was likely being paranoid. I wasn't about to get pregnant.

Peter took my hand in his and pulled me close. Then he kissed me tenderly.

He could fuck so wildly, and also be incredibly gentle.

"Let's go home," Peter said. "I have a surprise for you."

19

I was certain that Peter's surprise would be of the sexual variety, but when we got to his place and he insisted on covering my eyes while he led me to his second bedroom, I realized it had to be something else.

"What is it?" I asked, giddy and excited.

"You'll find out in a moment."

I could feel him stretching to open the bedroom door. Then he walked me inside.

"Okay. You can open your eyes."

I did. And was floored.

"Peter," I said in awe. In front of me was a large easel, a stool, and a table with an array of paints and brushes.

"Do you like it?" he asked.

I turned to face him, emotion filling my throat. "I can't...I can't believe you did this for me."

Peter's eyes were dancing. "So you like it?"

"I love it. And I love you for caring."

"I have a friend in Miami who knows someone with a gallery. Maybe you can pursue this dream after all."

I stepped toward Peter and placed a palm on his cheek. Andrew had never taken my "hobby" seriously—and here was Peter, encouraging my dream after I'd known him only a couple weeks.

"Thank you," I said. "This really means a lot."

I planted my lips on his.

And then we made love, nice and slow, on the bedroom floor.

I pretty much spent the next two weeks in Peter's bed—except for when he was at work—which was exactly where I wanted to be.

The sex was hot, frequent, intense and luscious. I honestly didn't know when I would grow bored of fucking Peter.

Aside from that one time outside Denny's, we always used protection. We didn't let our passion get in the way of common sense.

And things were changing between us. The more we had sex, the more it started to feel like making love. We were getting closer. I started to wonder if this was the beginning of something real with him.

He even gave me a key so I could come and go as I pleased.

He'd worked Friday, Saturday, and Sunday morning—another weekend gig out of town—and by Sunday evening, I was at his place. Not only did we have lots of sex, but we cooked together, cleaned together, and generally acted like a couple.

But by Tuesday morning, I knew I had to get going. My plan to go home Monday was waylaid when Peter had seduced me with more sex.

I twisted my head to see the digital clock on the night table at Peter's side of the bed. It was 7:53 a.m.

"You're awake already?"

Peter's question surprised me. I thought he was sleeping.

I eased back down. "Yeah, I'm gonna get going."

"Going?" Peter asked. "Where?"

"Home."

Peter's eyes narrowed. "Why?"

"You know. I'll check messages, clean the house, check the mail. There are some bills that have to be paid…"

"You need to do all that right now?"

"I may as well get an early start," I told him, and kissed his nose. "Especially since I'll be coming back later. And I also told my friend Marnie that I'd go shopping with her today."

"You can check your messages from here," Peter said. "And Marnie doesn't need you to shop, does she?"

"Theoretically, no. But it's more fun to go with a friend."

"I don't like to shop."

"That's because you're a man," I said, smiling.

Peter tightened his arm around my waist. "I don't want you to go."

"I'll come back."

"Just stay with me."

I eased myself out of Peter's arm. "I do have to leave," I said, climbing off the bed. "There's also my cat. She's got to be starving."

"Oh, your cat will be fine. It's true," Peter said. "They can survive for days without food. I know. I used to have one."

"Used to…in Italy?"

"Yes."

"I guess you left it there?"

"No, I drowned the bastard when it scratched me."

My mouth fell open in horror. "Peter!"

He grinned playfully. "I'm kidding, of course."

"That's an awful thing to say. Why would you even joke about that?"

"I'm kidding," Peter stressed, his tone light. "As far as I know, Madonna is still alive. She's what?—fourteen now—and lives with one of my sisters."

I found my panties on the floor and slipped into them. "That's good to hear, but I still have to go home and feed Peaches."

"Okay. Go home and feed your cat. Then come right back."

I felt a spurt of annoyance. It wasn't like I didn't spend enough time at Peter's place. Not answering, I pulled my dress over my head. Then I went back to the bed and leaned over to give Peter a kiss.

Wrapping an arm around my waist, he pulled me onto the bed with him. I started to protest, but as his lips worked magic over mine, I melted into his kiss.

I was truly starting to believe that I was powerless once Peter touched me. That with his hands or mouth on my body, I could no longer think.

"Let me make love to you, *bella*," he whispered in my ear, making my body quiver.

And when he pushed my dress and panties out of the way and buried his face in my pussy, I forgot all about the fact that I'd been planning to go home.

I didn't make it home until the next morning, and only then because Peter had to report in for work. Peaches greeted me at the door immediately, her meows definitely angry.

"I'm sorry, baby," I said, bending to stroke her. She let me pet her only for a moment, then started to trot in the direction of the kitchen, looking over her shoulder as she did. When she saw that I was following her, she kept going. Stopping in front of her empty bowl, she looked up at me with a pleading expression, one that seemed to beg, *Feed me!*

I quickly filled one bowl with water and the other one with food. Peaches rubbed her head against my legs and purred, showing me some love as I was about to give her what she craved most.

Once the food was set down, she attacked it.

The red light on the wall phone was flashing, so I checked my messages. There were five from Marnie, starting from Monday night, and ending about an hour ago. She wanted to know where I was and why I'd stood her up for our shopping trip.

I called her.

"So you're not dead," she said sarcastically when she picked up the phone.

"I'm sorry, Marnie. I totally didn't mean to stand you up."

"What happened?"

"I just...I lost track of the time with Peter."

"I called your cell. It went straight to voice mail."

I'd turned it off, wanting no distractions. It was weird, because when I was with Peter, the whole world was about Peter. I wasn't like that in my everyday life with Andrew.

Of course, my everyday life with Andrew wasn't primarily about sex.

I didn't want to confess to Marnie that I'd had my cell off to shut out the world, because it would sound...well, lame. So I said, "Let's reschedule. I *promise* I'll be there."

"I had a surprise for you, you know."

"You did?"

"Yeah. Robert."

"TRULYACUTIE? He was there?"

"Uh-huh. He came so he could finally meet the friend I always talk about."

"Oh, Marnie. I really am sorry."

"Robert was disappointed. He was looking forward to meeting you."

I didn't know what else to say to make this any better, so I said nothing.

Marnie broke the momentary silence. "You could have at least called. That's so unlike you."

"I know, I know. I was wrong. But let's make new plans. Hey, maybe we can all get together and hit a club this weekend."

"That's a good idea," Marnie said, her attitude finally warming.

"It'll be fun. Ask Robert if there's a place he prefers. I'll let it be your choice."

After that, the conversation went well, and when we ended the call, we were both looking forward to a double date.

But when I broached the subject with Peter that night after dinner, he couldn't have been less enthused.

"I don't think so," he said.

"Why not?"

"I don't feel like going to some club where other men will be staring at you, trying to touch you."

I frowned as I set our plates in the sink. "Well, we can go for dinner, then."

"Maybe." He didn't sound interested.

"We have to," I said, turning to face him. He was leaning against the fridge. "Marnie's already pissed off that I was a no-show for our shopping trip yesterday. Apparently, I was supposed to meet her new boyfriend."

"Why do you have to meet her boyfriend?"

What kind of question was that? "Because. She's my best friend. And now that she's got someone new in her life, she wants me to get to know him." I paused. "I want her to get to know you, too."

Peter's eyebrows rose as he stared at me. "Does that mean you think I'm special?"

"Of course I think you're special," I answered without hesitation. We hadn't had the are-we-dating-or-just-fucking talk, but I figured it was safe to assume, with as much time as we were spending together, that things were beyond the simply fucking stage.

Even if that was our favorite thing to do.

"Aren't we dating?" I asked casually. "Or is this just about sex for you?"

"It was never just about the sex," Peter said quietly.

"Good," I said. "I'm glad you feel the same way. That's why I think it's important for you to meet my friends. And I'd like to meet your friends as well. I realize you haven't spent much time with them since I've come along, but maybe they should meet the woman who's occupying all your time."

"I don't have many friends."

I'd kind of sensed he was a bit of a loner, perhaps because all of his family lived in Italy. But surely he had at least one good friend. "You must have at least one person you're close to," I said. "The way I'm close to Marnie."

"I'm close to you," Peter said. "You're all I need."

"The night I met you—who were you out with?"

"I was out by myself."

Okay, that was a little odd. But not completely unusual. Guys probably did that more than women, especially if they were looking to get laid. Women liked to go out with a friend or two—even to the bathroom.

"I think I fell in love with you that first night," Peter said. "The first moment I looked at you."

I actually giggled, thinking Peter couldn't be serious. But when I saw the solemn expression on his face, my laughter stopped.

"You're not kidding," I said.

"I never kid about love."

My God, he loved me. Or at least, he thought he did.

Peter moved toward me, slipped his arms around my waist. "Do you love me, Sophie?"

A few seconds ticked by. I didn't know what to say. But Peter was staring at me, clearly waiting for an answer.

"I love how we are together," I responded slowly.

Peter abruptly released me. "You love having sex with me," he said, accusingly.

"Well, yes," I answered cautiously. "Don't you love having sex with me?"

"My relationship with you isn't just about sex," he answered, and I could tell by his clipped tone that he was angry.

"It isn't just about sex for me either," I told him. "I care for you, Peter. Or I wouldn't spend as much time here as I do. But how long have we known each other? Three and a half weeks? Is that long enough to know that you love someone?"

"Yes," Peter answered without hesitation. "Don't you believe in love at first sight?"

This conversation wasn't going where I wanted it to go. It was far too serious, and I got the feeling that no matter what I said, Peter wouldn't be satisfied. All I knew was that I wasn't ready to have the "love" conversation with him, not when I was a married woman who was undecided about the future with her husband.

"My parents fell in love at first sight," Peter went on. "They were married within three weeks of meeting. They were married for thirty-four years before they died."

"That's such a sweet story," I said softly, pressing my palms against Peter's chest. After my parents' failed marriage, and my own issue with Andrew, I was feeling jaded about the whole happily-ever-after thing, but Peter's story about his parents was the kind that made me believe in love again. "To be honest, I've been trying not to think about love," I told him. "I've been burned more than once. First Chad, and then Andrew."

Peter framed my face. "I would never hurt you," he said, looking deeply into my eyes. "I love you."

Could he possibly be serious? Could he *really* love me— romantic love, not just lust?

"And I think you love me too," he went on, "even if you are afraid of your feelings."

Peter kissed me, and the one thing I wasn't unsure about—my carnal lust for him—stirred deep in my belly.

His phone rang, and we pulled apart. As he hurried to the living room to answer it, I took a moment to catch my breath.

Peter loved me.

Why did that news make my heart feel heavier rather than lighter?

I knew I liked him—a lot—and our chemistry together could not be denied. What I felt sexually for Peter I could honestly say I hadn't felt for another man.

But love?

"Yes, Omar," Peter was saying. "I already got the revised schedule. Don't worry."

I turned back to the sink and rinsed the dinner plates we'd used so I could put them in the dishwasher. I heard Peter end his call, and he ambled back into the kitchen.

I faced him. "So, are we on for dinner with Marnie and Robert Friday night?"

"Dinner will be fine."

"Good." I smiled. "I'll tell Marnie, and we'll figure out where to go. It should be fun."

"Fine. Now come here."

He wrapped his arms around me and pulled me from the sink. Though my hands were wet, he linked fingers with mine and started to kiss me.

Before I could even fill the dishwasher, we ended up naked on the sofa, screwing like Energizer bunnies who couldn't get enough sex.

More and more we were playing house—cooking together, cleaning together, watching movies on the sofa while wrapped in each other's arms.

But there was no doubt that in the game of house, the bedroom was our favorite spot.

20

I went to Peter's apartment early on Friday and used the key he'd given me to let myself in. He'd worked late Thursday night so I hadn't bothered to head to his place then, but I'd promised to be there before he got home Friday.

His place was fairly tidy, except for a few plates and some cutlery sitting in the sink. I put them in the dishwasher and started the load, then wiped down the counters and burned a vanilla-scented candle so the place would smell nice when Peter arrived.

When he wasn't home by six, I started to get concerned. He'd assured me that he would be home by five-thirty at the absolute latest so he'd have time to get ready for our dinner with Marnie and Robert. He was shooting something for a shoe company, and was supposed to start early to finish the job.

While I waited, I called Marnie.

"Hey, Soph," she said. "We still on for eight o'clock?"

"Definitely," I told her. "But, Peter's not home yet, so I'm calling to say we might be a bit late."

"Try not to be too late."

"I hope we won't be."

"Good."

I heard the doorknob turn. "Marnie, that's Peter. We'll see you later, okay?"

"Bye."

When Peter stepped into the apartment, he wore a scowl. I went to him immediately and gave him a hug.

"Hi, baby," I said. "Why do you look upset?"

"I had a shitty day," he explained. "There were a lot of problems at the shoot."

"Oh, no. Did everything work out okay?"

"In the end, yes. But I'm not sure I'll be working for that production company anymore."

"Why not?"

"I had a disagreement with the director."

"Why?"

Peter waved off the question. "Difference of opinion. But seeing you makes everything better." His body seemed to relax, and he rested his hands on my shoulders. "I like it that you're here when I come home. It feels right." He paused. "I've got a surprise for you."

"Oh?" I said, smiling.

"It's the reason I'm late getting home." Peter reached into his back pocket and produced a small blue velvet box. "Here."

My stomach fluttered as he extended the box. "Peter…"

"Open it," he said.

Drawing in a deep breath, I lifted the lid. And gasped when I saw a pair of earrings with what looked like diamonds set in a circle around a champagne-colored stone.

"Peter!"

"They're diamonds," he said. "Even the stone in the middle. Set in white gold."

I stared at the earrings in awe.

"They're only one third of a carat. Next time, it will be more."

"They're beautiful," I told him, and gave him a soft kiss on the lips. "I love them."

Other than the bracelet Andrew had given me on our first anniversary, he had never surprised me with a gift like this. Flowers on occasion. A box of chocolates for Valentine's Day. I'd given him some serious hints about a tennis bracelet I wanted for our eighth anniversary, but he'd gotten me chocolates and a pair of shoes instead.

"I'm glad you like them," Peter said, grinning. "Put them on."

I slipped off my gold hoop earrings and put on the new ones.

"Beautiful," Peter said. "Just like you."

I went to the mirror beside the apartment door. The diamonds sparkled. "They're stunning."

Peter came behind me, met my gaze through the mirror. I watched and felt as he kissed my cheek.

"Now, what would you like to have for dinner?" he asked. "I make a very nice chicken parmigiana, with grilled vegetables. I can run to the grocery store and pick up everything I need."

"Oh, no," I said. "We have plans, remember? With Marnie and Robert."

"That's tonight?"

"Yes, that's tonight," I said, sounding a little exasperated. I couldn't believe Peter had forgotten. "And we've got to be there for eight o'clock, so if you're going to shower, you have to do it now."

"I'm not sure I'll be good company," Peter said. "Like I told you, I had a bad day."

No, no, no. This wasn't happening. "Being out will cheer you up," I said, my voice as upbeat as I could make it. I suddenly got the feeling I was going to have to twist Peter's arm on this. "Marnie's really funny, and she speaks highly of Robert. I bet you two will hit it off."

Peter shrugged, as though I were asking him. As though we hadn't agreed on this date two days ago.

"If you want," I said, my mind scrambling, "we don't have to stay out that late. We can come home early...for our own special dessert."

Peter didn't answer. Just strolled into the kitchen and pulled a bottle of beer from the fridge.

Marnie would hate me if I didn't show up tonight. Well, if not hate, then she wouldn't forgive me. Not if I blew her off twice in a row.

"I brought my clothes to change into," I said seductively, "and figured we could shower together before going out..."

Peter lowered the bottle of beer from his lips, one eyebrow arching with interest as he looked at me. "You want to shower together? Right now?"

"We've got a bit of time," I said, adding a little wink. Maybe sex would put Peter in a better mood, and in a better mood, I wouldn't have any trouble getting him to our dinner date.

Peter put the bottle of beer back in the fridge, then smiling like a cat with a canary in its mouth, came toward me. He enveloped me in his arms, and as our bodies pressed together, I could feel that his cock was already hard.

We were both naked before we hit the bathroom. Peter released me to start the shower and adjust the temperature. Then he got into the stall and offered me his hand.

I got in with him and closed the shower door behind me. Warm water splashed across my face and body. Peter rubbed his hands over my breasts, squeezing my nipples. Then he moved both hands lower—one to my pussy, and the other to my ass.

I reached for his cock and began stroking his impressive shaft. We started to kiss, the warm water sluicing over our bodies.

Releasing me suddenly, Peter reached for the bar of Irish Spring. He rubbed the soap over my breasts, building up a large amount of bubbles before lathering up my torso. When he reached my vagina, his fingers worked over me not just to clean, but to fondle, and soon, I was gripping his shoulders and breathing heavily.

Peter lowered his head to one breast and began to suck my nipple while his fingers tantalized my clit. I wrapped my arms around his neck and held on as his soapy hands pleasured me.

The combination of his mouth on my breast and his fingers on my pussy had sweet heat pulsing through my clit. And when he switched his mouth to my other breast and gently suckled my nipple, I started to come, my orgasm blasting through me like a bomb.

I gasped as I held on to him, my knees unable to support me. I thought Peter would spread my folds and drive his cock into me, but instead he lifted me in his arms and carried me out of the shower. The air-conditioning cooled my body as he exited the bathroom, but his hands had me hot. We kissed as he carried me to his bedroom. Kissed as he laid me on his bed.

"I want to eat you," Peter rasped.

"Let me please you," I urged. Peter always gave when it came to oral sex, saying that my pleasure pleased him more than anything else. But I wanted to have him in my mouth for a change, feel his body succumb to my touch.

"Climb on my face then," he said. "Let's do it together."

The thought alone had me moaning. Quickly, I straddled my hips over Peter's face and positioned my own face over his cock.

Overhead, the ceiling fan whirred, blowing cool air down onto our bodies. Goose bumps popped over my skin.

Within moments, though, my body exploded with heat as Peter gripped my ass and drew my clit into his mouth, and I was suddenly grateful for the extra blast of cool air from the fan. Groaning with delight, I took his cock in one hand and pumped it up and down, bringing it to full erection. Then, with Peter sucking my pussy, I slipped his cock into my mouth.

Up and down I moved my lips, trying to keep them steady between my euphoric gasps. I took him deep into my throat while pumping him, and Peter's groans grew louder, intensifying my pleasure. He was ravenous, delving his tongue and fingers into my pussy, sucking my juices as though he couldn't get enough of me.

I couldn't concentrate on giving Peter head, not while he was so skillfully eating my pussy. It was the sound of him sucking on his fingers that finally had me going over the edge. Heat exploded through my body with an intense, sweet orgasm.

He wasn't in my mouth, but Peter started to come as I was coming, his semen spurting upward, some falling on my hand. It was warm. I ran my finger over the tip of his penis, spreading the moistness around.

Moving my ass off of his face, Peter adjusted his body so that he was alongside me. He immediately began kissing me, then eased his body onto mine.

He was spreading my legs, settling between them.

"Peter—"

He silenced me with his lips and plunged his cock into my pussy. I wanted to tell him to put on a condom, but he kept kissing me, and then I simply couldn't form the words.

* * *

Peter fucked me hard, then slow and tender. At seven-thirty, I knew we were going to be late, and tried to tell him so.

Instead of listening, he drove his cock into my pussy until I was no longer thinking about the time.

We didn't stop fucking until nearly nine. Only then did Peter seem even mildly concerned about being late for our date.

"I have to take a shower," he said. "We won't be too late."

I don't know why, but his words pissed me off. He knew damn well we were too late for dinner, and I couldn't very well call Marnie and tell her we'd been fucking.

Peter went to the bathroom. I glanced at the clock. It was eight-fifty-eight.

Shit.

I got up and crossed the room to where I had the bag with my clothes for tonight. Maybe if we hurried, we could make it there within half an hour and Marnie wouldn't be too pissed.

I went to the bathroom door. "Hurry up," I called.

"What?" Peter asked from in the shower.

"Hurry up! Maybe we'll be in time for dessert."

But Peter didn't hurry. He showered as if he had all the time in the world. I put on my black dress and even did a quick coat of makeup, and still he was in the shower.

I was sitting on the armchair in his room, pouting, when he finally ambled out of the bathroom. He was rubbing a towel over his wet hair.

"Give me a few more minutes, and I'll be ready," he said. "Oh, I better brush my teeth."

It was 9:22 p.m.

When Peter had the gall to head back into the bathroom, I

lurched out of the chair. I grabbed my purse off the floor and headed to the door without saying goodbye.

I called Marnie when I was in the car. When she picked up, I said without preamble, "I'm sorry. I know you hate me, but I'm sorry."

"Where are you?"

I sighed. "In my car. Leaving Peter's place."

"You're on your way?"

I didn't answer right away. "Peter…he's still inside. I got pissed and I just left."

"Robert, give me a minute, okay?" I heard Marnie say. Then there were some shuffling sounds and, after several seconds, Marnie came back on the line. "What is going on?"

"I was ready, then Peter got home and was stalling. And…"

"And what?"

I said nothing.

"What, you ended up fucking or something?"

"Yeah," I admitted. What was the point in lying? "He was in a bad mood, so I just thought…and the time just flew." I couldn't completely blame Peter for our missing dinner. I was an adult. I had to take responsibility for allowing him to seduce me.

"What's going on with you?" Marnie asked.

"I don't think he really wanted to go out," I said. "It was like pulling teeth trying to get him to get ready."

"You know, sex is great, but not at the expense of a life."

"What's that supposed to mean?"

"You're not returning calls, you're standing me up. You never did that shit before."

"It won't happen again."

"I don't believe you."

"What?"

"How much do you want to bet that the next time we have plans, Peter will pull some shit like this. I think he wants you all to himself."

"That's ridiculous," I said. Marnie's comment did make me think. Peter and I spent pretty much all our time at his place, and most of that time, we were screwing like we'd invented the art of sex.

"You've changed," Marnie said. "And I don't like it."

A beat passed. "Do you still want me to meet you and Robert? I can come and have a cup of coffee or something."

"Don't bother," Marnie snapped, and she hung up.

"Fuck!" I screamed, and tossed my cell phone onto the passenger seat.

I drove home a little recklessly. Turning corners too quickly. Zipping in and out of traffic. Speeding.

I was angry. Angry at Peter for making us miss this prearranged date. Angry at Marnie for being pissy with me.

Angry at myself for acting like an immature teenager.

What *was* I doing? Marnie was right—sex was great, but not at the expense of a life.

I couldn't turn my back on my best friend just because I was having the best sex ever.

My cell phone rang, and I scooped it up. I saw Peter's number on the call display.

I didn't answer.

The phone rang two more times before I got home. Both times it was Peter, and both times, I didn't answer. I needed to put some space between him and me.

By the time I got to my street, I was calming down a bit. I would call Marnie in the morning and assure her that I would *never* stand her up again. Not unless it was a matter of life and death.

I was nearing my house when I realized the driveway wasn't empty.

My heart rate accelerated.

Andrew's SUV was there.

I pulled to a stop at the curb in front of my house, wondering what to do. Andrew had left me a few messages over the past couple of weeks, but I hadn't gotten back to him. I debated driving around aimlessly for a while, hoping that he would be gone by the time I returned. If Marnie wasn't out with Robert, I could have called her and swung by her place for a while.

And if I wasn't miffed with Peter, I could have gone back to his apartment.

As it was, I had nowhere else to go, and God only knows how long Andrew planned on sticking around. Sighing, I resigned myself to the fact that I may as well go inside and face him.

I pulled my car into the driveway beside his. Slowly, I got out and headed inside.

Andrew was sitting on the living room sofa, his arms spread wide across the back of the couch. The room was quiet, eerily so. The fact that not even the television was on told me he must have been waiting for me to get home.

He looked up when he saw me, but said nothing.

"How long have you been here?" I asked.

"Two and a half hours."

My heart pounded, but I walked farther into the room. There was no reason for me to be nervous in my own house.

"Your dress is on inside out," Andrew said, looking at my dress, not my face.

"What?" I quickly looked down at my dress, and indeed, I could see the seams. How had I not realized that I'd put my dress on the wrong way?

Andrew finally lifted his head and met my eyes. "So, you were with him?"

I didn't answer.

"What are you gonna do? Pretend you're not seeing someone? Or should I say, not fucking someone?"

"You're the one who told me to have an affair."

Andrew guffawed and looked away.

"What?" I asked testily.

Slowly, Andrew stood. "Why haven't you returned my calls?"

"Because I didn't want to talk to you."

"So, it's over? Because if it is, just tell me. Don't keep me hanging on."

I said nothing.

"I thought you were going to go have a fling, get even with me. Not dump me altogether."

"I told you...you don't get to make the rules." My chest was hurting. Just seeing Andrew was emotionally draining for me.

"Those are nice earrings."

Instinctively, I raised one hand to my ear.

"I guess he gave them to you." Andrew paused for what seemed like hours. "Are you in love with this guy?"

"No." I was surprised at how easily the word left my mouth. Surprised at how much I wanted to reassure Andrew of that fact, though God only knows why. "I'm not in love with him."

Andrew's eyes lit up with hope. "So you're going to end it?"

Now I hesitated. "When I'm ready."

"What do you mean, when you're ready?"

"When I'm ready."

"If it's not serious with him, then why keep fucking him?"

"I didn't say it wasn't serious."

"I'm confused," Andrew said.

"He treats me well. And you know what—the sex is amazing."

Andrew's jaw flinched at my unabashed statement.

"What's the matter, Andrew?" I asked, anger stirring inside me at the memory of his betrayal. "It was okay when you were screwing someone else, but I'm not allowed to have any fun?"

Andrew said nothing.

"You started this. Remember that. If you hadn't decided to have an affair with Isabel, we wouldn't be having this conversation right now."

"I told you I'm sorry. How many times can I say it?"

Sorry. As if that was supposed to make everything right. It incensed me even more.

"The sex I'm having now is so hot I don't believe this guy would ever cheat on me," I said, rubbing salt in Andrew's wound. But he deserved it. Deserved it for hurting me so deeply. "I do think I could fall in love with him."

That silenced Andrew. His lips pulled into a taut line. Then he moved away from me, starting for the door.

"Andrew." I followed him, suddenly regretting what I'd just said. I had wanted to hurt him, and I'd achieved that and then some. "Andrew, wait."

He didn't stop until he reached the door. Exhaling audibly, he faced me.

"I didn't—"

"I guess it's like you said. I don't get to make the rules. I just wish I knew what game we were playing."

I opened my mouth to speak as he walked briskly to his Escalade, but I couldn't find any words. What was there to say? I still loved him, I suddenly realized that. But I was also unsure that my love for him could sustain a relationship.

It hadn't stopped him from betraying me.

Stepping back inside, I closed the door, confused about what the future held for me.

Because as much as I still loved Andrew, I meant what I'd said. I *could* see myself falling in love with Peter, a man with whom I'd connected in a way I didn't know was possible.

21

Peaches was missing.

Before I'd gone to Peter's place on Friday, I'd let her outside, knowing that if I didn't make it home and she was hungry, she could at least catch herself a lizard. Or a bird.

Like a typical cat, Peaches enjoyed going out at night. But usually first thing in the morning she was at the door, ready to come back inside.

Not this morning.

Frowning, I closed the front door, wondering where she could be. I ambled into the kitchen and poured water into the coffee carafe. My phone rang as I was doing so, and I quickly set down the carafe and snatched the receiver off the wall.

"Hello?"

"Hello, Sophie."

Caught off guard, it took me a moment to recognize the voice. But then I knew who it had to be.

"Mom?"

"Hello, darling."

I smiled, pleasantly surprised. With the stress of seeing Andrew last night, plus Marnie's comments that I'd changed, it was nice to hear from someone who wasn't enmeshed in my current relationship drama.

"How are you, Mom?"

"I'm doing well, thank you."

My mother lived in California with her new husband, and we didn't speak all that often these days. We weren't as close as I would have liked, because of the decisions she'd made. Because of how she'd hurt my father.

My mother had left my father for another man. She'd waited until I was eighteen and heading to college, for my sake, she'd said. And she hadn't cheated on my dad—at least that's what she'd claimed. But my father had been heartbroken nonetheless when she announced that she simply didn't want to be married to him anymore. Less than a year later, my father died in a head-on collision with a semi, and witnesses had claimed there was no reason for his car to have swerved into the truck's path.

An accident, or suicide?

In my heart, I believed my father had committed suicide because he hadn't been able to deal with being alone. That after my mother had broken his heart, he hadn't seen much reason to go on.

My mother believed it was an accident.

"I suppose I'll get right to the point," my mother said, drawing me back from my trip down memory lane.

"Oh?" What did that mean?

"Andrew called me this morning, Sophie. He told me that you two have been having problems."

I didn't say anything. I couldn't believe that Andrew had called my mother to discuss our marriage.

My mother sighed. "I just want to say, don't make the same mistake I did, sweetheart. Don't…don't throw away your marriage."

"What are you talking about?"

"The affair," my mother said. "Andrew told me all about it."

"Really?" I asked, my tone sarcastic.

"He's afraid he's going to lose you, Sophie. Andrew's a good man. I know everyone has problems, but you have to try to work things out. See a counselor, the way so many people do these days. But don't throw away what you have with him."

I let my mother ramble on with her lecture, and it dawned on me that she was talking about *my* affair. The moment she was finished, I couldn't help asking, "Did he tell you that *he* screwed someone else?"

Silence.

"Of course not. It's not as easy to finger me as the bad guy if he confesses his sins."

I took a few minutes to fill my mother in on Andrew's affair, the threat of the lawsuit, and the fact that my husband had encouraged me to have sex with another man.

"So he's not as innocent as he'd like to claim," I pointed out. "Far from it."

"I didn't know all that," my mother said.

"Of course you didn't."

"But," she went on, "it doesn't change what I said. Andrew's had his fun, you've had your fun. I still think you have a good man. I'd hate to see you throw that away."

"What if I said my affair isn't just about fun for me? What if I told you that I've met someone I really like?" I didn't know why I was saying this, except for the fact that I was angry at Andrew for "tattling" on me. "Someone who might be better for me than Andrew?"

"You don't mean that," my mother said.

"What if I do?" What if Andrew calling my mother was a big sign that we weren't meant to be together anymore? I'd found a decent guy in Peter, someone who thrilled me in unimaginable ways. He loved me, and he believed in my dreams. A life with him wouldn't be so bad.

My mother sighed. "I'd say I thought the same thing once. And maybe I was wrong. Maybe what I did…hurt too many people."

Her answer left me speechless. It was as close as she'd ever come to admitting any responsibility for hurting my father, or even me. My mother had driven my father into a deep depression, and I'd always been angry at her on some level for that.

It was only in the past couple years that I'd started to warm to her, realize that my father was the one who'd ultimately taken his own life. There was no point in me being mad at my mother forever.

"I'm sorry I hurt you," my mother went on. "Sorry I hurt your father. If I could do it all over, I'd do things differently."

Suddenly I was crying. Not heavy sobs, but quietly. Tears were rolling down my cheeks.

"I don't know what's going to happen, Mom. Andrew and I have to work this out. On our own."

"I respect that."

I changed the subject, and asked about Hal, her husband, and Hal's twenty-year-old son. By the time we finished our conversation, I'd promised to visit them sometime soon.

I called Marnie right after I ended the call with my mother. Either she wasn't home, or she didn't want to answer my call.

"I don't blame you for not wanting to talk to me," I said after her voice mail picked up. "But I hope you can forgive me for being a totally insensitive bitch and call me later. Please."

Then I went back outside to look for Peaches.

I didn't find her, and was starting to get really worried. I'd driven around the neighborhood, fearing I'd see her remains, but I saw nothing. I went back home, hoping she was still roaming around somewhere, and that she'd return to the house soon.

My phone was ringing as I stepped in the door. I raced to get it, but when I saw P. Bacchio, I let it go to voice mail.

I couldn't have been more startled when, half an hour later, Peter appeared at my door.

"Peter," I said, the surprise unmistakable in my voice.

"Hello, Sophie."

"What—what are you doing here?"

Peter didn't answer, just stepped forward, forcing me to step backward. He entered my house and closed the door behind him.

He looked somber, and that worried me. That and the fact that he was at my house when I hadn't told him where I lived.

"You haven't been answering my calls."

"I'm not feeling well," I said, which wasn't a lie. "My stomach's a bit upset. I think I'm about to start my period." I was due for my cycle. In fact, it was a few days late.

Peter didn't say anything, just began to pace the floor in my foyer.

"How…how did you know where I lived?"

"I looked you up."

I frowned. "I'm unlisted."

"There are ways, Sophie," Peter said.

I studied him, feeling slightly apprehensive. Was it because

Andrew could show up any minute? I definitely didn't want a confrontation between the two.

Stopping, Peter stared at me—so hard, it unnerved me. Something was bothering him.

"What's the matter?" I asked.

"Are you leaving me?"

"W-what?"

"You left me last night, you didn't call." Peter paused. "Are you reconciling with your husband?"

I narrowed my eyes as I stared at him, wondering where he'd gotten that idea.

Suddenly, Peter was on his knees in front of me, pressing his head into my abdomen. Not in a sexual way, but in a pleading way.

"I was wrong last night, Sophie. But please don't leave me."

"What are you talking about?"

He looked up at me, his face contorted with sadness. He held on tight to my waist, as though he didn't want to let go. "I'm sorry, Sophie. I'm sorry. Please don't leave me."

"I just needed a little space," I told him. "Yeah, I was a bit pissed, but everyone gets pissed now and then."

Peter got to his feet, hope evident in his eyes. "You weren't planning to never call me again?"

"Of course not."

Exhaling in relief, Peter planted kisses all over my cheek. "I was worried, Sophie. So worried."

Hadn't he ever been in a serious relationship? One disagreement didn't mean the end of the world.

"Look," I said, taking his hands in mine. "I don't want to be doing this here. My...Andrew might show up or something."

Peter's eyes darkened. "He's still living here?"

"Absolutely not. But he has a key. We haven't sold the house." I didn't bother telling Peter that Andrew still wanted our marriage. I was more ambiguous than ever about what I was going to do. Last night, I realized that I still loved Andrew, but I didn't like the fact that he'd called my mother behind my back.

"I would never hurt you," Peter said. "Not like your husband."

I believed that. I really did. Perhaps because the sexual chemistry was so strong between me and Peter, I didn't see him going anywhere else for sex.

"I know that," I said softly.

"I don't like that your husband can come here whenever he wants. What if he hurts you?"

"He wouldn't do that," I said.

"You can come live with me. I think you should."

"Me and my cat?" I asked. "Speaking of which, I can't find Peaches."

"You and your cat. Your dog, your rat, whatever. As long as you're with me." Peter slipped a hand into the waist of my shorts, not stopping until he reached my pussy. A groan rumbled in his chest. *"Bella..."*

I placed my hand over his. "No, Peter. Not here."

He stroked me through my panties. "Then come home with me. And why don't you bring some clothes so you don't have to keep returning here?"

"I have to return home, at least periodically. I've got to keep looking for Peaches."

Peter kissed me and stroked me, as though to make me change my mind, and I knew how this would finish. Before we ended up on the floor, I tore my lips from his. "Let's go to your place." No way did I want Andrew to come home and see Peter here. "Let me just put some food out for my cat. In case she returns while I'm gone."

"Okay." Peter gave me a brief kiss before releasing me. I went to the kitchen, filled bowls with cat food and water, then put both outside the front door.

As soon as I was finished setting the bowls down, Peter offered me his hand. "Come on. Let's go home."

22

I was starting to get a slightly odd feeling about Peter.

At first he insisted on driving me to his place in *his* SUV, saying it didn't make sense to waste gas. I got his point, but reasoned that if I went with him, I wouldn't be able to go home when necessary. He finally agreed to let me drive my own car, but he didn't seem happy.

It wasn't his suggestion that bothered me. It was the fact that he seemed upset that I didn't want to ride with him.

Five minutes into the drive to his apartment, I pushed the feeling aside, telling myself that I'd likely misread his reaction. I was stressed about Peaches, and I think Peter was clearly feeling a little worried about our relationship, given that I'd walked out on him the night before. It was the first time that had happened, and I guess he was a bit unsure where he stood.

That had to be all that it was.

When Peter went to work on Monday morning, I went back to my place. I was glad for the breather, the time away from him.

All through Saturday night and Sunday, Peter had kept me close to him, either always holding me or watching me keenly if I was out of his grasp.

Once, he'd come out of the bathroom and looked visibly relieved when he saw me still in the living room, saying he thought he'd heard the sound of the door opening.

He had, but it had only been the pizza deliveryman.

For lack of a better word, Peter seemed paranoid.

It had me wondering if he'd driven by my place on Friday night when Andrew had been there. Had he seen Andrew's SUV in the driveway and jumped to the wrong conclusion?

More and more, I thought that was likely the case.

One thing was certain—things couldn't continue much longer the way they were. Without me making some sort of decision. Peter's feelings for me had evolved. Deepened. Andrew wanted me back.

And I was ambiguous.

On the one hand, I told myself that maybe I'd met Peter because he could be the next great love of my life. On the other, I wondered if all we really had in common was our sexual chemistry.

My heart was still tangled up with Andrew, that I couldn't deny. It was hard to cut the ties after being with him for so long, but it wasn't impossible. People moved on after divorce.

If we got divorced.

It was all I could think about as I drove home, but once I got to my driveway, I put Andrew and Peter out of my mind. I hurried out of my car and rushed to my front door.

Peaches's food and water remained untouched.

I was really starting to worry. It wasn't like Peaches to take off and not return. Once, she'd been gone for more than twenty-four hours, but this was longer than that.

I consumed myself with painting so I wouldn't have to fret about the cat. Not that I could truly erase the unease over my cat's fate from my mind.

At five-thirty, Peter called my cell. "Where are you?" he asked me.

"I'm at home," I said.

"No, I'm home, and you're not here."

"I mean my home. I'm at my house."

"Why?"

"I had to see if my cat came home."

"And did it?"

"No. She's not here." Her bowl of food on the front step remained untouched, a sure sign that the cat hadn't been back. I didn't want to, but I feared the worst. There was a lake not too far from our house, and I'd heard more than one rumor that a gator lived there, and that it was responsible for more than one pet's demise.

"Maybe your husband took her."

"He would have left a note if he did," I said.

"Not if he wanted to scare you."

"Scare me?"

"I don't trust him," Peter said.

I did believe that Peter didn't trust Andrew, but not because of any real concern that Andrew might hurt me, or use the cat to get to me. Peter was clearly concerned that I was going to end up reconciling with my husband.

"I want you here," Peter went on. "Where I can protect you. Will you come? Now?"

"Okay," I said. "I'm on my way."

I went mostly to pacify Peter, because for whatever reason, he was suddenly insecure about me and Andrew.

Peter opened the door for me before I could even knock, indicating he'd been looking out the window, anticipating my arrival. He pulled me into his arms and hugged me for several seconds before releasing me.

"Peter," I said softly. "You seem a little—I don't know—stressed, maybe? Like you're worried about me."

"Remember when I told you that I came to Orlando to meet a woman?"

"Yes."

"Well, she left me. While I wasn't at home. She packed up her things and left without so much as a goodbye."

"Oh," I said, for lack of anything better to say. "That was really lousy."

"So yes, knowing that you still speak to your husband…I guess I am a little concerned."

"I promise you," I said, "that I would never do that to you." At the very least, if I ended my relationship with him, I'd be mature enough to tell him it was over.

Peter gave me one helluva kiss, suctioning his lips to mine, tangling his tongue with mine, as though he hoped to fuse our mouths together. When we pulled apart, we were both breathless.

Taking my hand, he tucked it through his elbow. Then he led me to his bedroom where he proceeded to strip me out of my clothes. Slowly. Lovingly. When I was naked, his eyes roamed over my body with genuine tenderness in their depths.

"I love you, Sophie," he said. "And I know that in your heart, you love me too."

I didn't answer. I don't think he wanted me to, because he started to kiss me. Slowly, sweetly. With a level of emotion he hadn't displayed before.

His hands played over my breasts, kneading my skin, tweaking my nipples to erection. I arched into his touch, moaning softly. Every time Peter touched me, I was convinced that in his arms was exactly where I wanted to be.

Peter lowered his head, suckled each nipple, then dipped his head lower to kiss my abdomen. He skimmed his fingers over my pussy, almost with reverence, then stood and kissed me on the lips once more.

"Turn around, *bella*."

I did, feeling sexy and aroused by the fact that I was completely naked while Peter was still fully clothed. A shiver ran down my spine as he kissed the back of my neck.

When I no longer felt his hands or mouth on me, I turned to see what he was doing, and saw that he had a piece of cloth in his hands. Approaching me, he slipped the material over my eyes.

"Do you trust me?" Peter whispered, and a wave of sexual longing flowed through me.

"Yes," I said.

He took my hand, led me to the bed. And then he left me there.

"Peter?"

In a moment he was back, taking one of my wrists in his hand. I felt him wrap something around it. Not a rope, but something silky. He pulled it so that it was tight but not painful.

Peter moved his body over me, and then he was on my other side, circling a piece of material around my right wrist.

Tugging on my left wrist, I found that I could move it only a short distance. He must have tied me to the headboard.

Whatever Peter had done to my left wrist, he did to the right one. And then he was off the bed.

I writhed around a little, pulling on my wrists as I did.

"You're so beautiful."

He took my right foot in his hand, kissed my big toe, flicked his tongue over it. Then he tied both ankles and secured me to the bed.

I could feel the heat of Peter's gaze on my body, hear his heavy breathing, and desire coursed through my veins. He'd never blindfolded me, never tied me up. I'd never been quite at his mercy like this.

And my God, it was exciting.

The room was hotter today. Humid. Or was that just my body?

No, I didn't think so. The air-conditioning wasn't on. But the ceiling fan above the bed was going.

As I waited for Peter's next move, I suddenly realized that I could no longer hear him. No longer sense him.

Was he still in the room?

I angled my head to the right, in the direction of the bedroom door, as though that would help me hear better.

"I'm right here, *bella,*" Peter said softly, and my head jerked to the left, where I thought I'd heard his voice. "I think I could look at you and come, without touching myself. That's how much you excite me."

And then I heard him moving. Toward me. I swallowed, anticipating his touch.

Something skimmed my neck. Then my cheek. Not his finger, but something soft. It brushed across my neck again, then along the underside of my jaw.

"Do you know what I'm touching you with?" Peter asked.

I wasn't certain, but I had a pretty good idea. "A feather?"

"Yes, *bella.* A feather."

The tip of the feather inched its way along my bottom lip. Such a light, wispy touch, but it sent a jolt of heat through my body, causing me to part my lips and emit a shuddery moan.

Another stroke. This time across my upper lip. My naked body quivered.

Quivered with anticipation of the pleasure that was to come.

The feather traveled lower, over my chin, then crossed the expanse of my neck from left to right. Right to left. All with agonizing slowness.

Then it stopped. Abruptly. Five seconds went by. I held my breath, waiting for what would come next. The blindfold over my eyes prevented me from seeing, but also heightened my sense of excitement. I could hear every sound in the room, smell everything. Mostly, I heard only my own raspy breaths and the whirring of the ceiling fan above the bed. But I could smell the desire in the room, clinging to drops of warm moisture in the air. I could smell the sweat dampening his skin. The scent was musky and heady.

And arousing.

When the feather caressed my left nipple, my body jerked, making my wrists and ankles pull against the ties that bound me to the bed.

"Do you like that?" he asked.

"Yes," I responded, surprised to find my voice faint. "Yes," I repeated, louder this time.

Once again, nothing. My hips writhed. I groaned softly. I was eager for his touch now. Desperate for it.

"Patience, *bella*," he murmured.

"Easy for you to say," I told him. "You have total control over my body right now." *Total control over my pleasure*.

"Have I disappointed you before?" he asked.

"No," I answered honestly. "Never."

"And I will not disappoint now."

The feather touched down between my rib cage, then traveled

south, where it dipped into my belly button. It continued its lazy journey into my strip of pubic hair, then stopped—just when I wanted it most.

I whimpered. "Please, don't make me beg."

He didn't say a word. Several seconds passed and nothing. I strained to hear past the *woo-woo* sounds the ceiling fan was making.

Soft footfalls on the carpet, then the creaking of the bedroom door.

What? Was he leaving me here?

I counted ten more seconds, and when he didn't return, I began to struggle against the ties that bound me. The headboard rattled as I pulled and yanked. Futilely. The knots were too tight, preventing my escape.

And then I heard the sound of footsteps again. He was coming back into the room. I exhaled audibly.

"Look at you," he said. "Your body writhing. Did you think I was going to leave you here while I went and watched a baseball game?"

I didn't answer. I suddenly felt foolish. I *had* been afraid that he'd left me here, totally exposed and helpless to escape until he freed me. I'd been under his complete control before, yet this was the first time I'd felt such a moment of panic.

Why?

Because he seemed different today. From the moment I'd arrived, I could sense a certain intensity level in his looks and his touch.

Something darker.

"I wouldn't leave you," Peter said. "I would never leave you. You and I, we're connected in a way we can't control."

I swallowed. Did I sense something ominous in his tone? Or was I a little unnerved because I was bound and blindfolded?

How could a person be unnerved and extremely aroused at the same time?

"Do you trust me?" he asked. He was very close to me now. Maybe a foot away. I could tell by the sound of his voice.

I gyrated my hips, a motion that would please him, given the view he had of my pussy with my legs spread the way they were. "Touch me," I said. My chest heaved with each breath. "Touch me before I die."

"Do you trust me?" he repeated, and I felt the weight of his body on the bed, but I couldn't tell where he was.

"Yes. Yes, I trust you."

"Completely?" he asked, his warm breath suddenly tickling my clitoris, and my God, I almost came.

"Yes, yes. Completely, I trust you. Please touch me. Baby…"

I cried out when something cold and wet stroked my clit. What? The sensation had me confused. I'd expected the warmth of his tongue.

The cold and wet brushed against my inner thigh now, and I finally placed what it was. A cube of ice.

He stroked my pussy again with the ice cube. My nub clenched. My hips jerked.

"I wonder if I could make you come like this," he said softly, and stroked me with the ice again.

"I don't know. It feels good, but it's so cold…"

The bed squeaked as he got up. Where was he going now? "Baby, please," I protested.

His lips brushed against mine. They were cold and wet. From the ice. My body writhed, my not so subtle cue that I wanted him. On top of me. Inside me. Fucking me until I collapsed from sheer exhaustion.

He kissed my jaw, then trailed his tongue to my earlobe and suckled. He whispered, "Do you love me?"

"You know I love everything that you do to me," I quickly replied, and that was the absolute truth. I craved this man's touch in a way I wasn't sure was healthy. "Even if you make me wait for it."

The ice cube circled my nipple, and my flesh tightened instantly. A moment later, I felt the flick of his hot tongue. Just a flick though, not nearly enough. I arched my back, pushing my breasts forward.

"Do you love me?" he repeated.

Slowly, I lowered my back. He *was* different today. Why was he suddenly asking me about love, knowing my situation? Knowing the circumstances under which we'd come together?

"I know you love this." He began stroking my clit with his thumb. Back and forth. Back and forth.

"Mmm, *yes*. I love that." I began to pant, close to the edge. "I can never get enough of your hands on my body."

"What about my tongue?" He adjusted his body between my legs, and I bit down on my bottom lip in anticipation. The moment his tongue came down on me, my hips bucked and I started to whimper.

"Baby, I love your tongue. I can't get enough of your tongue. *Ohhh*."

He suckled me until I was crying from the pleasure and on the verge of exploding. Then he pulled back, denying me my release.

"No, no. *Please*," I begged. "I need you, baby. I need—"

"Do you love me?" he asked again.

"Yes!" I cried out. "I love you. I love you."

"Oh, baby. I love you, too." Hastily, he untied my legs and hooked them over his shoulders and began to devour me. He sucked, he nibbled, he buried his tongue inside me. He ate greedily, as though my pussy was the last meal he would ever have.

My whole body convulsed as my orgasm gripped me, gripped me harder than anything I'd ever experienced before. It zapped me of my energy. Stole my breath. Left me shuddering as though a speeding train had just rocketed through my body.

Even through my pleasure, I was aware that something had changed between us.

I wasn't sure it was for the better.

23

Two days later, Marnie called me in the early evening and told me to turn on the television to Channel 4 News.

"Why?" I asked.

"Do it quickly," she said, not answering my question. "The story's coming up."

Holding the cordless receiver to my ear, I went into the living room and turned on the television. It was about five-fifteen, so the lead stories had already passed. "What am I watching for?" I asked. "Other than this commercial about fabric softener."

"Just hold on. You'll see in a minute."

And I did see, the moment the news came back on. A picture of Teddy, the man who had harassed me the night I met Peter, flashed on the screen. The news anchor, an attractive black woman, took on a serious tone as she began to speak.

"Police this evening are looking for the man who attacked and nearly killed Theodore Granger." The normal picture of Teddy changed to one where his face was bruised and bloodied. "Granger was attacked last night while out at CityWalk. He has described his attacker as six feet two inches, with dark, wavy hair. Possibly Hispanic, or possibly biracial, with an accent. Granger was punched and slashed several times with a knife, but was able to fight off his attacker before the man fled. If you have any information on the possible identity of the assailant, Orlando Police urge you to call them at 1-800-555-TIPS."

Frowning, I hit the mute button. "That's the guy from the club that night," I said. "Why did you want me to watch that?"

"What do you think?"

And then I got it. Exactly what was going through Marnie's mind. "Marnie, you can't possibly think—"

"Hell, yes, I think," Marnie said before I could finish my question. "Attacked while outside of CityWalk? The same guy who was harassing you?"

"It could have been anyone," I said.

"That description is Peter to a *T*. And you know it."

I didn't respond. Yes, I could see why Marnie believed that, but he wasn't the only biracial or even Hispanic man in the state of Florida. Hell, there were thousands who fit that description, right down to speaking with an accent.

"How many Cubans live in Florida?" I asked Marnie. "And others from Mexico, Central and South America…"

"It was Peter," Marnie said. "I know it was."

"Four weeks after I met him?" I said doubtfully.

"I don't know. I've got this feeling."

"What do you want me to do—call the cops?" There was a hint of incredulity in my voice. Surely Marnie didn't expect me to call the police with her suspicion that Peter had attacked Teddy. It was wild speculation at best. And it kind of pissed me off that she'd jump to such a conclusion about the man I was involved with.

Yes, I was starting to feel that he was a bit too clingy. But so what if he didn't want to hang out with Marnie and Robert? That didn't make him a violent person.

"I guess I want you to be careful," Marnie said.

"I am being careful," I told her. "And promise me you aren't going to call the cops about your suspicion. You wouldn't do that, right?"

"No," Marnie said after a moment. "But I thought you should know. So you can maybe get some…perspective."

"What kind of perspective?" I asked testily.

"You've changed, Sophie. You've changed since you've been with this guy. We hardly see each other anymore."

"You're dating Robert. That's just the way it is when you start seeing someone new."

"Yeah, but I don't like that he doesn't want to meet any of your friends. And what do you really know about his family?"

"His family is in Italy," I said. "And I think he's just a bit shy. Not everyone is outgoing. Some people are more reserved. What do you know about Robert's family?" I challenged.

"I know they're from Jacksonville, and both his parents are teachers. He has two sisters, twins, who are eighteen months younger than he is. And I'm meeting his family in a couple weeks at a family reunion."

"Oh," I said, her answer not what I expected. "Well, like I said, all of Peter's family is in Italy. It's a totally different story. Just because he's shy and we like to stay in and have sex…is that a crime?"

"All right," Marnie said, a hint of defeat in her voice. "Maybe I'm jumping the gun. I saw Teddy's picture at the top of the newscast and heard he was beaten and I thought…I'm just worried about you."

"I know. I do appreciate your concern." My call waiting beeped. A quick glance at the display told me it was Peter calling. "Marnie, I've got to go. That's Peter."

"All right, sweetie. Remember, I love you."

"I love you, too. Talk to you later." I pressed the button to link over to the other line. "Peter?"

"Bella."

My breath caught in my throat, and already, I felt a pull of desire.

"I have a surprise for you," Peter said.

"What kind of surprise?"

"The kind of surprise that you must come here to see. Right away."

"Right now?"

"Yes. Right now."

"Okay. I'm on my way."

As I got into my car, I thought about what Marnie had said. That I'd changed since I'd gotten involved with Peter.

Here I was getting in a car to head to his place because he'd asked me to do so. Did that mean I had changed?

I shook my head. No, it didn't. I was having the best sex of my life. I was addicted to that sex, to the feeling of giving myself completely to Peter and he to me. It was intoxicating, and unlike anything I had ever experienced before.

What I did understand was that the longer I was involved in a relationship with Peter, the more complicated it would be to get out of it. He was in love with me. I loved the way I felt when with him, but wasn't sure I wanted a long-term commitment with him.

But for right now, I wasn't ready to walk away from him. Didn't want to.

I concentrated on the fact that Peter had a surprise for me—not Marnie's words of warning—and I smiled as I drove to his place.

Butterflies danced in my stomach as I knocked on his door. He opened it almost immediately, his eyes dancing as he stared down at me.

I loved that about him. How he genuinely seemed so happy every time he saw me.

"Bella." He pulled me into his arms and kissed me deeply. "You got here quickly."

"I want to know what my surprise is."

"Ah." His eyes crinkled as he regarded me fondly. Yes, Peter might be a little obsessed with me, but that didn't make him capable of violence. Why had Marnie jumped to such a conclusion?

"Well, I will not keep you waiting," Peter said, pulling the door open wide. "Come in."

I waltzed into the apartment, staring around as I did. I didn't immediately see anything that might be for me.

Perhaps it would be in a little blue box. More dazzling jewelry?

Peter took me by the hand. "Come."

He led me to the bedroom, and I narrowed my eyes, wondering if his surprise was of the sexual variety. The last time, he'd tied me to the bed. Did he have something even more risqué planned for this time? Perhaps a whip, or some toys?

But when we got to the bedroom, I saw nothing out of order on his neatly made bed except for the medium-size cardboard box.

Did I just hear something? A faint meow?

Peter led me to the bed, still smiling proudly. "This, *bella,* is your surprise."

He gestured to the box, which had holes cut in the top of it. I knew now that I hadn't misheard. Yes, there was a faint meow coming from inside the box.

"Open it," he said.

So I did. A tiny black kitten all but leaped into my hands, dying for freedom from its makeshift cage.

"Oh, hello," I cooed. I lifted the kitten, likely eight to nine weeks old, holding it up to my face. "Hi there, little fellow."

"It's a girl."

The tiny cat began to purr. "Oh, my goodness, she's precious." I beamed at Peter. "Absolutely adorable."

"You're happy?"

I held the kitten to my chest. "Yes."

Peter slipped his arm around my waist and kissed me on the cheek. We both laughed when the kitten swatted at my necklace, already trying to hone its hunting skills.

"Now you don't have to worry about your other cat," Peter said. "You have a new one."

The comment took the edge off of my happiness. "I still need to find Peaches," I said, meeting his eyes. "Just because you've bought me a new kitten doesn't mean I'm going to forget about the pet I've had for years."

"I think it's time you accept the fact that your cat is gone, Sophie. This kitten is a new beginning for you."

"I'm still going to look for Peaches," I stressed, feeling a stirring of annoyance in my gut. I appreciated this new kitten, but it would never make me forget my cherished pet. Parents who lost children to tragedy didn't just have more children and forget the ones who'd died.

"I was only trying to make you happy," Peter said.

I nodded my understanding. Perhaps Peter was just clueless. Or, perhaps like a man trying to "fix" a situation, he'd figured a new kitten was going to take away my sadness over losing my pet.

"I am happy," I told him. The kitten continued to play with the heart charm on my necklace, and I gently eased it backward, taking the charm from its claws. "Thank you."

"This kitten will stay here," Peter announced. "I want her to be *our* pet."

Our pet. Our meant a future.

"She's too little to be alone," Peter went on. "You'll have to be here when I'm at work to take care of her."

Something bothered me about the comment, but I let it slide without a response. Instead, I kept my attention on the kitten, which continued to purr, its little chest expanding and contracting.

"Now it's time to name her," Peter said.

"How about Ebony?" I suggested. "Since she's black. Or Onyx. Ooh, I like Onyx."

"Those are stupid names." Peter dismissed my suggestions with a wave of his hand. "Give her a name that suits her personality. Look at those claws. She is a little tiger." He kissed my neck. "Just like you. We should name her Tiger."

Why had Peter bothered to tell me I should name her if he already had something in mind? Now I was really feeling annoyed.

"Didn't you buy the kitten for me?" I asked.

"Yes."

"Then shouldn't I be able to choose her name?"

The humor in Peter's eyes went out as quickly as a person switched off a light. He was angry. "You want to name her Onyx. Fine. But I don't think it's a good name."

Peter walked out of the bedroom, leaving me wondering what the heck he was mad about.

Well, he could be angry all he wanted. If this was my kitten, I was choosing the name.

I held her up to my face again and nuzzled my nose with hers. "What do you think? Do you like the name Onyx?"

The kitten purred in response.

"Onyx it is."

I scrunched up foil paper and made it into a ball, which Onyx batted and chased around to her heart's content until she tired herself out. Then she curled up on the edge of the carpet, her eyes slowly drifting closed as she fell asleep.

Peter had put in a gory horror movie an hour ago, but I wasn't really into it. And when he moved his hand from my hip to my belly, I knew he wasn't into it either.

"Finally, little Tiger is sleeping," Peter said, slipping a hand beneath the waist on my jean shorts. "What about *my* little tiger? Are you sleeping?"

Just knowing that Peter wanted to fuck me had me already turned on.

"I don't know," I teased. "I think your tiger could use some special love and attention."

"And then will she purr? Or roar?"

I undid the snap on my shorts to give Peter easier access to my pussy. "Why don't you find out?"

Peter's hand delved into my panties, immediately separating my folds with his fingers and fervently stroking my clit.

I moaned.

"That was a purr," Peter said. "Let me see if I can make you roar."

He inserted his fingers, three, maybe four, and started to finger-fuck me. With his other hand, he pushed my tank top and bra up urgently, then brought his mouth down onto one of my nipples with a satisfying sigh.

He suckled me hard. Finger-fucked me without mercy. My moans grew louder as my pleasure built. Fuck, I was going to come, and I was going to come hard.

I was almost there, almost ready to explode, when Peter moved his mouth from my breast, quickly dragged my shorts down my hips and brought his hot and greedy tongue down onto my clit. He lapped at me hungrily, grazed my clitoris with his teeth. And that's when my orgasm gripped me. Absolutely overwhelmed me. I screamed with its intensity and soon ended up begging for mercy when Peter continued to devour me.

"Stop, Peter…I can't take it…"

He gave my clit one last suckle, then raised his face to mine. He wore a devilish grin.

"You roared."

I blushed. I *had* roared. "That's because you bring out the tiger in me."

24

The next morning, I woke up to find Peter gone. Onyx had slept on the bed near my pillow, but once I stirred, so she did, stretching her little body.

"Hey, there." I scratched the kitten's head, then lifted her. She was so light and small that she could almost completely fit in one palm. "You hungry? Want me to get you some food? And I'd better bring you to the litter box, just in case."

Peter had set up the litter box in the bathroom, so I brought Onyx there and set her down while I used the toilet. The kitten sniffed around the litter and beyond, but once I left the room, she darted out after me.

In the kitchen, I directed Onyx to her bowl of food, which she began to eat while I got myself some cereal and toast. The cat really was adorable, but made me miss Peaches all the more.

Peter had said that the kitten was our baby, and that I needed to be at his apartment to take care of her.

Well, Peter wasn't home. I wanted to head home and contact local animal shelters with Peaches's description.

I stared at Onyx, who was still eating her dry food.

I had a litter box at home. There was no reason I couldn't take her with me.

I called the S.P.C.A. and learned that yes, there were a few cats that had come in recently that fit Peaches's description. Leaving Onyx at my place, I hurried to the S.P.C.A. with hope in my heart.

That hope fizzled when I didn't find Peaches.

I was dismayed but told myself not to be distraught. I refused to believe I would never find my cat. She would turn up one day. I had to cling to that belief.

"This is a picture of my cat," I told a young male worker. "Please, if she shows up, will you call me? I'm desperate to find her."

The worker nodded and took the picture. Then I headed to my car, knowing there was nothing I could do but continue to search my neighborhood and wait.

I was nearing home when my cell phone rang. "Hello?"

"Where are you?"

Peter.

"I'm almost home," I told him, slightly irritated at his abrasive tone. "I had a few errands to run."

"What kind of errands?"

"I decided to check the S.P.C.A. to see if Peaches turned up there."

"And?"

"And no. She didn't."

"Do you see now, Sophie? Do you see why I told you you must move on?"

I didn't say anything. I knew Peter and I wouldn't agree on the issue.

"Where is Tiger?"

Tiger. I rolled my eyes. He had completely discounted the name I'd given the kitten. "Onyx is at my place."

"So you took the fucking cat and left me."

"I didn't leave, Peter. I had things to do."

"Is it too much to ask that when I come home, I find you here? You're always leaving, Sophie. Why?"

"I told you why."

"I know what you said. But maybe you are seeing your husband while I'm at work. Is that it, *bella?*"

"No, Peter. I am not seeing my husband behind your back. I'm not seeing anyone else."

"Are you home yet?"

"I'm just pulling into the driveway."

"Then get the cat and get over here."

I sighed, exasperated. "I don't know, Peter. I'm tired. I've got a headache. And you seem…I don't know—like you're in a bad mood."

"I've had a stressful day. I need you, Sophie. Please come home."

"All right," I said, giving in.

As I hung up, Marnie's words sounded in my ear. *You've changed.* Maybe I had.

Peter grinned like a man victorious when I got to his door. I'm not sure why, but something about that pissed me off.

In a second, I knew why. On the phone, Peter had been angry with me, but now he was as happy as a clam. It suddenly felt that he was playing some warped game with me. Could he make me do what he wanted when he wanted me to do it?

You've changed.

Peter had said that he'd had a bad day, but as he wrapped his arms around me and nuzzled his nose in my neck, he didn't seem at all like a man stressed about work. And I didn't believe for a moment that the "stress" had simply evaporated the moment he'd laid eyes on me.

"*Bella.*" Peter framed my face as he pulled away from me, then stroked Onyx's head. She was cradled in my arms. "I'm going to make a nice dinner for you. What would you like?" His eyes lit up with mischief. "Or…maybe you would like to go back to that Denny's?"

I said nothing, just stepped past him into the apartment.

"How about a homemade pizza?" Peter suggested. "You can help me. My parents loved to make pizza together."

I didn't want to be here. I wanted to be home—alone—taking some time for myself. I wanted a moment to grieve about Peaches in some damn privacy—the only exception being that I wanted Onyx around to help lift my spirit.

"I don't want pizza," I said to Peter as he came around to stand in front of me.

"Then what? Anything you want, I'll make it for you."

How sweet, I thought sourly.

He guided me to the sofa, where he slipped my purse off my arm and urged me to sit. "I'll get you some Prosecco."

I closed my eyes as I sat, trying to get past my irritation. I concentrated on the warmth of Onyx's body, the only thing giving me any comfort.

Peter was back in less than a minute with a champagne flute. "Here. Drink."

I accepted the glass from him, took a reluctant sip.

"I picked up some movies," Peter said. "I didn't know what you would want to watch, so I got a comedy, a dramatic film and something scary."

He had the whole evening mapped out, but I didn't want to be part of it. "Why am I here?" I asked.

Peter looked confused. "Because I love you."

"You said you were stressed. That you needed me."

"I'm not stressed anymore, now that you're here."

"I'll bet you weren't stressed at all," I said as I stared up at him. "You just wanted me over here, and for what—more sex?"

Now Peter's lips pulled into a taut line. "I want you here because I love you. Because you are my family. You and Tiger."

"Her name is Onyx," I snapped.

Peter rolled his eyes. "We went through this yesterday. We decided that Tiger was a better name."

"*You* decided that."

"Is that why you're mad, *bella?*" Peter asked, a look of humor now on his face. "Because of the kitten's name?"

He had the nerve to chuckle, belittling my feelings. I put the champagne glass down on the coffee table, then abruptly stood up. "I'm leaving."

Now his eyes darkened. "What?"

"I'm going home."

I started out of the living room toward the apartment door, but Peter hurried there before I could reach it, bracing a hand on it to prevent me from getting out.

"Get out of my way," I told him.

"You want to leave because you're angry about the cat?" he asked, incredulous, and clearly angry himself.

Well, he could be mad at my leaving all he wanted, but I wasn't a prisoner in his house. Surely he couldn't expect me to spend every waking minute at his place and never leave unless he approved my errands in advance.

"I'm leaving because I'm not in the mood to be here right now." He didn't need more of an explanation than that.

With lightning speed, Peter's hand moved from the door to my neck. I gasped, startled, and he began to apply pressure.

"Who are you going to see?" he demanded.

"No one."

"Your husband?"

He applied more pressure. "No."

"I'm the only man who's never hurt you, never betrayed you. And yet you want to leave me to go back to that bastard who broke your heart?"

I wriggled to free myself from Peter's grasp. It didn't work. "Peter, stop! You're hurting me!"

A moment passed, and something seemed to register in his irate expression. He let me go but didn't step backward.

"Did you lie about being raped, Sophie?"

"What?"

"Did you lie when you said you were raped?"

"No! Of course not." My eyes narrowed in confusion as I stared at Peter. "Why the hell would you ask me that?"

"Have you ever lied to me, Sophie?" Peter's eyes were cold. So much so that I felt a chill.

"Because I want to go home you think I've lied to you about everything?"

"Have you lied to me!" he yelled, so loud that I took a hasty step backward. *"Have you lied to me?"*

"No!" I shouted back.

"You're not still fucking your husband, the nights you don't spend with me?"

"No!"

"Are you sure?"

"Yes, I'm sure." I drew in a shaky breath. I finally understood.

"Why don't you just ask me what you want to ask me? I think you drove by my house the night we were supposed to go out with Marnie, and you saw my husband's car there. He just showed up, Peter. He wanted to talk but I sent him away."

Peter studied me. "I don't believe you."

"Believe what you want."

I wanted to get the hell out of here, but I remembered that Peter had taken my purse from me. He must have put it in the kitchen. Without a word, I went there, and saw my purse on the counter.

I grabbed my purse and walked back to the door.

"You're going to leave," Peter said, disbelief in his tone.

"Yes. We'll talk later, but tonight...I'm not in the mood."

Peter shrugged, accepting my decision. I opened the door and went downstairs. Only when I got to my car, I couldn't find my keys.

"What the hell?" I asked aloud, my fingers searching every crevice in my purse as it rested on the hood of my car. My keys *had* to be there. I'd dropped them in there en route to Peter's door. I knew I had.

Unless...

A weird feeling crept down my spine. Had Peter taken them out in the kitchen? The idea seemed ludicrous. Perhaps they'd dropped on the ground while I was heading up the stairs.

I retraced my steps, searched diligently. But my keys were nowhere.

I had no choice but to go back to the apartment.

I didn't knock, just opened the door. Peter wasn't in the foyer. But when he heard the door, he appeared from the kitchen.

"You're back," he said.

"Where are my car keys?"

Peter moved toward me slowly. "Why are you leaving me?"

"Because I need a break from you tonight." *Maybe forever.* The way he'd so easily put his hand around my neck… "We both need a break from each other. Please, just give me my keys."

"I don't know where they are," he said.

I frowned. Was it possible? But I'd looked outside. They weren't there. And he'd taken my purse from me when I'd gone into his apartment.

No, Peter had taken them. I knew he had. "This is stupid," I said. "Just give me my keys."

"I don't like that you leave me when you're upset," Peter said. "My parents never went to bed angry."

My anger flared. "You can't just take my keys!"

"And you are running away again!"

"I'm going to go home sometimes. There are things I need to take care of."

"I want you to move in with me."

"I leave when I want to leave," I spit out. "You don't control me."

Peter advanced quickly, grabbing me by the shoulders and pushing me backward until my back was against the wall. Cold fear coursed through my veins.

"Just tell me the truth! You're going to fuck your husband, aren't you?" Peter demanded.

I tried to wriggle free of his grasp carefully, because I didn't want to hurt Onyx. But he wouldn't release me. "What is wrong with you?"

He stared at me. Stared hard. In his eyes, I saw a person I didn't recognize.

A person who could have savagely beaten Teddy?

"You want the keys—you give me the cat."

My eyes grew wide with alarm. "No!"

Now Peter put his hands around Onyx's neck and started to tug.

"Stop it!" I screamed, tears springing to my eyes. The kitten squealed in protest as we both fought to hold her. "For God's sake, Peter!"

I twisted my body, shielding Onyx as best I could with both my arms. "We just need to take a break from each other," I said, my voice cracking. "Please."

"Fine." He abruptly let Onyx go. "Leave if you want."

I stayed against the wall, my breathing ragged, as Peter left the room. Several seconds later, he returned and threw my keys at me. They hit my thigh, stinging me.

Tears filled my eyes as Peter stormed off to his bedroom without a word.

25

The next day, a deliveryman came to my door with a huge arrange-
ment of red roses. My first thought was that they were from Andrew.
And then I opened the card.

Bella,
I am the world's biggest jerk. I don't know what got into me last night.
I love you so much that I can't imagine life without you. I know I
scared you. It will never happen again. Please call me, my love. I'm
very, very sorry.
Peter

I didn't call.

I did, however, want to call Marnie. Wanted to share with her
what had happened last night at Peter's place. But I stopped myself
from doing so, because I didn't want to hear her chastise me for
having changed and not listening to her when she'd tried to warn
me about Peter.

I looked down at my left thigh, fingered the bruise where my keys had hit me. What I needed ultimately was to spend some time alone with my thoughts. Try to get some perspective on my relationship with Peter.

Think was all I could do that night, and by the next morning, I was still confused. While I'd originally been terrified that Peter could put his hands on me in anger, I'd softened somewhat, accepting that even the best person in the world could lose emotional control. I know I'd wanted to claw out Andrew's eyes for hurting me.

But despite being able to allow for Peter's momentary outburst of anger, I was wondering more and more if it wasn't best to cool things off completely with him. Our relationship had begun with lust and heat, perhaps too much for either of us to handle.

The next day, a courier arrived with an oversize card from Peter professing his undying love for me, and once again asking me to call him.

I was tempted. In fact, a big part of me missed him and I *did* want to call.

But I didn't.

The phone woke me up after eleven that night. I'd been sleeping, but bolted upright and grabbed the receiver from the night table beside my bed.

"Hello," I said groggily.

A beat. Then, *"Bella."*

Peter's soft voice made the anger and uncertainty I'd felt start to ebb away. "Hi."

"I'm sorry," he said. "I was very stupid and very wrong."

I didn't say anything.

"I hate arguing. I reacted badly. Like a jerk."

The edges of my lips began to curve in a smile.

"Are you there?"

"Yeah, I'm here," I said softly. "And I'm sorry, too. I got to your place in a bad mood, and that didn't help anything." It was true. What Marnie had said had weighed heavily on my mind as I'd gone to Peter's place that night, and in retrospect, I think I'd gone there pissed and wanting to prove that he wasn't in any way controlling me.

"I miss you, *bella*."

"I miss you, too," I found myself saying.

"So everything's okay between us?" Peter asked.

"Yeah." The word seemed to escape on its own.

"Will you come over tomorrow evening?"

"Yeah."

"Good." I could hear the smile in Peter's voice. *"Buona notte, bella."*

"Good night," I echoed in English.

I was grinning as I replaced the receiver.

No sooner had I hung up than the phone rang again. I quickly snatched up the receiver. "Hello?"

"Why don't you come over tonight?"

"Right now?" I asked, already feeling a rush of desire.

"Yes, right now."

"I'm on my way."

I was at Peter's place within half an hour, and we fell easily back into our world of hot and frequent sex. Once again, I felt like everything between us was right, and that I was right where I needed to be.

Peter had to be up for eight, so by one-thirty, we were finished having sex and lying in each other's arms. I thought I'd sleep the entire night, but shortly after six, I was up.

And puking in the toilet.

Peter came into the bathroom with me, rubbed my back while I sat hunched over the toilet. Only when the wave of nausea passed did I get to my feet and head to the sink.

Peter turned on the water, and I splashed it over my face, then drank some. "Ugh, I must be coming down with something. I hope you don't get it."

"Maybe you're pregnant," Peter said.

My eyes flew to his. "Oh, God. Don't say that."

Peter didn't say anything for a moment as he studied me. "Would that be so bad?" He looked hopeful. "If you had my baby inside you?"

"I can't get pregnant now, Peter. I have work, which will be starting soon. And…I'm still officially married, you know…"

His hopeful look disappeared instantly, replaced by something dark. Angry. "So you're concerned about how this will affect your divorce—or how it might upset your husband?"

I didn't like Peter's tone or his body language, and I didn't answer. But I found myself wondering why I'd gone against my judgment last night when I'd figured I should keep my distance from him. How could I feel so comfortable in his arms only hours ago and now be feeling wary in his presence?

"I think I'm just sick, that's all. I've been feeling a little off for a few days now." Which was true, though I hadn't felt feverish. And the nausea seemed to come and go, sometimes when I smelled certain foods. Like eggs. And chicken. And, oddly enough, steamed asparagus.

Oh, God. *Was* I pregnant?

How could I have been so stupid? I chastised myself. Getting caught up in the moment, letting Peter fuck me without protection at least twice? Not only did I know better, that kind of behavior wasn't like me.

"Come here, *bella*." Peter wrapped an arm around my waist and drew me to him. I let him hold me, let him stroke my hair.

Suddenly, he squeezed one of my breasts, and I yelped.

Now Peter grinned. "Your breasts are more sensitive than normal. And they're heavier. Yes, bella...I think you're carrying my baby."

Peter kissed my cheek, then led me to the bed, where he tucked me under the covers. He was smiling the entire time, as though he was the happiest man in the world. I forced a smile as well, but inwardly, I felt a sense of dread.

Please, God——don't let me be pregnant.

Sending up a prayer was likely blasphemous under the circumstances, but I did it nonetheless. I didn't want to be pregnant with Peter's baby.

Peter got into bed beside me, and gently placed a hand on my stomach. "I'm going to take care of you for the next nine months."

The walls were closing in. I was feeling trapped.

"I want you to stay here while I go to work," Peter said. "I want you home when I return. I will take care of you."

A simple statement...but was it a statement, or an order? Once again, I was getting that gnawing feeling in my gut that Peter was trying to control me.

"I have to go home and see if Peaches came back," I told Peter.

"Forget about the cat," Peter said in an annoyed tone. "You'll never find her."

I gaped at him. "That's not a nice thing to say."

"I think some well-meaning family took her in." His tone was warmer again. "I'm sure she's fine. How can you worry about a cat when you're about to have a baby?"

My stomach twisted. Nausea, or dread? "We don't know that that's true."

Peter kissed my lips slowly and passionately while rubbing my belly. "I do," he said when he ended the kiss. "My mother said that my father was the one to realize she was pregnant the first time. And *bella,* you're pregnant."

I'm not sure when I drifted off to sleep, but when I woke up again it was after ten and Peter was gone.

Even as I'd slept, I'd dreamed about his words. *I want you here when I get home.*

He wanted me around always, hardly liked to let me out of his sight. It wasn't normal, even if he lusted after me with the unbridled passion of a teenager. His love for me was smothering me—and if I was pregnant...

"How could you have been so stupid?" I asked myself. The thought that I might be pregnant made my head throb, it was so distressing. So distressing that I told myself not to entertain the idea of being with child. Not even consider it as a possibility.

But that was easier said than done. My breasts *were* tender. Was Peter right? Was I going to have a baby?

A baby would tie me to Peter indefinitely, something that suddenly seemed terrifying. If he was already smothering me with his intense feelings, what would happen with a child in the mix?

Hot sex I could handle. His love I could deal with, even if I was still married to Andrew. But his need to control me?

No way in hell.

I lay in Peter's bed and tried to imagine what life would be like with him and a baby. Would he freak out if he came home from work and I'd gone with the baby to the mall? Would he call numerous times a day to check up on me?

It would happen. I knew it would.

And knowing that helped me make an instant decision. I couldn't continue a relationship with Peter, not for another second. I needed to end things with him, do it cold turkey.

I felt a pressing urgency to get out of his apartment as fast as I could, so I got up, got dressed, and headed for the door. But before I left, I decided to write him a note.

It was the chicken shit way to end a relationship the way his ex-girlfriend had done. But now I understood the woman's reasoning. Instinctively I knew I couldn't have this conversation with Peter face-to-face. Especially not now that he believed I was pregnant.

He wouldn't *let* me go. That's why I couldn't give him a choice.

I found a piece of paper and a pen, and began to write.

Dear Peter,
I was feeling better and decided to go home. I didn't want to stay away from Onyx for too long. Peter, I really do adore you, but I think it's time for us to cool things down. Until I resolve the issue of my marriage, I think that's the best thing.
Sophie

I frowned as I reread my note, not knowing if I'd chosen the right words. I didn't want to hurt him, but I also didn't want him believing I'd be coming back.

I decided to leave the note as it was. Then I left for home, hoping Peter would accept my decision.

I should have known better.

26

Before I even got to my house, my cell phone rang. Peter's number was illuminated on the caller ID.

How the hell did he already know I wasn't at his place? That fact alone told me that I'd done the right thing by leaving. Peter wasn't giving me any room to breathe.

Onyx greeted me when I got to the door. I lifted the kitten and nuzzled her nose against mine.

Peaches hadn't returned, but I put new food and fresh water in her bowls on the porch. Peter's comment that maybe a well-meaning family had taken her in had got me thinking. Maybe a kid had found her. Peaches was very friendly, the kind of cat who would roll onto her back and offer strangers her stomach to rub. Andrew and I liked to joke that she thought she was a dog.

It was time I made some posters and put them throughout the neighborhood. If someone had given her a home, thinking she was stray, surely he or she would return her once they saw that Peaches actually had a loving owner.

But first, I went to bed because fatigue got the better of me. When I woke up, it was after noon.

I forced myself out of bed, feeling unusually groggy. I got the coffee brewing and considered making eggs. But the thought alone made my stomach churn, so I opted for toast instead.

My coffee in hand, I went to the computer and set about designing a poster with Peaches's picture. Satisfied, I printed off fifteen posters. Then I ambled into the kitchen and called Marnie. Maybe she'd come over and help me put up the posters.

And help me with something else.

"Marnie?" I said softly when she answered the phone.

"Sophie." She paused. "Long time."

"I know. I know."

"What's going on?"

I swallowed. "I'm wondering if you're still my best friend."

"Sophie, you know I'll always be your best friend. Even if you put me on the back burner because of a man."

"I'm sorry. I really am." I started to softly cry.

"Hey," Marnie said. "Sophie, I didn't mean that."

"Yes, you did."

"Maybe I did," Marnie said honestly. "But I didn't mean to make you feel bad. Look, I've been busy too."

"I ended it with Peter," I said, getting to the real issue I wanted to talk about.

"You did?"

"He was smothering me, and I thought…I don't know. But a few days ago he put his hands on my neck and—"

"What?"

"He didn't really hurt me, but I knew then it was over. He was jealous about Andrew and even accused me of lying about being raped."

"Sweetie, why didn't you call?"

"Because I didn't want you to say *I told you so.*"

"Oh, Sophie." Marnie blew out a loud breath. "I'm sorry you didn't feel you could call me. No matter what's going on, you can always turn to me, you hear?"

"Yes," I said, nodding. "He scares me, Marnie. He took my keys the other day so I couldn't leave. That's not normal."

"Jesus."

"I don't know if it's that he's just insecure because he thinks I'll go back to Andrew…"

"Girl, trust your instincts. Once I realized Peter was trying to keep you all to himself, I started to get a bad vibe about him. I still think he beat up Teddy."

A thought entered my mind then—what Peter had said about his cat in Italy.

I drowned the bastard when it scratched me.

"Sophie?"

"Peter once told me that he drowned his cat. Then he said he was joking. But… Peaches is missing." I stifled a moan. Had I printed the posters for nothing? Would Peaches never be found? "Maybe I'm stretching here, but…he never liked me coming home to feed my cat. Do you think he could have done something to her, just to make sure I could always be with him without distraction?"

"It sounds crazy," Marnie said. "But who knows?"

Conflicting thoughts went through my mind.

Peter was dangerous.

I was overreacting.

He was insanely jealous, even of my cat.

I was jumping to a ridiculous conclusion.

With the phone at my ear, I paced the kitchen. That's when something caught my eye. A bouquet of lilies on the living room coffee table. "Marnie, hold on a second."

I put down the receiver and walked into the living room, my stomach fluttering a little. The bouquet was absolutely stunning.

My hand instantly went to the small envelope amid the bouquet. I opened it and read the card.

I didn't want to wake you, you were sleeping so peacefully. I hope these flowers brighten your day.
Andrew

I held the card to my heart, my chest tightening with emotion. I was completely torn. I loved my husband, but a part of me hated him for what he'd done to me. To our marriage.

And yet, the flowers stirred feelings within me that I'd all but repressed in the past month. I couldn't remember the last time Andrew had sent me flowers. And I appreciated the simple message. It reminded me of the Andrew I'd started dating ten years earlier, the one who was gentle and thoughtful and knew that a kind word or gesture could make my day better.

It was what I'd needed at the moment—from a place I hadn't expected.

My phone rang at least once every twenty minutes for the next three hours, each time the caller ID displaying Peter's cell number. Sometimes the calls were one right after another. Peter had to be at work, so how on earth did he have the time to call me so damn much?

Shortly after four, my doorbell rang. Wary, I moved quietly to the door and peered through the peephole. I saw a man holding a clipboard and a small package.

I opened the door.

"I have a delivery for Sophie Gibson."

"That's me."

The man extended the small box to me. "Sign here, please."

I signed, then retreated into the house and opened the package.

I gasped when I opened the box. Inside was a necklace.

I love you, bella, the accompanying note said.

How had Peter arranged to send this to me in the hours since I'd left his place? He must have called the store where he'd bought my earrings, since I could tell right away that the necklace matched them exactly.

I wanted to pull my hair out. I was home barely four hours and Peter was already freaking out, sending me a stunning piece of jewelry to ensure he wasn't losing me.

What would he do when he got home and saw the note?

I suddenly regretted writing it, fearing how unstable he might get after reading it.

I called Marnie but didn't get her, not even on her cell. I left a message that she needed to call me back as soon as she got the message.

"What's going on?" Marnie asked me when she called me an hour later.

So I told her. Told her that Peter had been calling pretty much nonstop, how he'd sent me a piece of jewelry that would have any other woman melting, but instead was pushing me away even more.

"What do I do, Marnie? If I keep the necklace, he's going to think—"

"It doesn't matter what he thinks. You can't call him back. That's what he wants. You have to cut the ties, cold turkey."

The urgent pounding on my door made the hairs on the back of my neck rise.

Peter?

"Marnie, someone's pounding on my door. I bet it's Peter."

"I'll stay on the line."

More pounding. My kitchen phone wasn't cordless, and I slowly lowered it so that it hung nearly to the floor.

My heart racing, I made my way to the door. Opened it and saw Peter standing there, looking harried.

"You left me," he said. "You said you'd never leave me, but you left me."

I didn't know what to say. I only knew that every cell in my body was afraid.

Peter stepped into my house without an invitation, looking inside suspiciously as if he expected to see someone else inside. Something about his body language set me on edge.

"I thought you loved me," Peter said.

"Peter, I've got to deal with my marriage. I can't keep…having an affair."

"An affair? Is that what you think this is?"

"That's the legal definition."

"Why are you worried about legal definitions? We have found each other. We have something special. I don't care that you're married." Peter's eyes suddenly widened with understanding. "Your husband. He's threatening you. What is he going to do—leave you penniless?"

"No, it's not that."

"I have money, *bella*. We can buy a place, maybe somewhere

else. Miami, if you want. Or we can move to another state. If it's your husband you want to escape—"

"Stop, please," I said. "Peter, you know I'm not feeling well."

"I know. I was worried about you. I called and called, but you didn't answer. The moment I got my lunch break, I went home to take care of you, and you were gone. I saw your note." He paused. "I wanted to come over right away but I needed to get back to the set, so I called the jewelry store and got the necklace sent to you. I hoped it would show you how much you mean to me. I hoped after you opened it you would return to our home." He took a much-needed breath. "I don't want you running back here every minute. Once your husband learns you're carrying my child, what if he hurts you?"

"Peter, I really doubt I'm pregnant." I said the words, hoping they were true.

"I bought a test. You can take it now. We can know for sure."

"No," I said. I didn't want to take a pregnancy test with Peter around. Something told me that if he learned I was pregnant, he would become more demanding, insisting I live with him. Not wanting to let me out of his sight.

And what I needed was time—time to figure out what I was going to do—*if* I was pregnant.

"Why not?" Peter asked.

"I was just about to put up some missing posters of Peaches."

"The cat, the cat! Forget about the fucking cat."

"No, I'm not going to forget about my cat."

"Are you planning to kill my baby?"

"I'm not pregnant. I'm certain I'm not." I needed Peter to believe that, because otherwise, he would never leave me alone.

"Come home with me," Peter said.

"No." I spoke quickly. Perhaps too quickly. "I—I just want time to think. I need to figure out what I'm going to do…about my marriage."

"You mean how you will break the news to your husband that you will be divorcing him."

I looked into Peter's eyes, saw his expectation, and knew I couldn't say anything to the contrary. He had to believe I would still be a part of his life, or he would never walk out my front door.

So I lied. "Yes."

My answer seemed to appease him, proving my instincts right. His chest rose and fell with a deep breath. "Sometimes I feel you're slipping away from me. I've told you so many times that I love you, but you say nothing in return."

I said nothing.

Something stirred in Peter's dark eyes. Doubt. Then anger. "You're lying to me," he suddenly said. "You don't need time. You *are* still fucking your husband."

"No, I'm not."

"Is it his baby inside you, *bella?*"

I didn't answer the question, instead asking one of my own. "Why are you being like this? This is what's bothering me, Peter. You've changed into someone I don't know. Someone who's possessive. Someone who scares me."

I hadn't meant to say the last part, but once I had, I knew I'd said the wrong thing. I saw it in the way Peter's eyes narrowed, the way his lips tightened. He was furious.

And I *was* scared.

"I told you I would never hurt you," he said, his voice low. And then suddenly, he knocked the flower vase off the table in my foyer—the roses he'd sent me—and the glass shattered on the tile floor with a loud crash.

I screamed. His hand flew to my neck and he squeezed. Hard. "But that was when I believed that you would never betray me! You *whore!*"

"Peter," I managed, my voice squeaky because he was squeezing my larynx. "You're hurting me."

He held me. Glared at me.

"Peter..."

Abruptly let me go. "Look what you made me do. You're making me crazy."

Crazy was right. Tears filling my eyes, my hand went to my injured neck.

"I've done nothing but love you," he said. "I would do anything to make you happy, *bella. Anything.*"

"I haven't betrayed you." My voice was weak, filled with emotion.

"Then marry me," he said.

I gaped at him, baffled. "One minute you're calling me a whore," I said slowly. "The next you want to marry me?"

"Even if you are not pregnant, what are we waiting for?" Peter asked as though he hadn't lost it moments earlier. "My parents got married after three weeks. They loved each other until they died together."

I said nothing.

"Do you love me, Sophie?"

I opened my mouth, but I couldn't speak. I couldn't tell him what he wanted to hear.

Peter backhanded me across the face. Screaming, I went flying and landed on the floor.

"You lied about being raped, didn't you? You have probably fucked a hundred men, haven't you? Let them come inside you, every one of them. *No one has ever made me feel like this before,*" Peter mocked, recalling words I'd once said in the heat of passion. His nostrils flared with each angry breath he took. "You're sickening. You disgust me. You fucked me but you didn't love me. You're a whore. A dirty whore!"

I was crying as I stared up at Peter. Who was this person? Why was he being so hateful?

I remembered that Marnie was on the line. At least I hoped she was. "Get out of here!" I yelled, hoping Marnie would hear me. "You can't talk to me like this in my own house. You can't hit me!" I grabbed a broken shard of glass. It cut into my skin, but I held it tightly. I would use it as a weapon if need be. "Get out!"

He didn't move, but there was something dark and dangerous in his eyes. "You're not fit to carry my child."

I wondered if he was going to hit me again. Or worse, kick me while I was sprawled on the floor. Instinctively, I moved a hand in front of my belly.

But Peter didn't kick me. He turned and stalked toward the door.

When he opened it, he faced me. An evil grin formed on his lips. "Ever find your cat, *bella?*"

And then he was gone.

Sobbing, I ran to the door and locked it. I looked through the window that bordered the door and saw Peter's SUV peeling out of the driveway.

My neck hurting and my face stinging, I scrambled the short distance to the kitchen, where I sat on the floor beside the dangling receiver. I grabbed it and put it to my ear.

"Marnie! You still there?"

I heard the steady beep of a phone that's been off the hook for too long.

I couldn't muster the strength to stand, and stayed on the floor, my back against the wall as I softly cried.

What on earth had happened to Peter? Why had he changed from a guy who was totally into me to one who now seemed to hate me?

Because he felt used? I'd never made any promises to him. And fine, maybe he'd fallen in love with me and now felt like I'd used him. Most guys would call a girl a bitch and walk away.

Not backhand her.

Or kill her cat.

"Peaches," I whimpered. Had he really taken her? Had he killed her?

My stomach lurched, and I barely made it to the kitchen sink before I threw up.

27

As I was rinsing the sink, someone pounded on the door.

My entire body froze.

"Sophie!" I heard.

Marnie.

Nausea still gripping my stomach, I hurried to the door. Marnie swept inside and pulled me into her arms. I cried against her shoulder.

"Is he gone?" she asked when we pulled apart.

I nodded.

"I raced over here as fast as I could. I was about to call the cops. Did that motherfucker hit you?"

I nodded.

"He's lucky he's not here. I brought my gun." Marnie patted her purse. I'd been with her when she'd gone for her firearms license, and she'd encouraged me to get a gun as well. Not being a fan of guns, I'd declined.

"He freaked out, Marnie. And I think maybe he killed Peaches!"

Marnie wrapped a hand around my waist and led me to the living room, where she sat me on the sofa. "Tell me everything."

So I did. But I left out the fact that I might be pregnant. For the moment. I told her that he hated me leaving his place, that he thought I was still screwing Andrew behind his back.

"I'm so sorry," Marnie said when I was finished. "He's insane, obviously. The kind of guy you don't know is crazy until things don't go his way."

"You think so?" I asked. "Crazy crazy?" How could he be crazy and I not realize that? "Maybe he just went into a jealous rage. Trust me, I'm not justifying him putting his hands on me—and I definitely never want to see him again—but some guys lose it when a relationship ends."

Marnie was slowly shaking her head. "He wanted you all to himself. I hardly heard from you, saw you even less. Because you were always with him—right where he wanted you to be."

I was silent as I mulled over Marnie's words.

"I know the sex was great...but did you really have more in common than that? What did you guys do that made you a couple?"

It was a good question. No, a great one. "We cooked together, watched movies, and..."

"And fucked."

"It was an affair, Marnie."

"I know. There's nothing wrong with fucking. But...did a day go by when you guys *didn't* fuck?"

I shook my head.

"Again, there's nothing wrong with sex. Robert and I like doing it—a lot. But we also have great conversations. We argue, too. And we go out in public."

I flashed a mock-scowl at Marnie.

"Seriously, Soph, when you think about it, is it normal to spend most of your time with a guy in bed?"

"The sex was great, what can I say. And in so many ways, it felt like more than sex. Like a spiritual experience. I know, you'll say I'm nuts—but I mean it." I paused. "Peter said he fell in love with me the first minute he saw me. Maybe if Andrew hadn't still been in my heart, I would have fallen in love with him, too."

"I think he's obsessed with you," Marnie said bluntly. "He's confusing his sexual obsession for love."

Marnie's words stung. I don't know why.

But perhaps she was right. I don't know why Peter and I connected so powerfully in the bedroom, but possibly we'd both gotten hooked on our sexual chemistry. Confused it with something more.

"I guess I was a bit obsessed with him, too," I admitted. Even now, thinking about the sex with Peter, I still felt the stirring of desire. Like an addict craving something she knows is bad for her.

"At least he showed his true colors now rather than later."

I felt a bout of nausea again, and quickly ran to the kitchen, where I threw up in the sink.

I puked not only what I'd eaten earlier, but kept dry-heaving until I started vomiting bile.

"Jesus," Marnie said.

"Marnie," I said softly, facing her. "I think I might be pregnant."

I'm not sure I would have had the courage to go to the drugstore without Marnie. We perused the various pregnancy tests, and I trusted her opinion on which one I should buy.

"You really think you're pregnant?" she asked when we were back in her car.

"Last week, I realized that I hadn't started my period when I should have. I didn't dwell on it though, because I've never been very regular. And all the stuff with Andrew, plus I've been so worried about Peaches." The thought that my cat might have met foul play at the hands of Peter made my throat clog with emotion. I didn't want to believe that Peter would hurt a harmless cat. "But I kind of noticed that some smells make my stomach feel a little woozy."

"Oh, sweetie."

"Then last night, when I was in bed with Peter, I also noticed that my breasts seemed extra-sensitive."

"Oh, boy."

"But I still think I might be late. Stress can do that, can't it? I've been so worried about Peaches..." I stifled a cry.

Thinking about my cat was preferable to thinking about the fact that I might be pregnant. The more I thought about it, the more I doubted that Peter could have hurt her. He didn't even know what she looked like.

Or did he?

Had he driven by my place on more than one occasion, perhaps seen Peaches on the front step?

Was Marnie right about Peter, that he was insane?

And if he was insane, just how dangerous was he?

Back at my place, Marnie held my hand while I waited the three minutes for the pregnancy stick to change color. Or not.

It did.

"A pink line," Marnie said softly when she returned from the bathroom. I hadn't had the guts to check the test. "That means—"

"I'm pregnant." I let out a soft sigh.

The phone began to ring as Marnie sat beside me on the sofa. It had been ringing pretty much nonstop since the moment we'd arrived. The caller ID had shown Peter's number the first few times I'd looked, and I was certain he was the one who continued to call every few minutes.

"Jesus," Marnie said. "Can't the man stop calling?"

His incessant calling only validated my decision to not see him again. His behavior was overboard. Unnatural.

Obsessive.

I would do anything to make you happy, bella. *Anything.*

I got a chill remembering Peter's words. Did his doing anything to make me happy mean trying to kill Teddy for harassing me the night we'd met?

I pushed the thought out of my mind. I didn't want to think about what Peter had or hadn't done, because what mattered now was my predicament.

"I can't believe I'm actually pregnant," I said.

"I don't know why, but I thought you overreacting or something. I mean, you and Peter were careful."

I said nothing, just stroked Onyx, who had climbed onto my lap.

Marnie's eyes widened as she regarded me. "Sophie...tell me you were careful."

I couldn't face her. Suddenly, I felt enormously stupid. I'd let my passion stop me from using my brain, and that was inexcusable. "We were careful," I began. "Most of the time..." My voice trailed off, ended on a groan.

"Oh, Jesus," Marnie said. "Sophie, this isn't like you. You made Andrew use condoms even though you were on the Pill when you weren't ready to get pregnant."

"I know, I know." I buried my face in my hands. "I'm a complete moron. For this to happen to me at my age? I know better."

"Well, you can't change it now."

Marnie gave my back a comforting rub, and we fell into silence. The seriousness of the situation weighed heavily on me.

"You think the test could be wrong?" I asked.

I knew I was grasping at straws, but I wanted Marnie to tell me that the test could have given a false positive. That perhaps when a person was stressed, her body gave off hormones that could be confused with pregnancy.

"I wish you weren't, sweetie," she said. "But you are, and you can't run from this. You have to decide what you're going to do."

Words I didn't want to hear. "This is the worst possible thing that could happen. The worst."

The phone rang again. Marnie bolted to her feet and charged into the kitchen. "Listen, you crazy asshole. Stop calling here. The police know you've been harassing Sophie, and if you don't stop this shit, they're gonna arrest your ass."

"Thank you," I said, as she made her way back into the living room.

"Hopefully that stops the asshole," Marnie said. "Crazy or not, no one wants to get arrested."

It was as Marnie was sitting back down that she suddenly said, "Hey, what's this?"

"What?"

She gestured toward a table behind the sofa that rested in the corner between the bathroom and master bedroom. A card envelope was propped up on the vanilla-scented candle that sat on the table. In my distraught state, I hadn't noticed it.

My stomach fluttered. "It can't be from Peter. He couldn't have gotten into my house."

Marnie reached for the envelope and offered it to me. I recognized Andrew's handwriting.

I opened the envelope, pulled out the card and read.

Sophie,

Maybe you don't believe me, but I am sorry for hurting you. I know that "hurt" isn't an adequate word to describe how you must feel. I know that, because now I feel it too. I don't want to lose you, Sophie. And if there's a part of you that still loves me, even a small part, we've got to try to work things out. Before it's too late.

The ball's in your court, and I won't pressure you if you can't forgive me. But I hope you'll call. Sophie, I want to save our marriage.
Andrew

By the time I finished reading the note, I was crying. Subconsciously, I pressed my hand to my belly.

Andrew wanted our marriage.

But would he still want it if he knew I had another man's child in my belly?

"I think you should call him, Sophie," Marnie said. "I'm sorry I tried to steer you away from Andrew. He loves you. He made a mistake—a big one—but he's not Keith. He's a good man."

I thought about Marnie's words, and wondered why she was so convinced Andrew was good for me when she'd made him for a player.

If I had a husband who could hit on my friends, then he definitely wasn't the right man for me. But if Marnie had somehow misconstrued Andrews words and actions...

"Marnie," I began slowly, "you didn't think Andrew was such a good man a month ago."

"I know, and maybe I was wrong about that."

"You didn't want to tell me what Andrew said when he hit on you...but will you tell me now? It's important."

Marnie nodded, drew in a deep breath. "Remember your

twenty-sixth birthday party? How Andrew had a bash for you in the backyard?"

"Yeah."

"Well, Andrew put his arm around my waist and told me that I was a very sexy woman, that any guy would be lucky to have me. He'd never really done that before, and…" She shrugged.

I pondered her words. "That was right after Keith filed for divorce."

"Yes."

"And you were feeling down," I went on, remembering. "I told Andrew to give you a compliment because you needed a bit of a morale boost."

"Oh, God." Marnie closed her eyes.

"I told him to say something that would make you feel better."

"You know." Marnie sighed. "I always wondered if I'd read him the wrong way, but after Keith…"

"After Keith was such a dog, you jumped to the wrong conclusion about Andrew."

Marnie nodded as regret flashed across her face. "Who's the moron now?"

I gave her hand a squeeze. "I'm glad you told me. Because yeah, Andrew was wrong to cheat, but it makes a difference that he *didn't* hit on you. That—I couldn't forgive."

"Call him, Sophie," Marnie said. "Work it out."

"I'm pregnant, Marnie," I said. "How can I call him now?"

The phone rang again, and I screamed in frustration.

Marnie answered the phone again, saying, "Call here one more time, Peter, and the police will be heading to your place to arrest you. Leave Sophie the hell alone."

"Maybe I should just ignore him," I said when Marnie had slammed down the receiver. Pissing Peter off could be bad. But perhaps if I ignored him forever, he would eventually go away.

What wouldn't go away was his child—our child—growing inside of me.

"I don't like that he won't leave you alone," Marnie said. "He's going to come back."

"I think you're right." In fact, I knew she was right.

"You're going to need my gun." Marnie withdrew it from her purse and gave it to me. "And don't be afraid to use it."

"Marnie, I don't like guns."

"I'm not going to stand by and watch another man hurt you," Marnie told me. "Take the gun. Put it in your bedroom, because that's when Peter's going to show up. When it's late, and you're in bed."

"I don't know."

Marnie took the gun from me, went to my bedroom, and was back in less than two minutes. "It's in the night table drawer. You don't have to look at it unless you need it."

I nodded. "All right. Now I need you to do me a favor."

"Name it."

"Take Onyx for me. I don't want her getting hurt...not the way Peaches did." My voice cracked.

I didn't want to believe it, but in my gut I knew it was true. That Peter had killed her. She'd gone missing the first night I walked out on Peter, the night Andrew had shown up at the house to talk to me. If Peter had driven by and seen Andrew's car, he could have easily lashed out at my cat.

The phone rang again. Both Marnie and I groaned.

"I'll do one better," Marnie said. "I'll take Onyx, but I'll take you, too. Peter doesn't know where I live. You're gonna stay at my place."

28

For the next few days, Onyx and I stayed at Marnie's place. I went home only to get mail and water my plants. I had to clear both my home voice mail messages and cell messages, because Peter had called so much, he'd taken up all the space.

He loved me, he said, why didn't I see that? All he wanted was a future with me. Even if I wasn't pregnant, he wanted us to get married. He would treat me right, never raise his hand to me again. He would go to counseling with me if I wanted.

He repeated the same things over and over again.

He was insane. I was sure of it now.

For three days, Marnie had put off seeing Robert because I was around. That evening, when he called, I told her to spend time with him, that I was a big girl who could handle a solo sleepover in her apartment.

So Marnie did and I, as much as I thought I'd be okay, was depressed. Depressed over being pregnant, depressed that I had to avoid my home because I didn't know what Peter was capable of.

I decided to head back to my place that evening. I continued to hold out hope that I'd see my cat on my doorstep.

I didn't find Peaches, but I did find three envelopes. I opened one, saw *"Bella,"* and knew all of them were from Peter.

I ripped the notes into small pieces and threw them in the garbage. Then I parked my car in the garage, in case Peter decided to come by.

Because tonight, I was going to sleep in my own bed.

Tonight, I wanted to feel normal.

Nothing was even close to normal. Every sound had me bolting upright. More than once in the night I crept to the window at the front of the house to peer outside.

Each time, thankfully, I saw no sign of Peter.

Late the next morning, Marnie called me on my cell. "What happened, girl? I came home to find you not here and I was terrified."

"I just wanted to come home. I can't hide out at your place forever."

"Sophie, I don't trust Peter. If you have to stay here for the next five months, that's okay with me."

"I parked my car in the garage," I told Marnie. "He won't know I'm here. I'm keeping a low profile."

"All right. Well, that's good."

"Plus, I don't want to intrude on your life."

"Oh, for God's sake," Marnie said. "You're my best friend. My sister, as far as I'm concerned. Keeping you safe is not intruding on my life."

"I'm okay," I told her. "I'm gonna paint. Spend my time and energy focusing on the positive."

I tried, through my artwork, to forget about my problems. But I couldn't. How could I forget about being pregnant? How could I forget about the fact that Peter was hounding me like a stalker?

By early evening, I was calling Marnie again, needing someone to talk to. "I just don't know what I'm going to do," I told her. "Pregnant?"

"Okay," Marnie said. "Enough. Tonight, you're not going to think about Peter, or Andrew. And you're not going to worry about the baby, either. It doesn't matter if it's Peter's or Andrew's—it's yours. And there's no crime in raising the baby alone."

Emotion made my throat clog. "I can't believe I'm really pregnant," I said softly. I sounded like a broken record but I couldn't help it. "Now, at the worst possible time. Andrew and I don't have a solid marriage anymore, but he wants to work on it. And now—"

"Didn't I just say you weren't going to worry about being pregnant?"

"I know, but—"

"No buts. Look, you're going to have to make a decision, but it won't be tonight. And whatever you do, don't choose to stay with a man if the relationship isn't what you want. Because a baby sure as hell won't help you grow closer."

Marnie was right. I wouldn't decide anything tonight. And I didn't want to think about my dilemma, because it was driving me crazy.

"What did you have in mind?" I asked her.

"How about that club Illusions on International Drive?"

"Girl, you want me to shake my pregnant behind?"

"You're only pregnant. Not dead. Besides, it'll be good exercise. May as well get a head start on that if you're going to gain fifty, sixty pounds."

I rolled my eyes, but I was smiling. "Thanks, Marnie, for giving me *that* to look forward to."

"Hey, I'm just telling it like it is." I could hear a smile in Marnie's voice. "You ready to go shake your butt and burn some calories?"

I didn't need any more convincing. A night of dancing was exactly what I needed. "What time?"

Marnie and I made plans to meet at ten. Early enough to avoid the major crowds that tended to show up around midnight, but not too early that the place would be a ghost town when we arrived.

The DJ was lively, playing an old school mix that had everyone in the club dancing. It was the kind of music that pushed everything but fun thoughts from your mind.

Marnie and I got silly on the dance floor, busting out moves we used to do in college. I laughed. She laughed.

It was just what I needed.

"You ready for a drink?" Marnie asked when the music slowed down in tempo. "Nonalcoholic, of course."

"Definitely," I told her. I fanned myself. "I haven't danced this much in ages."

"I promised you fun. Did I deliver?"

"You sure did."

I walked with Marnie to the bar. She ordered a margarita for herself, while I opted for a Sprite.

I noticed men looking at me, but I didn't make eye contact long enough to indicate I might even remotely be interested in getting to know anyone. And as a result, no one bothered me.

"Oh, my goodness," Marnie began when the music morphed into an upbeat song. "Heavy D!" She placed her nearly empty drink glass on the bar and pulled me by the hand. "I need to dance to this one!"

Giggling, I hurried with Marnie to the edge of the dance floor. She pulsed her hips, waved her hands in the air. I sipped on my Sprite, bopping my head to the beat beside her as opposed to dancing.

I was in the groove, enjoying the moment when all of a sudden I felt hands in my hair. Before my brain could process what was going on, my head was being jerked backward violently.

I was too shocked to scream.

"What the fuck are you doing, Sophie?"

The sound of Peter's voice in my ear made a chill pass through my body. What was he doing here?

He was pulling my hair so hard, tears filled my eyes and I lost my balance. I slipped and fell to the dance floor, my glass of Sprite crashing beside me.

I looked up then. Saw Peter's face filled with absolute rage. Then I looked at Marnie, whose eyes were wide with alarm.

She started for me, offering me her hand. But Peter grabbed me by my hair again, yanking me up.

I cried out in pain, the sound drowned out by the throbbing music. But some people around me noticed what was going on. Noticed, and were staring.

"Peter, let me go!"

His grip grew tighter, pulling at my roots until I couldn't help sobbing. Only then did he let my hair go and take hold of my arm. "We're leaving. Right now."

Marnie threw herself between me and Peter, trying to push him away from me. "What the fuck are you doing, Peter? Sophie's a grown woman. You can't come in here, grabbing her up like this. Like you fucking own her. She can do what she wants."

Peter released me, and I gasped with relief, grateful that Marnie's words had gotten through to him. But then he put his hand on Marnie's face and shoved her so harshly that she stumbled backward, slipping on her heels and falling onto her butt.

"Stop it!" I screamed, and pounded Peter on his chest.

He grabbed me by the wrist. Anger brewed in his eyes. "Is that what you're doing here?" he asked. "Doing what you want? Maybe flirting with other men? Deciding who you'll take home like you did with me?"

"It's over, Peter! Leave me alone!"

"And what the fuck were you drinking?" Peter kicked the broken glass I'd been drinking from. "You're pregnant!"

The glass went flying, hitting a woman's ankle. She whirled around with a pissed-off expression.

"You better leave, Peter," Marnie said as she got to her feet. "Because I'm reaching into my purse right now for my cell to call the cops."

Peter's lips curled in a smug grin as he regarded me. He must have seen the question in my eyes, the question that asked, *How do you know that I'm definitely pregnant?*

"You thought I would believe you when you said you weren't carrying my baby?" he asked. "I know you're pregnant, *bella*. And I know that *you* know it too."

Two bouncers suddenly appeared, one on either side of Peter. "Is there a problem here?" one of them asked.

"Yes," Marnie replied. "This guy is bothering my friend. The motherfucker needs to be arrested. He grabbed her by the hair like he's Tarzan or something."

"She's my girlfriend," Peter said, his eyes on me as he spoke. "She's pregnant with my child and she's out here flirting like a fucking whore!"

"All right, buddy," one of the bouncers said. It wasn't his job to mediate domestic disputes, just to squash any possible problems. "You need to leave now."

"Sophie, come on," Peter said.

Each bouncer took one of Peter's arms.

"Sophie."

When Peter didn't start to move, the bouncers began to force-fully pull him toward the door.

"Sophie! Come with me, Sophie!"

I stood and watched, tears streaming down my face, as Peter wrestled with the bouncers. He didn't stop making eye contact with me, and the expression on his face was one of abject disillusionment.

"Sophie!" he screamed at the top of his lungs.

The bouncers turned Peter around, twisting his arms behind his back, and picked up their pace as they led him to the door. I watched every second of the drama unfold, not breathing until Peter was out the door.

"What a fucking creep!" Marnie said, her chest heaving.

"How did he even know I was here?" I asked, though I knew Marnie couldn't answer the question. Instead of an answer, she put her arms around me and wrapped me in a hug and held me while I cried.

I pulled away from her, wiping at my eyes as I tried to regain control of my emotions. "How did he know I was pregnant?" I asked. "How did he know I was here? Is he checking my garbage, following me around?"

"All I know is that guy is totally off his rocker, so anything's possible." Marnie made a face as she shook her head. "He needs to be arrested. We can leave here and go to the police station, get some sort of restraining order."

"No," I said. I noticed that people were staring at me, and I wondered what they were thinking. Empathy for me? Anger? I blocked out the stares and concentrated only on Marnie. "I don't want to get into a long, drawn-out fight with Peter. I don't want this to get messy. If I ignore him, he'll eventually go away, right?"

"I don't know about that," Marnie said. "He's way too intense."

I looked around. Even though everyone around me was dancing again, some were definitely shooting sidelong glances at me.

"I want to get out of here," I said.

"No way. We can't leave yet. What if Peter is waiting in the parking lot?"

"Oh, fuck. You think so?"

"I wouldn't put it past him."

"You're right. Damn, you're right." I sighed. "But I don't want to be here anymore. Everyone's staring at me."

"If you really want to leave, I say we get security to walk us to our cars."

"Yeah," I agreed. "Let's do that."

Marnie and I made our way to the door, where the two bouncers who'd escorted Peter out of the club now stood. Marnie explained to the men that we needed their help in leaving, just in case Peter was still lurking somewhere, waiting for me to appear.

"No problem."

The taller and bigger of the two bouncers walked with us. "Where'd you park?" Marnie asked.

"At the far end of the lot."

"My car's right here." She pointed. "You can get in my car and I can drive you to yours."

We both surveyed the parking lot. Neither of us saw Peter anywhere, though there were several gold-colored SUVs.

"You two okay now?" the bouncer asked when we stopped at Marnie's Nissan Sentra.

Marnie nodded. "I think so. We should be all right."

The bouncer left. Marnie and I got into her vehicle, and I directed her to where I had parked.

I didn't see an SUV like Peter's near my car, and I was relieved.

I knew he could be anywhere, but I was getting the feeling he had probably left.

Thank God.

"Why don't you get into your car and follow me to my place?" Marnie suggested. "I don't want you going home."

"All right. That's a good idea."

I got out of Marnie's car and started toward mine. But I stopped abruptly when I took a good look at my Honda Civic.

Horror and disbelief washed over me.

"What is it?" Marnie asked, realizing something was wrong.

"My car," I said. Anger brewed inside me as I stared at my vehicle. "Peter slashed my tires."

29

My cell phone wouldn't stop ringing. It rang and rang en route to Marnie's place, and I finally shut it off.

I did, however, check my messages around midnight as I lay on Marnie's sofa. An automated message told me that my voice mail was full, and that I needed to delete any unneeded messages so that I could receive new messages.

I pressed the button to hear my first message.

"Sophie." A long beat. "Sophie, I'm sorry. You haven't been returning my calls, and...I miss you. I need you. Please don't be afraid of me. I'm sorry. I love you. I'm sorry, *bella*."

The next few messages were of the same variety, with Peter apologizing and asking me to call him. But the fifth message changed in tone.

"Sophie, did you ever love me? Or did you lie to me from the beginning? Perhaps you like to suck every guy's cock you meet. You pretend to be virtuous and sweet, but you fuck everyone. You tricked me, Sophie. You made me fall in love with you. I was good to you, but you betrayed me."

Then: "Sophie! Why don't you answer the fucking phone? It's your fault I got angry tonight. I didn't want to grab you, but you've made me crazy with your lies, by stealing my heart when all you really are is a whore. You're not fit to be the mother of my child. Answer the fucking phone!"

The last message terrified me. "I hate you, you lying bitch. You should be dead for what you did to me."

I wanted to erase every message, but I didn't. Something told me to keep some of them. At least the ones where Peter had sounded dangerous, threatening, and downright mentally unstable.

And then it came to me. The way I could be free of him.

The police were looking for the man who had viciously attacked Teddy. If I turned Peter in to the police...

That was exactly what I was going to do.

I closed my eyes, making a mental plan to contact them the very next morning.

The next morning, I arranged for a tow truck to get my car. The tow truck driver picked me up at Marnie's place and took me back to the club, then brought my car to a shop where I could have the tires replaced.

Marnie wanted to go with me, but I told her it wasn't necessary. I promised I'd call when my car had been repaired.

By the time the work was done, I was livid. How dare Peter treat me the way he had? I had done nothing to deserve his wrath.

But it wasn't wrath, was it? It was insanity. And a sane person would never understand what made a crazy person tick.

As I drove to my house, I was determined not to let Peter take anything else from me. Not my security. Not my home.

So the moment I got to my place, I called the Orlando Police

Department and anonymously reported him as the person who'd beaten Teddy. I told them Peter's full name, where he lived, his phone numbers, and when he would be home. I'd blocked my number when I called the tip line, just in case.

And then I prayed that my nightmare would be over. That the police would arrest Peter and that I would finally be free of him.

All that night, I was jittery. Afraid that the cop I'd spoken with was going to trace my number. Afraid that somehow Peter would know I was the one who had called to turn him in.

I was also tempted to drive to a pay phone and call Peter to see if he picked up. If he did, it meant the police had likely written me off as a viable lead. And if he didn't...

I did nothing that night, just curled up on my bed and watched television. My car was parked in the garage, just in case Peter was not in police custody and decided to drive by. After hours passed and Peter didn't call, I became convinced that he *was* in custody—either behind bars or being questioned for hours. Otherwise he would have tried to reach me.

I'd called Marnie earlier to tell her that I had called the cops. At eleven, I phoned her again. "I'm so nervous," I told her. "But Peter hasn't called. That has to be a good sign."

"I hope so. But just in case, you can come back here. In fact, I wish you would."

"No," I said. "I need to be here tonight. Just to really see. To really know. But, your gun is still here," I added, hoping that would put Marnie's mind at ease.

"Keep your night table drawer open for easy access. Just in case."

"I will." I paused. "I hope the cops lock Peter up on the spot, put him away without bail."

"He beat Teddy up pretty bad. It's clear Peter would have killed him if Teddy hadn't been able to fight him off."

"He'll get time for that, won't he?" I asked.

"If he doesn't, then there is something seriously wrong with our justice system. Oh, wait," Marnie suddenly said. "That's my other line."

She clicked over to answer her other line and, within a minute, she was back. "Sweetie, that's Robert."

"Oh, okay. You go talk to him."

"I'll call you back, if you like."

"No, it's okay. I'm gonna try to sleep."

"I'm glad you did what had to be done," Marnie said. "Call me tomorrow, okay? But if you feel threatened for any reason, you call me right away."

"I will," I told her. "But I'm sure I'll be fine. Tell Robert I said hi. And one of these days I'll meet him when my life isn't so messed up."

I lay down after I ended the call, but I was too anxious to sleep. I went to the kitchen and poured myself a glass of wine in almost total darkness, just in case Peter might be lurking outside. Then I remembered I was pregnant and shouldn't drink wine, so I opted for a glass of milk instead. I took it to my bedroom, where I once again curled up on the bed. I began to channel-surf, not finding anything that intrigued me. And when I reached what was clearly a movie, I lowered the remote and began to watch.

Glenn Close came onto the screen, and in an instant, I recognized the movie.

Fatal Attraction.

I actually shivered as I watched a scene where Glenn Close begged Michael Douglas's character not to leave her.

Coincidence, or was the universe sending me a message?

* * *

I got the sense that I was being watched.

My eyes popped open, and when I looked across the room, I was too startled to even scream.

Peter was sitting in the armchair in my bedroom, staring at me.

But how could he be in my bedroom? Confused, I looked around. Yes, this was my bedroom. Daylight streamed in through the cracks in the blinds. I closed my eyes, wondering if I was dreaming. But when I reopened them, Peter was still sitting there.

I didn't understand how. I hadn't given him a key to my house.

"*Bella,*" he said. His gaze didn't waver. I don't think he even blinked. The intensity in his eyes scared the crap out of me.

"P-Peter. H-how did you get in here?"

"Did you report me to the police, *bella?*"

Fear gripped me, making my heart spasm. I knew I had to lie, and yet I couldn't open my mouth to form any words.

Peter rose. Slowly moved toward the bed. "Did you report me to the police, *bella?*"

"N-no," I said, my voice a croak. "What for?"

Peter sat down on the bed next to me. I wanted to run from the room, but I was too afraid of him to do anything but lie there and act like his unexpected presence in my home wasn't creeping the hell out of me.

"Somebody reported me to the police. This person said that I attacked Theodore Granger, the man who was bothering you the night I met you at the club." Peter softly stroked my cheek, but there was nothing kind in his touch. "Was that you?"

"Why would I do that?" I asked, hoping my tone was even.

"Because you are mad at me, perhaps?"

"I—I'm not mad." And I wasn't. I was terrified—and wanted nothing to do with Peter anymore.

Peter slipped his hand beneath the covers and brought it to my crotch. "You're sure?"

He stroked me. Slipped a finger into my pussy as though he were here to seduce me, not possibly strangle me.

"Yes, I'm sure," I told him, hoping I sounded confident.

With the pad of his thumb, Peter stroked my clitoris, and damn it, I knew I was getting wet. I hated my body for betraying me. For getting even slightly aroused when I knew in my heart that Peter was dangerous. But his touch…fuck, his touch always made me weak.

That had always been the problem. I got so lost when he sexually aroused me that I had ignored all the signs that he was a madman.

Peter pushed his finger deep into my vagina, wiggled it around until I moaned despite myself. Then he pulled his finger out of my pussy and put it into his mouth. He sucked on my essence slowly.

I swallowed, conflicted. I was turned-on, yet I didn't want to be. And suddenly I was wondering if I'd made the wrong choice in turning him in. Not the wrong choice about leaving him—I couldn't be with him anymore, I knew that. But God only knows what Teddy would have done to me had Peter not intervened that night.

Peter placed a hand over my breast. Though the touch was casual, it very clearly said he owned me. Owned my pleasure. Something I couldn't deny, not even now.

"Oh, *bella*. You don't know how much I love to touch you. You love it too. I can tell."

I said nothing.

Peter stroked my nipple through my nightie. "I know I have acted badly, but it's just because I love you so much."

I moaned. Yes, the stroking turned me on, but something else in my brain had turned on. An idea.

The idea that in order to be safe, I had to pretend that I did still want Peter. Because if I didn't, there was no telling what he would do.

"You're afraid of what you feel for me," he said as he pushed my nightie up, exposing my breasts. "I know, because it scares me too. That's why you're avoiding me."

"Y-yes," I said.

"Because when you see me, when we're together, our bodies connect in a way that we simply cannot stop."

Peter used both hands to stroke my nipples. He stroked and tweaked until they were hard. He moaned his satisfaction, then began to suck my nipples in turn, arousing me even through my fear.

And proving that what he'd just said was one hundred percent true.

We connected so powerfully sexually that our bodies seemed to have a mind of their own.

When Peter raised his head, he kept his hands on my breasts. "Are you sure you didn't speak to the police?"

Peter had gone from sucking my nipples to asking me about the police. He might enjoy touching and tasting me, but he could just as easily wrap his fingers around my neck again, maybe this time slowly strangle the life out of me if I said what he didn't want to hear.

Goose bumps popped out on my skin.

"Of course I'm sure," I told him.

"If it wasn't you who turned me in, then it was Marnie," Peter announced.

My eyes widened slightly. "You can't assume it was Marnie. Lots of people were outside the club that night. Maybe someone saw us, and they know who you are, reported you to the police."

My explanation sounded pathetic. I only hoped it was enough to appease Peter.

"It was Marnie," he insisted. He abruptly stood. "That's all I wanted to know. That bitch."

What did that mean? Suddenly, I was worried for Marnie's safety. I don't know why, but I got the sense that Peter would hurt her, the same way he had hurt Teddy.

Hurt her for betraying him.

He turned and started for the bedroom door. I threw the covers off and jumped out of bed. "Where are you going?"

"I am leaving, *bella*."

"But—but—what are you going to do?"

His right eyebrow shot up. "You think I am going to do something...perhaps something bad?"

I didn't answer. He'd obviously read my mind.

"Why don't you ask me, *bella?*"

"Ask you what?"

"Ask me if I beat Theodore."

I paused. Then, "Did you hurt him?"

"Yes."

I was so surprised by the answer that I stepped backward.

"I saw him again at that bar. He said something crude about you. So I gave him what he deserved for disrespecting you. For hurting your friend. For wanting to hurt you."

I opened my mouth. But I didn't know what to say, so I stayed quiet.

"What do you think might have happened if I had not come to your aid?" Peter asked. "Do you think he would have hurt you? Perhaps tried to rape you?" Peter gave me a pointed look. "I protected you, *bella*. Protected you so that he would not dare to hurt you in the future. I protected you because I fell in love with you the first night I saw you. How can I not do everything to keep you safe?"

His reasoning made sense, and once again, I was confused. Maybe I *had* overreacted. Maybe I shouldn't have called the police. I *had* been afraid of Teddy. In my gut, I knew he would have gotten violent if Peter hadn't come around. He'd pushed Marnie to the ground, trying to get to me.

And Peter had protected me. Could I really fault him taking care of someone I knew was a problem? Even if Peter and I couldn't be in a relationship, calling the police might have been going too far on my part.

"Did you…did you admit to the police…"

"Of course not. The police held me for hours last night, but I refused to answer any questions without a lawyer. Now they want me to go in to do a police lineup."

"Now?" I asked.

"Soon. Maybe I will be arrested, for doing the honorable thing."

Oh, God. If Peter was picked out of a lineup—and he would be—surely he'd be pissed at Marnie.

I couldn't let her take the fall for the phone call I had made.

"Peter…"

"Yes?"

"I…" *Say it. Deal with the consequences.* "Marnie didn't call the police. I—I did."

I closed my eyes. Feared he'd unleash his rage on me. Instead, I heard him softly *tsk*.

"*Bella*. Why would you want to hurt me?"

"I'm sorry," I said, meeting his gaze. "I shouldn't have. I over-reacted. But…you scared me…." My voice trailed off as I began to softly sob.

Peter wrapped his arms around me. "No. It is my fault. You're right." He pressed a hand to my belly. "You reacted the way a good mother should. I can never fault you for that."

I expected Peter's uncontrollable rage. Not this.

"I'm sorry, *bella*. I hurt you because my feelings for you are so strong."

He said that as though it excused his behavior, but he didn't realize that he was verbalizing the exact reason I couldn't be with him. He was too volatile.

"I will never hurt you again, *bella*." Peter rested his hands at the nape of my neck. Was he going to strangle me? Finally kill me and be done with it? "But I need to know that you love me."

"I…I love you." I felt like I was in a movie, saying words that were scripted for me. I was no longer myself with Peter. Maybe I never had been. I knew I was saying what he wanted to hear, and I didn't want to test what might happen if I didn't say what he expected of me.

He kissed me. A hot, wet kiss. Then he pulled my silk nightgown over my head, exposing my naked body.

He was going to make love to me, right here in my matrimonial bed.

I didn't protest.

Because this was about survival.

30

I totally let go as Peter and I fucked, sharing my body with him the only way I knew how.

Completely. With abandon.

I didn't deny my body any pleasure. Nor did I deny Peter any pleasure. Our bodies took over, taking us to the heights of sexual bliss.

For about ten minutes after a serious fuck-fest, Peter and I lay in each other's arms, our bodies slick, our souls connected the way they always did after we made love. Honestly, I was beginning to scare myself with my wishy-washy feelings. One minute I was sure I didn't want to see Peter again, but the next…hell, the next I craved his loving like a drug addict craves cocaine.

I had let him bed me because my survival instincts said I needed to do whatever was necessary to make him believe I loved him and wanted to be with him. And yet, once he'd started to make love to me, I had quickly fallen under his sexual spell.

And he was no longer angry. Sex had softened him, and in his arms, I no longer felt afraid. When he left, I would do what I had to do in order to cut him out of my life, but for now, I had helped squash his anger, putting me out of harm's way in terms of his unpredictable wrath.

I pressed my lips against Peter's chest and gave his skin a lazy kiss, feeling a modicum of sadness as I did. I had cared for him deeply, shared the most explosive sexual encounters with him. And yet, this was the last time we would be together.

It had to be.

I kissed Peter's chest again, expecting him to stroke my hair, or kiss my forehead. Instead, he was still and quiet. I sensed a change in him even without looking into his eyes.

I did raise my gaze though, saw something dark in Peter's pensive expression.

"Something wrong?" I asked.

"Here's what you're going to do," he began matter-of-factly. "We're going to get dressed, and then we're going to the police station. You will tell them that you were the one who called."

"What?"

"Listen, *bella*," Peter said sternly. "You will tell them that you called to report me, but you will tell them that you are also a witness. You will tell them that you were with me the night I beat Theodore, but that I did so because he had attacked you."

I gaped at Peter. "But if I tell the police that, they're going to wonder why I called to report you in the first place."

"You'll tell them we had a fight."

I didn't say anything. But I was no longer feeling any sense of sadness over the fact that Peter would forever be a part of my past once we got out of bed.

"And *bella?*"

"Yes?" I met Peter's gaze. His eyes were void of anything. Vacant, and frightening.

"You need to be convincing. You caused this problem, and you need to solve it."

There was a distinct threatening undercurrent to Peter's tone. A do-it-or-else quality.

I was once again plunging downward on this emotional roller-coaster ride of a relationship with Peter. He could go from hot to cold, love to hate in seconds flat. How was it that one minute, as we'd been fucking, he had been eating my pussy and sounding so vulnerable as he begged me to come in his mouth, as if his very existence required that for sustenance? Then he was ordering me to the police station with the kind of coldness that let me know I had no choice in the matter?

Peter released me and got off of the bed. He put his clothes on while I watched him, not moving, not speaking.

"Get up, Sophie. We're going now."

I got up.

Did I have a choice?

At the police station, I felt like a complete moron. The kind of person who cried wolf for attention.

"So you're saying," the female cop with a severe haircut said, "that you turned this guy in, but that he actually was acting in self-defense when the assault occurred?"

I gnawed on the inside of my cheek. Shifted from foot to foot. "That guy was trying to get me to go with him. He'd been rough with me. He'd hurt my friend. He was being an asshole. Peter...he came to my aid."

The cop looked skeptical. "Then why would you anonymously turn him in?"

I hesitated. Lord, I wished I were anywhere but here. Nothing I said would make any real sense.

"I was mad at him," I said.

"Pardon me?"

"I was mad at him," I repeated, louder this time. "I shouldn't have made the call, but we had a fight. And, uh, I…"

"You what?" the cop prompted.

"I wasn't thinking. I'm pregnant, and emotional." I sighed. "I know that's not an excuse. I was stupid. I'm sorry."

The cop shrugged. "All right, then," she said doubtfully. "You'll sign a statement to that effect? That your boyfriend was acting in self-defense?"

I looked toward the door. Peter wasn't there. I knew he wouldn't be, because I was having a private meeting with this cop. Perhaps I could confide in this officer whom I was certain didn't believe me. Tell her that I was afraid of Peter, and that was why I was changing my story. Beg her to lock Peter up and throw away the key.

But I wasn't stupid. I understood the way the system worked. If Peter was arrested, he'd get a chance to be bonded out of jail. And if he got bonded out of jail…

He would hurt me. I was sure of it.

No, I couldn't do what I really wanted to. Not without risking my safety.

My life.

My baby's life.

"Yes." I nodded vigorously. "I'll sign a statement to that effect."

The cop handed me a sheet of paper and a pen. "You can write your statement."

I lifted the pen. Placed it on the paper to begin to compose.

"A word of advice. Next time you have a fight with your boyfriend, find another way to lash out at him. If you make a false allegation, you can get into serious trouble."

"It wasn't a false—"

"Not entirely. But you didn't come forward as a witness when you should have."

I got the point and shut up. The police didn't appreciate a person playing games, even if she was pregnant and hormonal.

A short while later, I left the police station with Peter. In the car, he gave me a kiss on the cheek and smiled warmly at me.

I forced a smile, though inside, I was tormented. I had written and signed an almost entirely false statement.

You've changed.

"Peter," I said after we were driving for a while. "I need to see my husband. To end it," I added quickly, when his eyes widened with alarm. "It's time. I need to tell him. Tell him about the baby. About my…my decision."

"Of course." Peter grinned. "I'll go with you."

"No." I linked fingers with Peter and raised his hand to my lips. "I appreciate that you want to be there for me, but I need to do this alone. It's only fair."

"I don't want him to hurt you."

The way you hurt me when you don't get your way? "I'll do it at his workplace, so I'll be fine." I smiled to assure Peter that I was telling the truth. "I'm pregnant with your child. My future is with you. You would never betray me, not the way he did. I know that now." I was pouring on the lies, making it good. I had to convince him. "You have my love, Peter. Forever."

Peter's face filled with warmth as he regarded me. He believed me, thank God.

"Okay," he said. "I suppose it's best you see your husband on your own, because I am once again traveling out of town for work."

"You are?" I tried to sound disappointed.

"Yes. I'm going to Seattle for three days."

Three days! The words were music to my ears.

"It is a good thing this police matter was resolved, or I might not have been able to travel."

Peter gave me a pointed look. I caught his meaning. "Yes," I said. "I'm glad, too." Even more glad because my statement to the police had enabled him to leave town for a three-day business trip. I would have peace for three whole days.

I was so happy, it might as well have been three years.

"All the ugliness is behind us now," I said. "We can move forward. Be a family."

In my driveway, Peter stopped his Navigator and reached for the glove compartment. I sucked in a sharp breath, suddenly worried that he was going to pull out a gun or a knife.

If he did, I was doomed.

But instead, he pulled out a small velvet satchel. He opened the satchel and withdrew a modest diamond solitaire engagement ring.

"This was my mother's," he said sadly. "My father spent every penny he had to buy it for her. I wanted to give this to you at another time, but if you are going to see your husband, I want you to wear it. Wear it so he can see that you have found the man of your dreams."

I swallowed. Peter held the ring out to me, waiting for my permission for him to put it on me.

"Will you marry me, *bella?*"

"Oh, Peter." I gasped as I offered him my hand. I was giving an Academy Award-winning performance. "Yes. Oh, sweetheart— yes."

Peter beamed as he slipped the ring on my wedding finger. It was a bit big, but not so much that it would fall off. "I'll have it resized for you," Peter said.

"Okay. But not yet. I want to wear it—like you said."

My words clearly pleased him. Peter kissed me. I put every ounce of myself into the kiss, because it needed to be convincing.

"I love you, *bella*," he said when we pulled apart. "I'll call you every day I'm gone."

"Oh. Peter." I framed his face. "I love you, too. I'm going to miss you."

"I will miss you, too."

I gave him another kiss, then opened the door to get out of his car. Peter reached for my hand, took it in his. *"Bella?"*

"Yes, sweetheart?"

"Make sure you keep a low profile. I want you safe."

31

Keep a low profile... What an odd thing to say as his parting words.

And they sounded strangely familiar. But why?

I opened my front door, then turned to wave to Peter, who was waiting until I got into my house. He returned my wave and drove off.

I closed and locked the door, then peered through the door's side window to make sure Peter didn't drive back around. I waited twenty minutes, to be sure. I had glimpsed the suitcase on the backseat in his vehicle, so I believed that yes, he was leaving town.

Confident that he was en route to the airport, I went to my bedroom and slumped onto the edge of my bed, the weight of my burden heavy on my shoulders.

I looked down at my hands. Studied the beautiful ring Peter had just given me. I yanked it off of my finger and placed it on my night table.

That's when I noticed a folded slip of paper with my name written in Andrew's handwriting.

I lifted the paper and unfolded it.

I love you now and forever.
Andrew

It was a simple message, but it held meaning for both of us. It was the same message Andrew had put on a bouquet of roses he'd sent me the day he had proposed.

It was the first time in weeks that it hadn't hurt to hear from Andrew. The first time I'd been able to smile.

I couldn't help thinking about him and the life we'd had. What had gone wrong? Or had we simply been too young when we'd gotten together? Maybe the answer wasn't anywhere near as simple as that. I thought we'd both be loyal to each other until death, but he'd been tempted.

I'd been tempted.

Now I knew how easy it was to get caught up in sex with another person. A person you hadn't vowed to love forever.

For the past several weeks I'd tried to push all thoughts of Andrew and our relationship out of my mind. Peter had been a fantastic distraction, but the awful turn of events with him had me realizing that it was time to deal with my life, not run from it.

If Andrew and I were ever going to get our relationship back on course, the time was now.

If he loved me, he would forgive me, right? The way he wanted me to forgive him?

I had to cling to that thought, because I knew now, without doubt, that I wanted Andrew back in my life. Knowing that he hadn't hit on Marnie was a huge relief. I did believe that he still loved me, that he'd made the kind of mistake he wouldn't make again.

I'd made a mistake, too—more than one. I had the child growing in my belly to prove it.

A tear rolled down my cheek. So much had happened in the past month and a half. And maybe there was no going back.

But there was only one way to know. I picked up the phone and punched in the digits to Andrew's work. But something gnawed at my memory, and I pressed the end button to hang up.

Keep a low profile…Marnie had said that to me while we'd been on the phone the night we'd gone to Illusions. The night Peter had shown up, knowing where I'd be.

Knowing, without a doubt, that I was pregnant.

I know you're pregnant, bella. *And I know that* you *know it too.*

Oh, my God. A chill washed over me. Did Peter have some sort of listening device in my house? On my phone line?

I couldn't be sure, but I knew that I couldn't call Andrew from the house phone. I got my cell phone and went to the backyard. I pulled out a seat at our deck table, then made the call.

After a few minutes, he came on the line.

"Andrew Gibson."

"Andrew. Hi."

"Sophie," he said, mildly surprised.

"I got your notes."

"I wasn't sure you've been around. You've been leaving food for Peaches outside."

Peaches. My throat constricted. I would tell Andrew about the cat later.

"I've been around," I said. "Can I see you, Andrew? So we can talk?"

"Of course. When?"

"What about in an hour? I know you're at work but—"

"That's fine. I'll take a break. We can go to the coffee shop across from the hotel."

"Okay. See you then."

Andrew's face lit up when I walked into the coffee shop and saw him, and my heart picked up speed. This was the Andrew I'd fallen in love with. The handsome man with the charming smile, who could, with one look, make me melt.

He stood as I walked toward him and drew me into a hug. "Hello, sweetheart."

It felt good being in his arms after all this time. Like returning home. "Hi, yourself."

He took a step backward and spread my arms wide so he could fully see me. His eyes took me in slowly from head to toe. "You look amazing."

"Thank you."

Now he pulled me close again, as though he couldn't bear to let me go. He nuzzled against my cheek. "I've missed you."

My eyes misted, something I didn't expect. "I've missed you, too."

"It's okay," he said, noticing my tears. "It matters that you and I are here right now. That's what matters, Sophie."

That was easy for him to say. He didn't know that I was pregnant.

"Sit," he said, and gestured to one of the two comfy chairs at the table.

I did, glancing around at the other people nearby. There was no one at the table beside us, and we'd have an adequate amount of privacy.

Still, I kept my voice low as I asked, "Andrew, what happened?"

He looked confused, so I said, "How could you have betrayed me and slept with someone else?"

A beat passed. "I was stupid," Andrew replied. "I've already said that."

"I need more than that, Andrew. Something I can understand. Or are you telling me you were simply tempted, and caved to temptation?"

"Sophie, there's really no excuse for what I did. Nothing I say can excuse it. Nothing will make it right. I can only tell you that it will never happen again. Ever."

"Did you feel we drifted apart?" I asked.

"I guess we both got comfortable," Andrew said. "We loved each other, but we fell into a pattern. The fire burned out. And I..." He sighed. "I've been thinking a lot about this. I think I saw you in a certain way, a certain role," he said, his voice low so no one else could hear. "You didn't really have any sexual experience when we got married, and neither did I, for that matter. And I kind of had this image of what a wife should be. What she should want to do or not do. I guess because of my own mother. In some ways it's complicated, and in other ways it's simple. Do you understand what I'm saying?"

I did. Andrew had to be talking about how he viewed me when it came to sex. I knew he'd been raised in a very conservative home, and that neither he nor his two older sisters had been allowed to date until they went to college.

"And with your rape...I always wanted to be sensitive to you."

"I get that, Andrew. But I'm not a piece of china. I won't break if you don't touch me in a delicate way. I know I've had my issues when it comes to sex, but I always thought we would get through them—together. I didn't expect you to screw someone else."

"Sophie, you're absolutely right. You didn't deserve what I did to you." Andrew's expression grew somber, resigned. "If you want nothing to do with me, I can't blame you."

I sighed softly. "I don't want that, Andrew," I said, speaking a truth I hadn't realized until that exact moment.

"Oh, Sophie." A glint of happiness sparked in Andrew's eyes. "I love you so much."

"If we're ever going to work things out," I began, "we need to take things slowly. Start dating again. Spend time together and re-discover what we had." I paused. "We can figure out if we're really well suited, or if we should go our separate ways."

"That's not what I want," Andrew said without hesitation. "If my life isn't with you—"

"I don't want that, either. But I don't know if love is enough to keep us together."

"Is it over with that guy?"

"Yes," I said. But I thought about the baby. This wasn't the time to tell Andrew about that.

"Good," he said. I was surprised that he didn't have any more questions for me. I'd expected some.

"What are you doing tonight?" he asked.

"Nothing."

"Then why don't we go out? Get dinner. You name the place."

I thought for a bit. Then I said, "Surprise me."

"Surprise you?"

"Uh-huh. I think one of our problems is that we lost the passion in our marriage. We were no longer spontaneous."

"You're right," Andrew agreed. "Okay, I'll surprise you. I can pick you up—"

"No, I'll meet you at the hotel. I want to treat this night like I'm a single woman meeting a guy I like for a date. And I certainly don't want the temptation of our bedroom. We'll get there…I just…I want to take our time."

Sex was important. But sex had also steered us both off course.

Andrew and I needed to reconnect on an emotional level. If we could do that, then everything else would fall into place.

"And so you know," Andrew began, "she's gone, Sophie."

I didn't have to ask who "she" was. I knew. "You fired her?" I asked, surprised.

"No, I didn't fire her. But I arranged for her transfer. To the resort in North Carolina."

I took a moment to digest the news. "And she went quietly?"

"She was given a helluva promotion, but at first, even that wasn't enough. She's getting a cash settlement. It's coming out of the hotel's insurance, for…cases like this. It's been messy, a headache, and I can't quite hold my head high at work anymore. But Isabel is gone. I hope she won't be a problem anymore."

"So she gets a promotion." I snorted. "Nice to be rewarded for being such a bitch."

"It was the only way we could get her to drop the threat of a sexual harassment suit."

"After she was the one to seduce you!" I gritted my teeth. "Although, if you had just said no…" I stopped myself because I didn't want the anger to surface again. Even though I wanted to move on, I was pissed at the situation, and still a bit pissed that Andrew had jeopardized much more than our relationship when he'd made the decision to cheat.

"I know that," Andrew said. "I learned the lesson the hardest way possible. And not because of the humiliation at work, but because I almost lost you."

"It certainly wasn't worth it, was it?" I asked, giving him a pointed look. My chest hurt from trying to keep my anger at bay.

"No." Andrew was quiet for a moment. "Sophie, do you forgive me? I know it's a lot to ask, but without forgiveness..."

One thing was certain—I had to let go of the anger if we were ever going to move forward. And there was only one way to do that. "Yes, Andrew. I forgive you."

"Then we have a chance."

32

The decision to forgive Andrew had lifted the burden in my heart. I knew that things had irrevocably changed between us, but offering my forgiveness gave me a renewed sense of hope. So much so that when I pulled into the hotel parking lot at five-thirty, I was excited. Andrew had called at three to say he was thinking about me, and I'd been grinning like a fool ever since. I hadn't answered when he'd called the house phone in case Peter had a way of listening to my conversations, but Andrew had then called my cell, which I had picked up.

I'd asked Andrew for a hint as to where we were going, and all he told me was that I should wear my sandals.

I have to admit, I was anxious—in a good way. This was exactly what we needed. Time to hang out like a young couple in love, instead of a married couple trying to get past problems.

And the fact that we could do that with Peter on the other side of the country…I felt like I'd won the lottery.

I was wearing gold sandals and a pink cotton dress with a wide skirt. It was cool and breezy—and would provide easy access if our necking evolved into petting.

But I was determined to make sure we didn't end up in bed. Sex was easy—and it wouldn't solve our problems. Besides, I wanted him lusting after me, and me lusting after him.

Andrew was waiting in the lobby when I entered the hotel, and he walked right up to me, took me in his arms and kissed me unabashedly. He wasn't concerned about the guests in the lobby or his staff witnessing his affection for me.

I liked that. A lot.

Before we were tempted to forgo the date and ended up heading to one of the hotel rooms, I now took a step backward and secured my clutch under my arm. "Where are we going?"

"You'll see."

"No hints?"

"No hints."

"Are we taking separate vehicles?" I asked.

"Only if you want that."

I shook my head. "I don't. I'm more than happy to ride with you. I trust you," I added with a smile.

Andrew took my hand, and together we headed out to his Cadillac Escalade. We separated only to get into the vehicle and, once there, resumed holding hands. Then Andrew leaned in close and kissed me. A deep, meaningful kiss that had my heart filling with warmth.

"Hold it there, cowboy," I said, but my voice sounded shaky. Despite what I'd told him about not having sex tonight, I suddenly wanted to drive to our place and do just that. Reconnect on a physical level.

But I didn't suggest that, because having a special date where we could talk, hold hands and reconnect emotionally was far more important after what we'd been through. And if we were both left a little sexually frustrated at the end of the date, then that would only give us something to look forward to the next time we went out.

Besides, I knew that jumping into bed with Andrew would be in part a way to try to push Peter out of my mind.

Sex, when we got to that, would be when we were both ready to take that important emotional step.

Once he drove out of the hotel parking onto International Drive, I asked, "Now will you tell me where we're going?"

"You're the one who wanted me to surprise you."

I faked a pout. "I didn't know you'd take me so seriously."

Andrew reached for my hand and drew it onto his lap. "Don't worry. You'll be impressed."

I got a hint as to where Andrew was going when he merged onto I-4 heading west. West was Tampa, and the beach. And Sarasota, a place we used to go on weekends early on in our marriage.

We listened to the soft jazz playing on the car's stereo, content with each other's company. We'd argued bitterly over the past weeks about what had happened, and I didn't want to talk about any of that anymore. Isabel was out of Andrew's life, and I was working on getting Peter out of mine.

From here on in, we would concentrate on each other.

About an hour later, Andrew pulled up to a parking meter along a beautiful stretch of beach in the Tampa area. He parked the Escalade, and we both got out. Then he went to the back and pulled out a large wooden picnic basket and blanket.

"A picnic on the beach," I said, grinning.

"When was the last time we did this?" he asked. "Maybe seven years ago?"

"About that."

We walked together to a portion of beach that was free. I helped Andrew spread the blanket on the sand.

"Sit," Andrew told me. "Then close your eyes."

"Okay."

I lowered myself onto the blanket and then shut my eyes.

"No peeking," Andrew said.

"I'm not. But don't keep me in suspense forever."

I could sense him going down beside me, hear him opening the picnic basket. Then I flinched slightly when I felt something cool on my lip.

"Open your mouth," Andrew told me.

I did. Something brushed against my tongue. It took me only a moment to figure out the slightly rough texture belonged to a strawberry.

"Take a bite," Andrew told me.

I did. The sweet flavor of the fruit filled my mouth. "Mmm."

"Keep your eyes closed."

"Okay, okay," I mock-protested.

A moment later, I felt something else brush against my lips. It was wet and cold.

An ice cube?

No. I smelled the citrusy scent of pineapple. I took a bite and moaned my approval. The pineapple was the right mix of tangy and sweet.

I chewed, swallowed, then spoke. "Strawberry and pineapple, my two favorite fruits. What's next?"

"The best surprise of all. At least I hope."

I couldn't help it, my eyes popped open.

"Hey," Andrew protested.

"Sorry," I said, and this time put my hands over my eyes.

The next several moments passed in silence, though I could hear Andrew's hands rustling around in the basket. I could also hear the sound of the waves crashing to the shore, and the cry of seagulls in the air.

"My hands are getting tired here," I said.

"It'll be worth it," Andrew assured me.

About a minute passed, but it seemed like hours as I anxiously waited. Suddenly, I felt something go around my wrist.

Was that—

Yes, it was. Andrew was undoubtedly fastening the clasp on a piece of jewelry he had just put on my wrist.

"Go ahead and—"

"Can I open my eyes now?"

We spoke at the same time.

"Yes," Andrew said. "Open your eyes."

Lowering my hands, I popped my eyes open. My focus went immediately to my wrist. And then I gasped.

"Do you like it?"

"Like it? Oh, my God, it's *beautiful*."

Beautiful was an understatement. The tennis bracelet was set in platinum, dazzling with rubies and diamonds.

I knew, because I'd seen it before.

"You wanted that for our anniversary," Andrew said, "and at the time…" His voice trailed off, leaving his statement incomplete. "I realize now that price doesn't matter, not compared with your happiness. When you're happy, I'm happy."

"Oh, sweetheart." I kissed him, hoping to convey not only my appreciation, but my love.

He poured champagne for both of us, and I almost didn't accept the glass. But now wasn't the time to tell Andrew about my being pregnant. I would have to, but not now when everything was going so well.

One glass of champagne won't hurt me, I reasoned.

"To a new start," Andrew said, and raised his glass in a toast. I clinked my glass against his. "To a new start."

I was feeling good about taking the step to save my marriage.

I knew it was time.

I was on a high that night when Andrew and I returned to the hotel parking lot. On a high when he gave me a kiss good night. I'd turned off my cell when I'd been with him, not wanting to take the chance that Peter would call, but once I was back in my car, I turned it on.

It rang immediately.

I glanced at the caller ID. Andrew's number.

I quickly opened the phone and put it to my ear. "Hey."

"Now and forever, Sophie," Andrew said. "I love you."

"I love you, too."

"Good night."

"Good night, Andrew."

Peter called about an hour later. I acted happy to hear from him, but also put on a weak voice, telling him I was sick.

"Is it the baby?" he asked.

"No," I said through a feigned-hoarse voice. "I think I'm coming down with a cold. I had some lemon tea with honey, and I'm going to bed. I'll be fine."

"I hate to say this, but there was a problem with the shoot today. I'll be delayed another day."

"Oh no."

"I wish I could get back to you."

"We'll be together soon," I told him.

"Did you speak with your husband?"

I paused. "Yes. I told him, Peter. He knows it's over."

"*Bella,* I am so happy. I wish I could be there with you to celebrate."

"We still have to deal with getting the divorce, and that's going to take some time. Maybe it will be messy."

"We'll get through it. And then we'll get married."

"Yes, sweetheart. But can we talk tomorrow? I'm very—"

"Of course. Get some rest."

I was relieved when he was finally off of my line.

33

The next day I felt even better, knowing that Peter would be out of town an extra day. I debated going back to the police station to tell the cop I'd spoken with that Peter was really dangerous and I was afraid of him. Not only did I debate it, I got in my car and drove to the police station. But when I got there I kept driving, then doubled back and returned home.

I didn't want the cops getting angry with me and deciding to charge me for obstruction.

Once home, I called Marnie from my cell and told her about my evening with Andrew.

"Oh, sweetie. That's wonderful."

"I think we're going to work things out," I said. "We'll put all the crap behind us."

"Did you say anything to Andrew about…about the baby?"

I sighed softly. "I couldn't, Marnie. Not…yet. Not when we're trying to get back on track. I know I should, but…"

"I've been thinking about your pregnancy. At least everything I've ever heard about pregnancy."

"What do you mean?"

"How do you know the baby's not Andrew's? You know you're pregnant, yes. But what if you got pregnant before we went to the Bahamas?"

"I had my period shortly before we went away," I said. "Though it was really light. I remember that. Once I got back, Andrew dropped his bombshell, and we definitely didn't have sex after that."

"I've heard stories about people having periods right until the time they give birth. You never know. What you do know is when you met Peter. You need to go to the doctor and arrange an ultrasound, see how far along you really are."

I wanted to cling to the hope that I might be carrying Andrew's baby, but it seemed far-fetched.

"One way or another, you need to know," Marnie said.

"I'll call my doctor now."

My house line rang before I had a chance to call the doctor. The caller ID told me it was Andrew calling from the hotel, so I picked up the receiver.

"Morning, Andrew."

"Morning, sweetheart. I have to tell you, I thought about you all night long. I hardly got any sleep."

"Is that right?"

"Uh-huh. And I can't wait to see you again."

My heart fluttered, and I smiled. "Me, too."

"How about tonight? I'm off tomorrow morning…"

"Are you now?" I asked, getting the hint.

"You know I'm off every Friday."

"Oh, that's right," I said, pretending I'd forgotten.

"So we can make use of tonight…if you want."

"Sounds intriguing," I said, and giggled. "Shall I buy some board games?"

"If you want...though we might end up playing another game."

I giggled again, enjoying this fun banter.

"Sweetie, I've got to run," he said suddenly. "But I'll call you later, okay?"

"Okay."

I hung up the phone knowing that I had to make an appointment with the doctor. First, I needed a professional pregnancy test. Then, like Marnie had said, I needed an ultrasound.

Something suddenly struck me. I wanted this baby. Even though it might be Peter's and that fact might be the end of my marriage, I wasn't even considering the other option available to me.

Abortion.

I was a grown woman, old enough to act responsibly. If I'd conceived a child with Peter, it had been conceived in passion and maybe something more. I wouldn't terminate the pregnancy simply because that might make things a bit easier for me.

I'd never be able to live with myself.

If Andrew chose not to forgive me for getting pregnant by my lover, so be it.

But the first thing I needed to do was figure out exactly when I'd gotten pregnant. Then I would go from there.

I was able to get an appointment with my doctor late that afternoon, and she confirmed what I already knew. Yes, I was pregnant. An ultrasound couldn't be booked until late the next week, however, which was disappointing, but there was nothing I could do about that. I resigned myself to the fact that I would have to wait to learn the exact time of conception.

What I debated, as I drove home, was exactly when to tell Andrew about the fact that I was pregnant.

I didn't want to lie to him, but I also didn't want to give him the news about the baby until I knew for sure who had fathered my child. If it was Andrew, then he didn't need to know I'd ever wondered if Peter could be the father. But if it was Peter…

"Cross that bridge when you get to it," I told myself as I turned onto my street. Realistically, in the scheme of things, one week wasn't too long to wait. But a week of Andrew wondering whose baby I was carrying…that could be too much for him, and too much for our relationship.

I spotted Andrew's SUV parked in the driveway. It was only after four, so he must have left work early to come home and surprise me. I found myself smiling. A bittersweet smile, given the secret I would have to keep for a week, and not knowing what the outcome would be. What I did know was that I was ready to see Andrew again, ready to repair our relationship. It would require work, perhaps lots of it, and I would do what it took to save my marriage. It wouldn't be easy, and there might be times when I wanted to walk away when the memory of his betrayal got to be too much. If the baby wasn't Andrew's he might not be able to get past that. But I hoped that we could overcome all of our obstacles.

Please, God—let me be carrying Andrew's baby.

I pulled into the driveway and parked beside Andrew's Escalade. My heart was racing as I got out of the car and hurried to my front door. It was nice to be excited about seeing my husband again.

As fast as I could, I tried the knob, found the door unlocked and threw it open. A little too harshly, because it hit the doorstop and bounced back toward me.

"Andrew," I called. "Sweetheart, I'm home."

Three simple words, words I'd used often over the years, but they meant so much more to me now.

Today, they meant a new beginning.

Andrew didn't reply, and as I stepped farther into the house, I saw that he was sitting on the sofa in the living room.

"Baby—" I stopped short when he turned toward me. The expression on his face...

He looked like someone had died.

I rushed toward him. "Andrew." I dropped myself onto the sofa beside him and drew his face into my hands. I'd never seen him looking so grim, so lost. "Baby, what is it?"

He turned away from me, leaving me facing his back.

Tentatively, I reached for him. Placed a gentle hand on his shoulder. "Andrew..."

"I thought you wanted me back. I thought..."

"I do. Of course I do. We talked about this last night."

There was a pause. "I know I messed up. More than messed up. But I hoped...maybe I was stupid."

"What are you talking about? Last night we had a great conversation. What's changed between then and now?"

Andrew turned to face me, his eyes misting with tears. "Are you in love with this guy you had the affair with?"

Where was this coming from? "No."

"You sure about that?"

Andrew's questions were reminding me of Peter's insane accusations. I couldn't deal with his doubt. Not now, after what he'd done and the fact that we'd gotten to this point where we'd vowed to start over.

"What's the problem?" I asked, anger rising inside me. "You can't deal with the fact that I slept with someone else? That was your idea, remember? You wanted me to 'even the score' so we could go on with nothing to hold over each other's head."

"You want me back, or are you just interested in the money I got from my father's will? Because if that's what you're doing——"

I slapped him. I couldn't believe the words coming out of Andrew's mouth. Never once had I been into him for money, and he knew that. He'd never known me to be materialistic in any way.

"How dare you?"

He picked up the remote from beside him on the sofa and switched on the television.

"What are you going to do? Shut me out? Turn on a friggin' football game?"

Andrew didn't answer. Instead, he also started the DVD player.

I got to my feet. "Fine. You want us to be over——"

"Sit."

Something in Andrew's voice made me do just that. "Andrew, I don't understand."

The words were barely out of my mouth before I heard the moaning. Moaning I recognized as my own.

Oh, my God.

34

Fear spread down my back and arms like liquid ice. Gripped my gut and squeezed.

Slowly, I turned toward the television. Even though I knew what I'd see, I still gasped at the sight. I was on my back on Peter's bed, my wrists tied to the headrest, my legs spread and Peter's face buried in my pussy. My back was arched well off the bed, my breasts bouncing around as I writhed in ecstasy.

I jumped up from the sofa and in front of the television, blocking the screen from Andrew's view.

"I've already seen it," Andrew told me. "Every last minute."

"H-how—"

"How did I get it? Your boyfriend brought it to me at the hotel today."

"What?" Peter was home? He knew where Andrew worked?

"I especially love this next part."

"Listen to me, Andrew. Peter—he's insane. I thought he was out of town right now, but if he's not, we shouldn't stay here. It might not be safe."

"Move out of the way," Andrew said, not in the least interested in what I was saying.

"Please don't watch this, Andrew," I begged. "I don't know what Peter was thinking. I didn't even know he'd taped this. But——" My loud moaning was suddenly too much for me to bear. "Turn it off. Turn it——" I quickly whirled around to shut the television off.

Immediately, Andrew turned it back on with the remote control.

"Don't do this, Andrew. For God's sake."

"Do you love me?" That was Peter's voice. Then more of my moaning.

Unable to stand another moment of this, I pressed the button to open the DVD player. The disc appeared, and I snatched it up.

"You told him you loved him," Andrew said.

I shook my head. It was all I could do.

"I heard you. And more importantly, I saw you."

"It was sex talk. It didn't mean anything."

"No? Then how does he know my father died and left me some money?"

So that's why Andrew made the comment about me staying with him because of the money his father had left him. "We were just talking," I explained. "About parents, and death. There was nothing sinister about it."

"You've never…" Andrew swallowed, as though he had to compose himself. "You've never been like that with me. The way you were moaning and moving around, the way you were trembling with pure ecstasy. I don't think we've ever… It's never been like that with us."

Though I wanted to, I couldn't argue Andrew's point. Sex with Peter had been one hundred percent uninhibited, partly because it had been taboo. Partly because he'd opened me up to a whole new world of sensation that I'd been afraid to explore earlier.

"And when you were with your slut, it wasn't enjoyable? You

told me you ate her pussy. I'll bet you loved that. You probably came in her mouth, or all over her face. Maybe both. I never wanted you to see me with Peter, but at least you know. I'll always have to imagine what you did with your lover, and I can guarantee you, my imagination is much, much worse."

"He told me you're staying with me until you get part of my father's estate."

I flew toward Andrew and dropped myself onto the floor in front of him. "Do you believe that? Because if you do, then maybe you never knew me at all."

Andrew didn't answer, but I could tell by the way his eyes lit up that he didn't believe what Peter had said.

"Peter— Well, he's a little off-kilter," I told Andrew. "I think he fell hard for me, which I didn't expect, because it was just an affair. But he wasn't happy when I told him it was over."

"Did he know that? That it was 'just an affair'?"

I opened my mouth, but I didn't say a word. It was a valid question. And for the first time I realized that I *hadn't* approached my affair with Peter as *just* an affair. At least, those weren't the ground rules that had been laid out at the beginning. I knew Peter was falling for me, and a part of me had been falling for him.

"Did he?" Andrew asked again.

"Did Isabel think you were only fucking her?" I shot back. "Both of us did things we shouldn't have," I went on. "Should I have handled Peter differently? Yes, I know that now. But it's over." Tentatively, I reached for Andrew's face. Caressed it. "You're the only man I love. Despite everything, I still love you."

"Then why did you tell him you love him?"

"Because—" Because he was playing with my pussy, holding my sexual release hostage until I told him what he wanted to hear. No, I couldn't tell Andrew that.

"It was sex talk," I said. "Please, baby. I don't want to talk about Peter anymore. Nothing good will come of it." I placed my hands on my husband's legs, ran them up and down slowly. Seductively. Maybe I needed to show him how much I still wanted him, our marriage.

We would make love, right here, right now. If Peter was lurking outside, surely he would have been pounding on the door by now.

No, he wasn't eavesdropping. He'd made sure to give Andrew a copy of the DVD, hoping that would be the last nail in the coffin on our relationship. And with Andrew out of my life, I would have no choice but to be with him.

But that wasn't going to happen.

"I want to talk about us," I said. I moved one hand to Andrew's groin and stroked his penis. "Or maybe we don't have to talk at all."

Andrew placed his hands on mine, stopping them. "You're not serious."

"Why shouldn't I be? I want to fuck you, Andrew."

"Sophie…"

"What? You don't like to hear me swear? Because it's dirty? Just like enjoying oral sex is dirty? I'm your wife, Andrew. We should be doing everything together. Oral sex, anal sex—whatever we want to do is not dirty."

Andrew jerked backward. "Did he fuck you up the ass?"

"No. No! All I'm trying to say is that whatever we want to explore is okay. That's what married people do."

"I need some time…"

"I need you to touch me." I took Andrew's hand and placed it on my breast. "I need you to taste me." Once again, I stroked him, stroked him until he grew hard. "I like that, Andrew. I like it a lot."

Andrew closed his eyes. "I keep seeing him doing that to you."

I pulled my blouse over my head, then unsnapped my bra. My breasts came free. "Touch me. Please."

Andrew opened his eyes. Opened his eyes but didn't really see me. He kept his attention on my face, never lowering it to my naked breasts.

"Pl—"

Suddenly, he covered a breast with his hand. "Yes," I purred. "Touch me, Andrew."

His hand moved over my breast. Slowly, like he was getting reacquainted with it.

"Play with my nipple." I played with my other nipple until it grew hard, something I hadn't done in front of Andrew before because I knew he would have seen that as too brazen. He definitely enjoyed my breasts, but he'd always taken the lead when it came to sex and I'd let him.

But now, he wasn't reacting with disapproval at me touching my own body. Instead, he looked from one breast to the other, his groans growing deeper.

"Oh, yes. Just like that, baby."

Andrew's breathing was heavier now. My panties were getting wet. Rising, I straddled him on the sofa. "Take my nipple in your mouth. Both, if you can. Lick them. Suck them."

Andrew gently kneaded my left breast before edging his head toward my nipple. I watched as his mouth got nearer. Then, as his lips slowly parted, a jolt of delicious heat shot through my pussy even before his tongue made contact with my skin.

"Baby…mmm." I closed my eyes and savored the pleasure of my husband's tongue on me. He moved slowly at first, gently flicking his tongue over my nipple. Around the areola. A little nip, a brief suck.

I purred. "Do you have any idea how good this feels?"

Andrew groaned, the sound ripe with his pleasure. Then he drew my nipple completely into his mouth and suckled me hard. Suckled me as though he hoped to swallow my nipple. Beneath my vagina, his cock grew into a hard, throbbing weapon. One I needed to conquer me.

He grabbed my other breast, none too gently, and pushed it toward his mouth. Then his tongue moved from one nipple to sample the other. He sank his teeth into my nipple. Not enough to hurt, but enough to give a small dose of pain with the pleasure. Then he went back to the other nipple and did the same thing.

"Yes, baby," I moaned. I wanted the same kind of wild, uninhibited sex with Andrew that I'd experienced with Peter. "Oh, God."

Rocking his cock against my pussy, he squeezed my breasts together and took both my nipples into his mouth at one time. As his tongue worked over my nipples in a frenzy, I lolled my head backward and moaned in ecstasy. I picked up the pace of our hip movements, the friction on my clit heating my entire body.

All of a sudden, Andrew whipped our bodies around so that I was on my back and he was between my legs. Moving his mouth from my breasts, he trailed his tongue down the center of my ribs. As he did, he undid my jeans and wrestled them down my hips.

"Yes, baby," I urged. I raised my hips so he could more easily move my jeans out of the way. He pressed his lips to the top of my pubic area. "Touch me... See how wet I am. How much I want you."

Andrew ran his thumb over me through my panties. "Damn, you really are wet."

"Take me in your mouth. Eat me until I'm screaming your name."

Andrew pushed my panties out of the way. I thought he was going to touch me, or lick me, but instead he just stared. I watched him as his eyes drank in the sight of my pussy up close and personal. He'd never really done that before. His mouth was so close to me, his warm breath tickled my clit.

Finally, he stroked me again. I shuddered.

"Play with me, baby. Touch me. Taste me."

He dipped a finger between my folds. "Like this."

I lifted my hips in response. "Yes. Now put your fingers inside me. All of them if you can."

Andrew slipped his middle finger inside me, a groan rumbling in his chest as he did. "You're so beautiful, Sophie."

He inserted another finger, and I gripped the sofa as waves of pleasure ripped through me. This pleasure was different than what I'd experienced with Peter, because it was ripe with love.

"So damn beautiful," he rasped.

"Finger-fuck me. Yes, just like that!" Andrew pumped his fingers deep inside me, wiggled them around, then pumped even harder. Soon, I was panting, my enjoyment so intense I could hardly catch my breath.

I gripped my nipples and thrust my hips upward, hoping he'd understand what I wanted most. Andrew's fingers felt wonderful, but I wanted his tongue. "Please taste me, sweetheart. I need to feel your tongue on me."

Andrew turned his face into my thigh and nibbled there. It wasn't what I wanted. "One touch, baby. One touch and I could come." I wiggled my hips, desperate now for his touch.

He moved his lips closer to my center, and just as I braced for the sensation of his tongue on me, he pulled his head back.

I moaned in protest. "No..."

"I can't." Andrew backed away from me.

The words crushed me, as surely as if I were a bug being squashed by the heel of someone's shoe. "Andrew, please."

"I can't. Not after seeing how you were with him."

"Don't do this," I said, softly sobbing. I got onto my knees and reached for him. "I want *you,* Andrew. Only you."

He got off the sofa and started from the living room. "I have to go."

"No!"

Andrew didn't listen. He sped out of the living room while I struggled to pull up my jeans. Once I finished, I ran through the living room to the front door. It was open, and I raced onto the porch.

Andrew was standing on the driveway beside his vehicle, as though he'd had a change of heart about leaving after all.

"Andrew," I said.

He turned to face me, his eyes growing wide with horror. As his gaze lowered to my breasts, I realized that I didn't have my top on. I glanced across the street, saw Mr. Warner looking my way with interest.

"Get back inside," Andrew said.

I quickly stepped backward, moving out of sight of nosy eyes. I was too defeated to be humiliated. "Please come back in," I said. "We need to talk about this."

"I'm coming," Andrew replied, his voice sounding strained.

The seconds ticked by. I would have moved back in front of the open door to see where he was, if not for Mr. Warner across the street.

Finally, Andrew crossed the threshold, and my shoulders sagged with relief.

But then I saw another shadow filling the doorway. I guess I sensed who it was before I saw. And fear trickled down my spine.

Peter stepped fully into the foyer, his gaze immediately falling on me.

As he looked my way and smiled, I saw the glint of a blade in his hand. He closed the door and turned the lock.

35

"Hello, *bella,*" Peter said. His smile appeared genuine, which, under the circumstance, only made it creepier.

I raised my hand to cover my breasts. I looked from Peter to Andrew, and then back to Peter. Rather, I looked at the knife in his hand.

"So here we all are," Peter said. "Maybe this is the way it needs to be."

"Let my wife put her blouse on," Andrew said.

"There is no need," Peter said. "I have already seen every inch of her body. Which you know, if you watched the video."

Andrew said nothing. Neither did I.

"Ah, Sophie," Peter said sadly.

"Wh-what are you doing here?"

"You mean, why am I not in Seattle?"

I think I nodded.

"I needed to know, Sophie. To know if you were telling the truth about us. And now I do."

My chest constricted, and I could hardly breathe. This had been a test. An elaborate trap. And I'd fallen right into it.

"Why don't we all go to the living room," Peter suggested. "Where we will be more comfortable."

I didn't budge. Neither did Andrew. But I saw Andrew's eyes moving around frantically, and I could tell that he was trying to figure out how to handle the situation.

Peter was wearing a long-sleeved shirt, and he had the knife mostly hidden beneath it. But now, he pulled it out, revealing a blade that had to be at least ten inches long.

"If you don't move," he began calmly, "I can assure you that this knife will go easily into your back. And once you're on your knees, I will slit your throat."

I gasped. If I'd had any doubts as to whether or not Peter *could* be a killer, those doubts quickly fled my mind.

"Go, Andrew," I said. Peter had murdered our cat, I knew he wasn't bluffing.

"You too," Peter told me.

Andrew began to move, heading toward the kitchen. I walked slowly behind him, my heart pounding frenetically.

"And if you even think about grabbing a knife, remember that I am just behind your wife. If you do anything stupid, I will slice her from ear to ear."

This wasn't an idle threat. I didn't want to believe Peter would hurt me, but I did.

"I won't do anything stupid," Andrew promised. He held up his hands as he continued to walk. "Look, you can see my hands. I'm not going to grab anything."

"Good," Peter said. "I would hate for this to turn ugly. All I want to do is talk."

In the living room, Andrew and I stood in front of the sofa. I reached for my discarded blouse and slipped it on.

When I was done, Peter said, "Sit. Both of you."

I lowered myself onto the sofa, never taking my eyes off Peter. Andrew sank onto the sofa beside me.

Peter positioned himself in front of the coffee table, then started to speak. "I wish we could be meeting under better circumstances, but love isn't always easy. Andrew, by now you have seen the video?"

Andrew hesitated, then nodded. "Yes."

"So you know exactly the depth of your wife's feelings for me. And mine for her. I'm here to ask that you let her go quietly."

I had no doubt that Peter had been spying on me while he was supposedly in Seattle. Watching to see if I met Andrew. Maybe listening in on my phone calls.

And even though he clearly knew that I *had* met with my husband during his supposed absence, Peter still held out hope that we would be together. In his mind, all he had to do was get Andrew out of the picture, and I would be his.

"Sophie," Peter said. "This will be easy. You will gather your belongings, all your clothes, your makeup. Whatever you need. You'll pack your things in suitcases and put them in my car."

I looked at Andrew. Swallowed.

"If you let her leave quietly, Andrew, then you will live. It's as simple as that. If you fight me, you will die."

This couldn't happen. I wouldn't let it. "And what if I don't want to leave with you? Will you kill me too?"

Peter's expression was almost that of a parent looking at a misbehaving child. A kind of loving disapproval. "I know you don't want to hurt your husband. You're a good woman. You feel guilty for leaving him. But it's the right thing to do, Sophie."

"Is that what you want?" Andrew asked me.

"No," I answered right away, and placed a reassuring hand on his knee. I didn't plan on it, but I couldn't help myself.

Which was why I knew I couldn't leave with Peter. I couldn't pretend anymore that I wanted to be with him. I was too emotionally spent to pull off such a ruse. Besides, I didn't want to. Not anymore.

Which meant Peter might kill me.

I faced him, debating what I would say to him. I decided that all I could do was plead. Hope that the love he'd felt for me would allow him to do the right thing.

"Peter," I began softly. "Don't do this."

"Did you tell him?" Peter asked, and the way he looked at me made dread fill my stomach like a lead weight. I started to shake my head, my eyes imploring him not to ask the question, but Peter continued. "Did you tell him that you're carrying my child?"

I buried my face in my hands. *Oh, God, no...*

"What!" Andrew exclaimed.

I couldn't look at Andrew as he tugged on my wrists, forcing my hands from my face. "Is that true, Sophie?"

Andrew sounded downright terrified. Tears filled my eyes.

"Tell him, *bella*." Peter wore a smug smile.

"Are you pregnant with his baby?"

I began to softly sob.

"My God," Andrew said, and he slowly got to his feet. "You *are*."

"I don't know that it's his," I quickly said. "The baby...it might be yours."

Andrew began to pace. "Jesus Christ."

I glared at Peter. "How could you?" I asked. "How could you do this?"

"Your husband needs to know. He needs to know that we conceived a child in love. Do you think he will be with you now? He won't, Sophie. Because he can't forgive you." Peter took a step toward me. "But I forgive you, Sophie."

Through my tears I stared at him in confusion.

"I know what you were trying to do before I got here. It's why you were topless and your jeans are still unbuttoned." He kept moving, getting ever closer. "But I forgive you. Because I love you. Without you—without our child—my life is nothing."

I threw a glance at Andrew, imploring him to look at me, imploring him to understand that it didn't matter who the biological father of my child was. As far as I was concerned, Andrew was the father. I didn't care what the tests might say.

"Your husband saw the video of us together," Peter went on. "Do you think he can accept that you were with another man? No. And why not? Because he feels he owns you. Look at him. He's like a caged animal, ready to strike out. Maybe he would hit you if I weren't here."

I stared at Andrew, who stopped pacing and looked from me to Peter. His nostrils flared as he breathed heavily. He was glaring. Though I didn't want them to, Peter's words got to me.

Was any man, pushed beyond an emotional limit, capable of violence?

No, I couldn't believe it. Andrew was angry, yes, but never had he raised a hand to strike me.

"If he loved you," Peter said, "he would forgive you and welcome you back with open arms."

I tried to swallow but found it difficult around the lump that had lodged in my throat. I met Andrew's gaze. Held it. Then he looked away.

Was Peter right? Was Andrew unable to move past my affair? Even though he'd been the one to push me into the arms of another man, would he never be able to forgive me?

I turned away, unable to look at Andrew, knowing that it was truly over.

"I do forgive you."

Andrew's voice. Spinning around, I faced him, my heart filling with hope.

"I forgive you," Andrew said. "None of this would have happened if it weren't for my mistake. And if you're pregnant, I'll raise the baby as mine."

"Oh, Andrew." I began to cry harder, knowing without doubt now, that he *was* the love of my life.

"I meant what I said, Sophie," Andrew went on. "Now and forever."

I started toward Andrew, but then Peter was there, stepping between us. His eyes flashed fire as he stared at me. "That is the wrong decision, Sophie."

Very calmly, Peter turned—and slashed Andrew across the chest.

"No!" I screamed, and leaped for Peter's arm. Easily, he threw me off him then turned the knife on me.

"I'll give you one more chance to change your mind," Peter said. "Next time, I'll slit his throat."

Shakily, I nodded. "Okay. Okay."

Peter offered me his hand, and slowly I gave him mine. He pulled me to my feet.

My eyes quickly went to Andrew. He was on the sofa now, clutching his chest. Blood stained his white dress shirt.

"I'm okay," he said. "The wound isn't deep."

"Let's stop wasting time," Peter said, stepping backward. "Get your things. Now."

I was shaking, terrified. But something suddenly clicked.

The gun Marnie had given me was in the bedroom.

If I went there to pack my things, as Peter wanted me to do, I could get the gun.

"I will," I said to Peter. Then I turned to Andrew. "He's right. I fell in love with him. I didn't want to hurt you, but…I don't want to be with you anymore."

Something flashed in Andrew's eyes. Hurt? Did he believe my words?

"I'm going to leave with Peter," I went on. "But Peter, you have to promise not to hurt him. There's no need. The police will be involved, then we can't be together." I forced a smile.

"I've already thought about this, and I know where I can put the body," Peter assured me. "It's where I would have put Theodore's, had I been able to kill that filthy pig when I tried."

So Peter wasn't planning to let Andrew live, despite what he'd said. Surprise must have registered on my face, even though I didn't want to show any sort of alarm. If Peter sensed I doubted him, he would kill Andrew—and me—before I had a chance to get the gun.

"Yes, *bella*. I was going to kill that awful man for you, the way your husband should have killed your rapist. But your husband wasn't man enough. He's not strong enough to protect you. I will always protect you and our child."

What had happened to Peter to turn him into such a monster? The brutal sting of rejection? Or was violence a part of his nature, the way others were kindhearted, or mean-spirited?

Ultimately, it didn't matter. I needed to get to the gun.

"I know you'll always protect me," I said to Peter. And for good measure, I approached him, gave him a soft kiss on the lips. "I'll get my things now."

I went to the bedroom and left the door open. I didn't want Peter getting suspicious. My heart was pounding a mile a minute, and my hands were trembling so badly I didn't know if I'd be able to shoot the gun.

I knew it was loaded. Marnie had told me that it was.

I rummaged around in drawers, threw clothes onto the bed. I made the sounds of a woman packing her things. But with every second that passed, I feared Peter would finish Andrew off with the knife.

The man was unpredictable.

Crazy.

Glancing behind me, I couldn't see Peter. Which meant he couldn't see me from this vantage point. Slowly I crept to the night table where the gun was. I eased the drawer open....

"Bella."

My heart jumping, I whipped around. Peter stood in the doorway.

"Do you love me?"

I forced a smile. "Yes. Yes, Peter. I love you. I think I loved you right from the beginning."

His lips pulled in a grin. "Do you need any help?"

I saw movement past Peter, and my eyes flitted in that direction. Andrew was trying to move slowly across the room to the kitchen.

Peter's smile instantly vanished and, following the direction of my gaze, he whipped his head around.

"Son of a bitch!" he exclaimed, moving quickly into the living room. "Get back on the sofa!"

"Yo, I'm sorry, man," Andrew said. "I just wanted to stretch my legs."

"You think I'm joking?" Peter bellowed. "You think this is a game?"

It was now or never. Before Peter killed Andrew.

I didn't waste another second. I reached into the drawer and pulled out the gun.

I eased back the safety the way Marnie had shown me, then I hurried out of the bedroom.

Andrew stood with his hands outstretched, hoping to keep Peter at bay. Peter had his fingers curled around the knife and was slowly raising it.

"I told you not to try anything stupid," he said to Andrew. "I almost wasn't going to kill you because of Sophie...but now you're going to die."

"Don't touch him!" I yelled, and Peter turned to face me. Andrew, too.

Peter's eyes widened in alarm, then settled as understanding registered.

"*Bella,*" he began, the hint of a laugh in his voice. "What are you doing?"

"Step away from my *husband,*" I said through clenched teeth.

I guess Peter didn't want to see if I was serious or not, because he took a few steps backward.

"Andrew, come beside me. I don't want you to get hurt."

"What—you're going to shoot me?" Peter asked, his tone incredulous.

Andrew came to my side. "I'll take the gun."

"No." I shook my head. In the moments it would take for the gun to change hands, Peter could leap over the sofa and stab at least one of us. "I can do this."

"You really believe you can *shoot* me?" Peter asked. "There is something undeniably special between us, *bella.* We are as one. The way God meant for a man and woman to be."

I didn't answer Peter's question. Instead, I asked my own. "Did you kill my cat?"

"Don't you remember how I made you feel in bed, *bella?* Everything we did—that was love. We made a baby because of our love."

"Did you kill my cat?" I repeated, slower this time, my breathing loud and labored.

"The cat. The fucking cat!" Peter spit out. "Every minute you were running home to feed the stupid thing."

Fresh tears sprang to my eyes, but I blinked them away. I needed to see Peter clearly when I shot him.

"And that's why you killed her?" I asked. I had to know.

"It's amazing how easily you can wring a cat's neck. It was fast, *bella.* You don't need to worry that she suffered."

"You son of a bitch!" I screamed.

And then Peter lunged around the sofa, the knife raised.

I squeezed the trigger. And squeezed.

The bullets struck my target, and blood popped out on Peter's chest. I saw confusion pass over his face before his eyes seemed to lose focus.

But he wasn't dead.

Another squeeze. Another spurt of blood. Clutching his chest now, Peter stumbled backward.

I squeezed the trigger again. This time a bullet pierced his forehead.

He went down at the side of the sofa. I started crying hysterically, but moved forward. I had to make sure he was dead.

Suddenly I felt Andrew's arms around me. He clasped his hands over mine and forced them down.

"It's over, Sophie. He's dead."

"He killed our cat," I sobbed, hysterical now, meeting Andrew's gaze. "The fucking bastard killed our cat!"

"Shh, sweetheart. It's okay now."

I threw a quick glance Peter's way, just to be certain he wasn't finding the strength to rise the way villains do in the movies, no matter how many times they've been shot.

"It's okay now," Andrew said again, reassuringly, and took the gun from me. He placed it on the decorative table behind us. "Sophie, it's okay."

Then he drew me into his arms and held me while I cried.

epilogue

Andrew was right. The wound he'd suffered had been superficial. He would have a scar across his chest, but he would be okay.

Well, as okay as anyone could be after nearly being killed. After enduring the wrath of a madman and living to tell the tale.

I thought I'd be an emotional wreck after taking a man's life, but I was strangely at peace with what I'd done. I wasn't happy by any means, and I cursed the day I'd ever met Peter, but I could live with myself.

Because I knew in my heart that it could be no other way. Peter *had* to be dead. Andrew and I would always have to look over our shoulders if he were still alive.

With him dead, we were free.

Perhaps having come so close to death, Andrew made the fast and easy decision that he no longer cared what had happened between me and Peter, even if the child I was carrying wasn't biologically his. He assured me that he meant what he'd said as Peter had threatened our lives—that he would raise the child as his, no looking back.

I loved him even more for that.

We both agreed that we would sell the house. Once we replaced the bloodstained carpet, we would put it on the market. I knew I couldn't live there anymore, raise my child there, and Andrew felt the same.

A new house would be a fresh start.

A week had passed since I'd shot and killed my lover. A crazy week with questioning from the police and intense media attention. I didn't admit to the reporters my affair, only my friendship with Peter, but I'd had to tell the police everything. The media reported that Peter had been a friend who'd become obsessed with me, and had wanted to kill my husband in the hopes that he could have me for himself. I'm sure that at least some people would be skeptical of the media slant and draw their own conclusions, but I didn't care what they thought.

I had my family to think about.

That family included a baby. One whose paternity I needed to determine.

I was surprised when Andrew told me Thursday night that he wanted to go with me to my doctor's appointment on Friday. On one hand, I wasn't—he'd spent pretty much every moment with me since the incident with Peter. But I knew that despite his bravado, he had to be worried that the baby wasn't his, and for that reason, I didn't expect him to want to go with me while I had my ultrasound.

But he did go with me, and even held my hand as the technician applied the cold gel and ran the probe over my belly. We both cooed when we saw and heard the baby's rapidly beating heart.

"I meant what I said," Andrew began softly when the technician was out of the room. "I consider this baby mine."

I placed my palm on Andrew's cheek. I wanted to say something, but my emotion filled my throat. Here we were in a predicament I wouldn't wish on an enemy, and yet, Andrew and I were closer than ever. If only we hadn't had to hurt each other to get to this point.

"I love you," I finally said. "And I'm so sor—"

Andrew placed a finger on my lips. "No looking back—remember?"

Slowly, I nodded. "No looking back."

The sound of the door turning had both Andrew and I looking in that direction. The ultrasound technician, a blonde, came back into the room.

"So," I said, anxious. "How far along am I?"

"From the size of the baby, it looks like about ten weeks."

"So the light period I told you I had?"

"Spotting is common with some women during pregnancy," the woman explained. "Especially early on."

My chest filled with warmth. "I'm ten weeks along. You're sure?"

"I'm sure. Your due date is March twenty-seventh."

Andrew let out a whoop of joy. Looking at him, I saw an expression of happiness I'd never seen on his face before.

"Our baby," I said softly. "*Our* baby."

The technician approached me and Andrew and handed us a small, square piece of paper. It was a picture of the image we'd seen on the screen. "I figured you might want this," the woman said, smiling fondly at us. "And that's it. You're free to go."

Accepting the picture, I gazed at the image of the baby through happy tears. It was small, but the shape was clear. I could see the distinct form of a tiny, tiny baby.

"Our baby," I repeated, looking from the picture to the man I loved. "It's not Peter's," I went on, now that the technician had left the room.

Beaming at me, Andrew placed his hand on my stomach. He had to have been worried and now he literally looked like the happiest man on earth.

"I love you," he said, and he kissed me. Kissed me through his own tears and laughter.

Giddy, we pulled apart, and once again stared at the picture of our child. "I think it's a girl," I said.

"A girl," Andrew echoed, his tone filled with awe.

"Yeah. A little girl. I feel it."

Andrew nodded. "I feel it too."

"Oh, my God—we're going to be parents."

"The best damn parents the world has ever seen."

I took Andrew's hand in mine. "Our baby."

"Yes, Sophie—*our* baby." He pulled me to my feet and kissed me again, a kiss that was full of love and the promise of a happy future. I knew we had a long road ahead of us to repair the damage we'd both done to our marriage. But Andrew's kiss proved to me we could get through it.

Smiling from ear to ear after we ended the kiss, Andrew led me to the door. "Come on," he said. "We've got some house hunting to do."